THE SECRET LIFE OF ROBERTA GREAVES

a novel by

ANN BIRCH

inanna poetry & fiction series

INANNA PUBLICATIONS AND EDUCATION INC.
TORONTO, CANADA

We gratefully acknowledge the support of the Canada Council for the Arts and the Ontario Arts Council for our publishing program. We also acknowledge the financial support of the Government of Canada through the Canada Book Fund.

Cover design: Val Fullard

The Secret Life of Roberta Greaves is a work of fiction. All the characters and situations portrayed in this book are fictitious and any resemblance to persons living or dead is purely coincidental.

Library and Archives Canada Cataloguing in Publication

Birch, Ann, author
    The secret life of Roberta Greaves / Ann Birch.

(Inanna poetry and fiction series)
Issued in print and electronic formats.
ISBN 978-1-77133-325-2 (paperback). -- ISBN 978-1-77133-326-9 (epub). --
ISBN 978-1-77133-327-6 (kindle). -- ISBN 978-1-77133-328-3 (pdf)

        I. Title. II. Series: Inanna poetry and fiction series

PS8603.I725S43 2016   C813'.6   C2016-904859-4
                                                  C2016-904860-8

Printed and bound in Canada

Inanna Publications and Education Inc.
210 Founders College, York University
4700 Keele Street, Toronto, Ontario M3J 1P3 Canada
Telephone: (416) 736-5356   Fax (416) 736-5765
Email: inanna.publications@inanna.ca Website: www.inanna.ca

MIX
Paper from
responsible sources
FSC
www.fsc.org   FSC® C004071

To Nicholas, John, and Hugh

"How do I love thee? Let me count the ways."
—Elizabeth Barrett Browning

1.

A S ROBERTA GREAVES OPENS THE DOOR of the hall closet, the aura of *eau de cheval* assails her. "James," she says to her husband standing behind her. "I wish you'd keep your jodhpurs in a separate closet."

"Just hand them to me, please. I don't need the lecture, and we're running late."

He sheds his jeans, grabs the jodhpurs, and pulls on his gear while Roberta buttons her favourite orange summer jacket. Perhaps the open air will dissipate the stink. She ducks just in time to avoid the riding helmet that crashes down from the closet shelf as James reaches for it.

At the front door, their two sons wait. Roberta notices that Ed has taken time to shave, while Charlie's stubble is still apparent. "What the hell, Ed," Charlie says, tucking in his T-shirt. "Do you understand old people? They get us up at the crack of dawn, and then we're the ones who have to—"

"Okay, okay, we're gone," James says, flipping the car keys to Ed. "You drive. I've got to sit in the back and try to keep calm."

As he climbs into the car, he smooths back his auburn hair, still abundant though he's forty-six years old. Roberta recognizes it as a gesture that betrays his nervous excitement. She moves in beside him and reaches for his hand.

Fair Hills is two hours' drive north of Toronto, and it's eight a.m. by the time they get there. The day looks as if it will be sunny, although clouds hover on the horizon. Already the parking is almost full. James takes off at a run down a gravel road toward the red-roofed stables while Roberta and the boys follow close behind. Roberta still thinks of them as "boys" even though Ed is twenty-five and Charlie, twenty-two.

"I've learned to trot," Charlie says. "Too bad I don't get a chance to participate in the day's events. But I know, I know. Four legs good, two legs bad." He has a fund of quotations that he produces at appropriate moments. Roberta had once hoped that he might become a teacher or perhaps a professor, but he's chosen to be a chef. And that's okay. Everyone in this world must surely appreciate good food.

"It bugs me sometimes the way Dad speaks of Bucephalus as if he was a pal," Ed says. "'He has such a nice smile,' *blah, blah.*" He puffs a bit as he tries to keep pace with his brother. Ed is articling with a major Toronto law firm, and he spends long hours sitting at a desk reading correspondence and talking on the phone. He's tall and thin, like Charlie, but Charlie is in better shape because he rides his bicycle daily to his chef classes at George Brown College.

Roberta laughs. "I know what you mean, but I tell myself, it's silly to be jealous of a horse."

"Yeah, but what about the expenses, Ma?" Ed says.

"I put up with them."

Ed's the practical one, and he's absolutely right about the expenses. There's the boarding, the vet, the farrier, the tack — all that stuff. Though she and James are both university professors and make decent salaries, there are times when she thinks, hey, can we really afford all this? For the last year, Bucie's comfortable stall in Fair Hills has had to be paid from her account.

And besides the expenses, there's the time commitment James makes to the sport: all weekend, every weekend, year round. But she recognizes that he needs excitement and charging over barricades and tearing up turf seems to keep him happy.

"I'm glad you never went in for riding, Mom," Charlie says, laughing.

"She knows the lingo, though," Ed says. "I've heard her talk to Dad about cantles and pommels, snaffle bits and nightingales—"

"Martingales, please. Oh yes, I know the lingo. But I don't have the guts for riding. I now make a confession. I did get up on an eleven-hundred-pound lump of brute force once when I was a kid, but they had to lift me off, pronto. I couldn't even remember the steps in dismounting. Except for the first one, of course: 'Bring your horse to a complete stop.' Which wasn't that difficult since I'd never got the beast started up in the first place."

"Just as well, I'd say. Wouldn't you, Charlie?"

When they get to the stable, they see that James is already inside the first stall on the left near the open door.

"Quick," Charlie says, pausing just outside the door, "deep breaths, guys." But it's too late. The stench of horse shit has already invaded their lungs.

James has just pulled an apple from the pocket of his riding jacket, and Bucephalus has drawn back his soft velvet lip to accept it. He makes gentle whuffling noises. He's a tall, chestnut thoroughbred with four white stockings, the favourite gelding of James's horse-breeder uncle who died two years ago, leaving his beloved possession to his nephew.

They have come to the Fair Hills site for the big competition that always takes place on the Civic Holiday weekend in early August. Though Roberta and her sons seldom join James on his weekend adventures, he wanted them along for this one. Eventing, he calls it. It involves three tests: dressage, cross-country, and show jumping. "Cross-country is where the fun is," James says, as he leaves Bucephalus munching his snack. "So let's get moving. I've got to walk over the course and have a look at what's what."

"Isn't Bucie coming along?" Charlie says.

"No way. We'd be in trouble with the officials. He's expected to race it blind."

So they walk the course together. "Oh jeez, Dad," Charlie says. "Those fences are something else."

"And don't you love their names?" Ed looks at the map of the terrain as they make their way around. "Elephant Trap, Bounce, Palisade, and Coffin. I especially love that last one. Is it just so much hype, Dad, or do people really die on cross-country?"

"I think the fences are mostly named for effect. But people have died."

"I checked it out on the Internet yesterday," Roberta says. "Someone posted a blog saying that six riders in England had been crushed to death last year when their horses fell on them going over jumps. It's an absolutely crazy sport when you think about it."

James stops for a moment to look back at the fence named Coffin. "I'll bet the riders got a decent send-off—priest, incense, and liturgy—but some of those poor lovely beasts probably died too, and *they'd* be fed to foxhounds— in great, bloody chunks."

"Yikes!"

"But it's all part of the scene, as I told you. It's the challenge that provides the fun."

"Galloping your horse full tilt at fences he's never seen before?" Roberta says. "That's fun?" She turns toward the line of spectators that's beginning to form. "Come on, boys. Let's give your dad a chance to get tacked up. We'll go find ourselves a place to stand before the crowd overwhelms us."

From the row of spectators along the barricade, they watch as James and Bucephalus move to the starting point. Roberta loves the way James looks in his riding gear, when she can't smell it, that is. One lock of red hair has escaped from his helmet, and the jodhpurs and tall boots show off his long legs. The horse seems to be in high gear, like a souped-up racing car. He's pacing forwards and back, making snorting noises. Roberta can tell that James is nervous by the way he whacks his riding crop against his right leg. He's the first competitor, and she remembers how he always prefers to be drawn late, so he can watch the other competitors and learn from their mistakes.

He and Bucephalus take off at top speed and ace the first half of the course. James seems to be rising to the challenge.

By the time they come up to the Elephant Trap, Roberta can see that James has conquered his nerves. He's leaning forward over the horse's neck and smiling. Bucephalus appears to be enjoying himself too. He seems energized by the crowd, or maybe it's the touch of the beloved hand on his shoulder, or the sun on his hide and the gentle August breeze behind him, nudging him forward.

And perhaps that's what goes wrong at the Elephant Trap. He's having *too* much fun. As he approaches the fence, Roberta sees him lengthen his stride without waiting for James's signal. He takes off into the air, soaring over the trap like Pegasus. But James is unprepared for his sudden upward rise. He loses his centre of gravity over Bucephalus's back, upsetting that perfect balance between horse and rider. Their landing is skewed. Roberta watches as James struggles to get himself properly balanced for the gradual left turn that leads into the downhill slope. She can tell that his weight is still behind the horse's centre of balance.

Within seconds, horse and rider arrive at the next jump, a high vertical fence placed halfway down the hill. Bucephalus is galloping flat out. They watch as James tries to slow him down, but Bucie is not listening.

"Christ! It's a disaster," Roberta says as she grabs Charlie's hand.

She has a clear moment of recognition. It's her Friday Classics in Translation class right here in Fair Hills. It's Phaethon's fatal plunge with the horses of the sun god. James and Bucephalus close in too fast on the base of the fence. The horse sails into the jump, but he's too near to clear it. He hits it with his chest, flips over it, and crashes onto his back. And James—oh merciful heaven—falls clear, landing ten feet beyond the fence.

Roberta and the boys push their way past the line of spectators who are crowding onto the field to get a closer look. James struggles to his feet. He holds his neck at an odd angle, and his left arm hangs, useless. He stumbles over to Bucephalus who tries to get up. A jump judge has already grabbed his reins. As the horse flounders, Roberta can see that something is terribly wrong. "Look," she says to her sons. "He can't seem to put any weight on his left hind leg. And your dad is hurt—"

James is screaming now. "For God's sake, get help!" But a second jump judge has already used his cellphone to summon the horse ambulance. It careens down the track from the parking lot. James runs towards it, and there's a hurried consultation with the vet. Then a brief examination of Bucephalus. The vet shakes his head.

"Oooh, it's the end for that horse!" says a woman beside Roberta. There are mutterings of excitement from the crowd. They are lusting now for the *coup de grâce*.

Roberta and the boys rush over to James. Tears are running down his cheeks, making tracks through the dirt on his face. "Bucie has a hip fracture, but by God, he's not going to provide the day's entertainment for jerks," he says, looking at a woman who has run out onto the course to get a closer look. "Let's get him out of here."

James keeps his right hand on Bucephalus's neck as four cross-country attendants struggle to get the horse into a sling and on board the ambulance. He doesn't struggle much. He seems subdued as he faces the end. The back doors of the ambulance close, and Roberta, Charlie, and Ed run after it, back to the stables.

James tries to help as the other men ease the horse gently from the back of the ambulance and lay him on a soft bed of straw. "What now?" Roberta asks, feeling totally useless.

"I won't have the bolt." James is sobbing now. "I won't have the bolt. It would tear apart his beautiful head."

"Barbiturates," the vet says. "An intravenous injection will do it."

As he opens his kit and prepares the syringe, a strange thing happens. The other horses in the stable stop their stamping and nickering. They stretch their heads toward the dying horse and prick their ears forward. "It's like they're mourning," Charlie says. "I wouldn't believe it if it wasn't happening right here before me." He wipes his eyes on his sleeve.

James seems to have a broken collarbone. There's a bone jutting out beneath his skin. He holds his head with his right hand and eases himself down into the straw beside Bucephalus. He tries to stroke the horse with his left hand, but he cannot seem to make his fingers work. Probably he has a fractured arm as well. Charlie gets down beside his father and pats the animal's glossy flank. Bucephalus appears to be comforted by the friends beside him. His brown eyes seem fixed on James and Charlie, and they close gradually as the barbiturates take effect. It is a quiet death.

For a moment, the only sound is James's sobbing. He struggles to his feet with Charlie's help. Then, three pairs of arms encircle him.

2.

ROBERTA HAS CLIMBED CAREFULLY onto the dining-room table to clean the chandelier. The table is a solid mahogany structure, but the two leaves added to it make it a bit unsteady in the middle. From her perch, she looks across the hall to the living room where James is slumped in his chair reading *The Gazette*. He is wearing the same blue sweater he's worn for several days.

"Wish you'd do this for me," she says. "Of course, I know you can't, but I feel so teetery—"

"Get down before you break *your* collarbone and arm, too. Why don't you leave it for Ed or Charlie?"

"Good idea." She climbs down onto a chair, then onto the floor. She waits a minute, adjusts the cotton bandana that holds back her long, wavy blonde hair, takes a deep breath, and climbs back up onto the tabletop. "I've got to get it done. But as soon as that cast and sling come off, the job is yours."

She and James bought the chandelier in Venice. It filled the back seat of their rented Volkswagen on their honeymoon tour of eight countries, and when they came home, they had to unwrap all of its eight-hundred tiny crystal drops for inspection by a fascist customs officer.

Now, she concentrates hard on each piece, spraying and polishing, until it shines pink and glows like the sunsets she and James watched from the *vaporetto* on the Grand Canal. "It wasn't all romance and glowing sunsets though, was it, James?"

"Huh?"

"Our honeymoon. Remember that guidebook we had? *Venice on $50 a Day?*"

"Yeah. Didn't it recommend sleeping in a moored gondola?"

She laughs, happy that he is playing along with her now instead of sleeping or reading the paper. "We did stay in that hotel they described as 'a favourite hostelry of Garibaldi's Red Shirts.' Remember the one?"

"Yes, it had that lumpy mattress — not that we cared on our honeymoon. And the cupboard was lined with filthy oilcloth, and the windows were dirty, and there was no bathroom. And didn't you come down with Garibaldi's Revenge?"

"'The Red Shits,' you called it, and that exactly described it. And there were only two bathrooms in the whole place: one on the first floor and one on the second. Do you remember what you did for me that day?"

"Sort of."

She is stretching now to the top crystals, and the table rocks a bit under her, so she waits until it steadies, then continues. "Remember the bathroom on our floor? It had a broken lock on the door, and my loperamide pills hadn't taken hold. So you brought the rickety chair from our room, and posted yourself outside the door, and sat reading for one whole morning while you rerouted the traffic to the downstairs toilet. Oh James, I loved you for that."

There is no response to this. She gets down from the table and looks at him. His chin is on his chest, the bag of ice for his collarbone has slipped into his lap, and he seems to have fallen asleep again. She touches his shoulder gently.

He looks up, his brown eyes unfocused, his red hair greasy and too long over his ears. "Sorry, Roberta. I can't stay awake."

"Want to take a slow hike around the block to get some fresh air? I could go with you now that I've done my complete housewife shtick."

"I'm happier asleep, really."

"Why don't we have someone to dinner next Friday night? It might cheer you up. How about Carl Talbot and his wife? We haven't seen them for a while."

"Go ahead. Invite whoever." He gets up. "You're right. I need some exercise. I think I'll hike up to my study. I should get working on my article on Trollope for *The Victorian Reader*. I've got one reasonably good arm. I'll probably miss the deadline, but they may cut me some slack."

A few minutes later, Roberta hears the gentle swell of music that heralds the opening of his computer. Finally, he is doing something constructive. She puts in a call to Carl.

It's six p.m. and the Talbots are due to arrive in an hour. Ed and Charlie are out on Friday night dates with their girlfriends, and Roberta is stuck in the kitchen, her least favourite spot in the house. James's cast came off his arm earlier in the day, and she hoped he would offer to do the meringues, but no luck. "Got to get that damned article written," he said. "Sorry about that, Roberta, but I've no alternative." He's been in his study for hours. He usually gives her parts of his manuscript to read over, but so far there's been nothing. She hopes he hasn't fallen asleep over the keyboard or become involved in one of those games of solitaire.

She has whipped the cream, licked the beater, and now it's time to get the meringue shells out of the oven. The oven mitts have gotten lost somewhere — she's been so distracted by James's problems she can't keep track of anything — so she takes a tea towel and yanks the oven door open. "Shit!" As she grabs the cookie sheet, the heat sears her fingers and the damn meringues slide off and smash into a hundred pieces on the kitchen floor. She sweeps the mess into a dustpan, looks at the clock. Half an hour to come up with an alternative idea for dessert, get the steaks out, and make gravy.

First, she has to get the disaster out of the way. She is at the garbage pail outside the back door, tipping the waste into the bin when a voice calls to her over the cedar hedge that separates her from her neighbour, Mrs. Schubert. It's John, Mrs. Schubert's middle-aged son, who comes over periodically to help his mother with her garden and lawn. He is the major book critic for *The Gazette*.

Just last month, Roberta came out with her pruning shears to cut off a dead branch in the hedge and caught him on the other side of the cedars in a close embrace with his mother's young cleaner, just out of range of Mrs. Schubert's back windows. The girl seemed to be trying to pull away, but Schubert had her trapped, like a mouse that's felt the metal clamp close down upon it. When she saw Roberta, she broke free and ran back into the house.

Remembering this, Roberta answers Schubert's greeting and turns away, hoping to avoid further conversation.

"Roberta, have you got a sec?" He does not wait for an answer, just comes through a gap in the hedge and corners her. "You're looking a bit flushed, dear, but it's becoming. Makes you look thirty again. But here I am, running off at the mouth, so I'll get to the point. I've just finished reading *The Very Birds Are Mute*. You do have a talent. Some of your poems are quite excellent. But there are others—well, I just can't relate to them. Still — pretty good for a first book of poetry. I'll try to give it a good review. Congrats, by the way. But *where* did you get the title? A teeny bit on the pretentious side, don't you think?"

She can feel more heat rising in her cheeks and knows that Schubert is probably enjoying the moment. She can see the way his pale eyes scan her face. "Thanks for your thoughtful, perceptive critique, John. But I'm a teeny bit surprised that an eminent theatre and book critic doesn't recognize a line from one of Shakespeare's most famous sonnets." She slams the lid down on the pail. "Or maybe you worked too long at that quack journal? Forgot all your Shakespeare?" And without looking back, she stomps into the house, banging the door behind her.

11

Five minutes later, she regrets what she has said. Maybe Schubert *did* recognize the source of the title. Perhaps it *is* pretentious? And why did she have to bring up his former editor's job at *Your Health*? He has always been sensitive about it. "Unabashed self-promotion by health-food outlets," he told her once.

She goes out the back door to find him and apologize, but he is already in his car, backing down the driveway, tires screeching.

3.

A T LEAST THE STEAKS ARE GOOD. Fortunately, everyone likes them medium rare, so Roberta has not had to fuss. They have settled into second glasses of wine, and she has just told them about the meringue disaster and her contretemps with Schubert.

"I totally understand," Carl Talbot says. "I might have said the same thing." Carl is a tall man, like James, but he has broad shoulders and more heft. He has grey hair and blue eyes, and braces on his teeth. Roberta admires that. It takes courage to have braces when you are Carl's age. Early fifties, she would guess. She and James met him when they were at Trinity College together. He was their TA in the Dickens-Eliot-Trollope course that James now teaches. James always gives Carl credit for sparking his interest in an academic career. At college reunions, people still talk about Carl. They remember his rewrite of the last chapter of *A Farewell to Arms* in the style of Dickens: "The funniest thing I've read in a long time," someone always says.

"I'm with you, too, Roberta," James says. He turns to Carl. "Schubert is a schmuck. Roberta caught him groping that young cleaner his mother hires. Not a thing the poor girl can do about it, I guess, since she probably needs the money she gets from the old lady. But he's also a powerful critic, and it wasn't a good idea to attack his ego, to remind him of his roots in yellow journalism." James seems a bit livelier tonight. He has washed his hair and put on a clean shirt. Perhaps immersion in his scholarly article has put some enthusiasm back into his life.

"I know what you're both thinking but not saying. It's bad policy for a writer to irritate a book critic. John Schubert's got a lot of clout in the literary world. He's moved into the role of God, and he loves it. In fact, that's one of the reasons I can't stand him. He looks down from his throne in the empyrean, and he hands down his version of the Commandments. Of course, I won't make any money from the poetry book anyway, so it doesn't really matter what pronouncement he issues about it. Perhaps it might be more to the point if we took some action on the sexual harassment he seems guilty of. At the very least, perhaps make Mrs. Schubert aware of what's going on."

Roberta thinks for a moment about what she's said and sighs. "Small revision to my earlier comment: It is foolish of me not to admit that it *would* be nice to get a good review. I've told the people at the Christian Mission that any royalties from the book go to the educational programs they offer to street kids."

"Roberta's doing volunteer poetry-writing workshops with those kids," James explains. "It's a huge departure from her academic world at Trinity, but she seems to find it worthwhile."

"The most challenging teaching experience I've ever had," Roberta says. "And last week, I got it so very wrong. I thought it might be a smart idea to introduce them to haikus. Only seventeen syllables and one compelling image to tie those syllables together. What could go wrong?"

"Let me guess," Carl says. "They didn't know what a syllable was?"

"Right. But what made them really angry — pissed them off was the phrase they used — was the three-line format of seventeen syllables. A 'fucking control freak' was what they called me."

"So why do you put yourself through that?" Claire asks. She is a wisp of a woman with black hair, pale grey eyes, and a puffy face.

"I don't know. It started with some smug, misbegotten notion I had of bringing creativity into their sad, deprived world. The reality is that some of the time it's more like warfare: me versus them. Though come to think of it, two or three of them actually caught on and started counting out the syllables. It was a small beginning."

"Brava," Carl says. "Sometimes, small beginnings develop into major triumphs. Perhaps I'm idealistic, but I think you're doing something really worthwhile."

"Back to Schubert and his reviews," James says. "You don't want him slamming *The Cretan Manuscripts*, my love. That's big stuff. It's bound to hit the academic world with a *bang*. Come to think of it, it may be so big that a dismissive review by Schubert wouldn't do major damage."

"Where's the launch going to be?" Carl asks.

"Strachan Hall, Trinity, next Thursday. Hope you and Claire can make it."

"I don't think I can," Claire says in a low voice. "It's chemo day." She puts her hand up to her ear and makes a small adjusting movement with her fingers. Now that Roberta looks at her again, she realizes the black hair is a wig. And there is a strange chemical smell, something like the nuts from a ginkgo tree in the fall. Roberta had no idea that Claire was sick again. Last time she saw her — was it two months ago? — she seemed to be in remission.

"And of course, I can't be there, either. Chemo days are miserable, and I need to lend a hand when Claire gets home." Carl puts his arm around his wife's frail shoulders. "But I want to buy a book, Roberta, and I want you to write something nice in it for me."

They finish their steaks, and then Roberta faces the problem of her diminished dessert offering. "Don't worry about the meringues," James says, as he helps Roberta carry the dinner plates to the kitchen. "Why don't we just have a bowl of whipped cream? I love it."

ANN BIRCH

"Good thought. I've some canned apricots we can put on top."

The apricots and whipped cream look pretty in the gold-and-red Royal Crown Derby dishes Roberta inherited from her grandmother. "Good china can detract from bad food, or so I fondly hope," she says, setting the dessert in front of her guests.

"Just as a bad farrier can cripple a good horse," James says out of the blue. Well, it's an effort at least, and Roberta is happy to see him steering the conversation onto a topic that interests him. He goes on: "Some riders are actually giving bare-footing a trial."

"They're not wearing riding boots these days?" Claire asks. "That must be dangerous."

"No, no. I mean that some riders are not putting shoes on their horses."

There's a long pause. Then Carl says, "I'm sorry about your horse having to be put down. That must have been a horrible shock."

"Bucie was a special friend. You know, he was eight years old when my uncle left him to me in his will. He'd never done eventing before, but he had the heart and the temperament to try anything with me. I'd even say he had the *soul* if you wouldn't laugh at me."

"No one's laughing," Carl says. "We've all had animals we loved. I remember my English setter—"

"He didn't like dressage any better than I did," James cuts in. "But he saved my skin once. I was so bored in the dressage ring — I was thinking about the cross-country — and next thing I knew I couldn't remember anything about the canter. I completely blanked out. But he put himself right into position, did the whole weight sequence: one hind leg, two hind legs and one foreleg, one hind leg and diagonal foreleg, one hind leg and two forelegs, one foreleg, then all four legs in the air."

"Ah," Carl says. "It's called the moment of suspension, isn't it?"

James smiles, confident that he has got someone who speaks "horse." If he would just leave it at that, Roberta thinks. But no, he's onto the different means of euthanasia, and then he segues into the burial pit in which Bucephalus was placed. The animal must be covered with at least a metre of soil. There is more, much more, but Roberta stops listening.

She is watching her guests closely. Claire has just taken a quick peek at her watch. Carl is wiping his mouth with a napkin. Or is he covering a yawn?

"Shall we move to more comfortable seats?" she asks.

In the living room, Carl helps Claire into a comfortable high-backed chair, and then, over coffee and Grand Marnier, Roberta asks Carl about his current life as head of an English Department at a west-end high school.

"Yesterday, one of the kids I teach told me when I was on cafeteria duty, aka pigpen patrol, that he'd enjoyed *Macbeth*. I was pleased because we'd had to rush through it to accommodate the new curriculum. 'Nothing wishy-washy about Shakespeare,' was what he actually said. I was so surprised. That old-fashioned adjective was perfect. I took it personally, patted myself on the back for the rest of the day." At this point Carl takes out a spotless linen handkerchief and wipes his eyes. "A teacher's grief is sometimes insupportable."

"Tell Mama and Papa all about it," Roberta says, looking at James to include him in the banter.

"I marked two essays. The first one informed me that Macbeth went down to Great Neptune's Ocean and tried to wash his hands, but the bloodstains wouldn't come off."

"Obviously, you didn't put across the concept of metaphor. And the second?"

"That one takes a bit of explanation. Do you by any chance remember the character Pat in *Hamlet?*"

"Hmm. Pat? I don't think so." Then Roberta gets it. "Wait. Is it Pat as in 'Now might I do it pat, now he is praying'?"

"That's it. One kid — name's Joey — asked me in class when

we were doing the prayer scene who this Pat was, and I told him, 'She's Hamlet's sister. Doesn't appear often in the play. In fact, only when Hamlet needs her advice.' So, in his essay, he told me that Pat should have told Hamlet to stick the knife into Claudius right then and there!"

"Serves you right for being a smartass with a poor kid."

"Thanks for the sympathy, Mama. I feel so much better."

Roberta and Carl laugh. Then, looking around, they realize that James and Claire are not joining in the fun. In fact, they are both asleep. James has started to make gentle snorting noises, and Claire's mouth has fallen open.

"She's dying, you know," Carl says to Roberta, leaning forward and speaking in a whisper. "I don't know what I can do to help her through these last weeks."

"Dear Carl, you hover over her like a guardian angel."

"And I notice a big change in James, too. He's just not the same lively person he used to be. Is it that disaster with the horse?"

"Yes. He blames himself for the accident. I'm worried."

"Does he need to get a new interest?"

"Ed and Charlie think so, and I agree."

"Remember that trip Claire and I took with your family so long ago? The hike along the Antrim Coast?"

"How could I forget? I was miserable most of the time, clinging to farmers' fences on the inside of the path while the rest of you hung over the cliffs. I could have sworn you were all seeing how close you could come to the edge without falling over the rocks into the sea."

"I was scared myself when we got to Carrick-a-Rede. Claire and you and I all sat on a bench while—"

"James and the boys raced across the rope bridge from the mainland to that little fishermen's island. It's a horror movie in my mind."

"I can still see the bridge swaying all those feet above the chasm—"

"And those Irish teenagers crawling back to the mainland on all fours, too scared to stand up—"

"It was insane. And yet, I could see James laughing all the way across. The boys were so small they probably didn't see the danger. But you were furious." Carl sets his liqueur glass on the coffee table.

"I didn't speak to James for the rest of the afternoon." She remembers thinking that he would wipe out her whole family in one hare-brained escapade.

"It's the type of adventure James enjoys. I'm not suggesting anything crazy, Rob, but maybe if he could find a safe thrill." He laughs. "*Is* there such a thing as a safe thrill?"

Claire stirs and opens her dark eyes. "Oh dear, I didn't mean to be such a klutz, Roberta." She touches the side of her head and begins to claw at her wig. "I hate this," she says and yanks it off to reveal tufts of hair sprouting here and there on a shiny bald head.

Carl gets up and leans over her, touching her shoulder. "You're tired. It's time to go home." Claire begins to shiver. He helps her to rise from the chair, takes off his suit jacket, and drapes it around her.

The activity wakens James. "Sorry, sorry," he says. "Too much food has a soporific effect on me."

A couple of minutes later, Carl and Claire are in their car and backing down the driveway.

"It wasn't your good dinner that put me to sleep, love," James says as he and Roberta stand in the doorway to wave goodbye. "Carl's become a bit of a bore, wouldn't you agree? I just couldn't keep my eyes open. Sorry."

"You seem so tired and depressed all the time, and I understand that. But don't blame Carl."

"You're right. Why blame Carl? I need to get charged up again, that's what I need." He glances at the staircase. "Maybe I'll just have a go at my article before bedtime." From the top of the stairs, he calls down. "Give me a cheque for ten thou, will you? I've got to cover the tree takedown, the new roof, and the taxes."

"Sure." Long ago, they decided not to keep a joint account. They each have a separate chequing account, and they have an informal way of paying bills. It's her turn this month. Last month, James paid for the eavestroughs and the new kitchen cabinets. Their big old house needs lots of upgrades, all of them expensive.

Roberta calls up to James. "By the way, will you phone the cabinet people and tell them to get their records straight? They left a message on the answering machine today saying we hadn't paid them."

She stacks the dishes, puts the food away, writes the cheque, and climbs upstairs to bed. Through the half-open door of the study, she gets a glimpse of the blue light from James's computer. She sees him hunched over the computer, intent on his work. She doesn't disturb him. At last, he's focusing on something worthwhile. Now, perhaps, she can stop worrying about him day in and day out.

4.

ROBERTA SITS IN THE BATHTUB looking at her notes for the evening. It is one of her "Big Days," as she calls those times when she has major public performances. The hot water and lavender bath oil soothe her. There is a knock on the door, and James comes in with a glass of white wine on a sterling silver butler's tray. He has a snowy white towel draped over his left arm, the arm that is now free from the troublesome cast.

He sets the glass on a corner of the tub near her left foot. "Anything else for Madam?" he says, bowing

"No thank you, Jeeves. But why do you put my drink way down there?"

"So madam must sit up in order to reach it. That way, madam will not fall asleep and drown." He shifts the towel to his other arm. "The Hermès scarf has been ironed, Madam, and the red dress brushed and laid out upon the bed. May I make a suggestion?"

"I'm listening."

"Madam's present undress is so much more attractive." He gets down on his knees beside the tub, pulls her left foot out of the water and kisses her toes. While she enjoys this, she cannot help noticing how his dry scaly hands scrape against her skin.

"Don't knock over my wineglass, you idiot," she says, laughing. "How much longer do I have?"

"About thirty-five minutes to finish in the tub, put your dress on — if you must — and then eat your supper. I have it ready."

"Better get some of my cream on those hands," she says. But he's out the bathroom door, heading for the stairs. Perhaps he didn't hear her.

When she goes into the dining room, she finds he has prepared her favourite comfort food: macaroni and cheese, warm gingerbread and applesauce. It's all served up on pretty Royal Garden plates with one of her mother's hand-embroidered napkins next to her fork.

"We've got the car ready for you, Ma, whenever you're ready," Ed says coming through the front door with Charlie. "I'll be chauffeur, and Charlie will sit in the front with me. You and Dad can sit in state in the back." Ed is handsome in a new three-button Italian suit with a gold silk tie that sets off his auburn hair. He is the one people always say is the spitting image of James.

"You guys look great," James says. "I'm used to seeing you in a suit, Ed, but Charlie — my God — I didn't know you *had* a suit. I'm impressed."

"Come on, Dad, get real. You've seen it before. It's been to two funerals, six weddings, and four graduations." He pats the lapels. "But this is its first book launch." He smiles at them, and for a moment, his blue eyes and wavy ash-blond hair remind Roberta of her father. She likes to think that her father would have approved of her sons, even Charlie's long hair, which he has slicked back into a ponytail.

Ed parks the car in the "Reserved" space in the tiny Trinity parking lot. Roberta looks at the dashboard. She has half an hour to check out the mike, make sure her books are laid out on an accessible table, go to the toilet near her office, and fix her hair. "Lots of time," Ed says, watching her. "But not space enough to have a spaz."

"We'll check out the food while you do what you have to," Charlie says.

"He means, inspect the waitresses, and I'd be happy to help him do that."

"Servers, they're called now, bro. Just to update you."

"And I'll be in my office," James says. "Call for me at the end of the evening. Good luck, Roberta."

"What's up, Dad?" Ed asks. "Come on, Trinity expects every man to do his duty."

"Yeah," Charlie adds. "Think Sydney Carton: 'It is a far far better thing I do—'"

"Sorry, gang," James says. "Got work to do."

"I wish you'd come." Roberta touches his sleeve. "But I know you're not really interested in the schmoozing. Thanks for my favourite food and the glass of wine. I needed that."

"Impressive spot, this," Charlie says when she joins the boys in Strachan Hall. "Didn't you used to eat here, Ed?"

"Yeah, we had to wear our academic gowns for meals. And there was a head table. I think we had an unwarranted sense of superiority over the great unwashed at the other colleges."

Roberta remembers her first dinner in the room. She'd been seventeen. For a kid from the boondocks of Summerton, it had all been intimidating. The heavy oak tables. The portraits of long-dead provosts staring down from above the wainscoting. The frosh dinner of corn on the cob, spareribs, and blueberry pie. She'd been unable to enjoy the food, worried about the grease on her chin and the kernels stuck in her blue-stained teeth. Now, she'd eat it all with gusto, swipe at her chin with a napkin, and pick out the corn with her fingers whenever people were looking elsewhere. There are bonuses to being middle-aged.

"I imagine the whole place looks a bit like Oxford, Mom?"

"Imitation Oxford. It was built in nineteen twenty-five, I think. But I do like the mullioned windows and all the dark wood. I even like that oil of Bishop Strachan looking down on us like a deity. Over the top, I know, with those silk robes and billowing linen sleeves, but he seems to be delivering a message to us earthlings: 'Eat, drink, and be merry, but remember that education is important.'"

She sees a large woman — one of the College's donors — bearing down on them.

"The deluge cometh," Ed says. "We'll get you a glass of wine, Ma, to show the Bishop that we're listening to his first bit of advice."

"My dear, so wonderful, so prestigious an honour." A huge bosom presses against Roberta, and she sucks in a fug of cleaning fluid and lily-of-the-valley perfume. But she manages to return a kiss on one side of the woman's fleshy jowls. And Charlie comes with a glass of wine, just in time to create a diversion. "What a handsome young man," the woman says as she moves away.

"You're too young, boys, to remember the good-old-days when a handshake was the accepted mode of congratulation."

"All those years ago," Charlie says. "But I can't say I like all this kissy-kissy stuff myself. And now here comes Rudolph Red Nose. Fortify yourself, Mom. Take one of these shrimps off my plate and stick the pick into him."

Another embrace. And another. And another. Roberta is conscious of the boys watching her. Ed says, *sotto voce,* "It's probably a good thing Dad's not here. He'd have been jealous to see you in that clinch with Old Baldy."

Charlie looks over at the buffet table. "Hey," he whispers into her ear. "See that moron at the end of the table? He just took a bite from his carrot stick, and now he's dipping it in the guacamole. Gross. The first thing they tell us at George Brown, 'No double dipping.' Too bad the Board of Health can't put a red sticker on his forehead."

"Isn't that Mrs. Schubert's son, Ma? You can't miss that black hair with the white stripe. Like a skunk."

John Schubert walks over to them, a copy of her book under his arm. "May I speak to you for a few minutes, Roberta, dear? Get some info from you for my piece in *The Gazette*? You'll excuse us, boys?"

Roberta and Schubert move to a quieter corner of the hall. He stands close to her, so close that his cologne overwhelms her: earthy, like a patch of uprooted fungi, truffles maybe, though she's never really smelled a truffle. "You look marvellous, Roberta. You do minimalist so well. So many women your age overdress. Look at that one over there. Sequins and lace *and* that ghastly droopy hemline that draws attention to her nasty fat legs."

"I thought you were *The Gazette's* book editor, John, not their fashion guru."

"What makes you so rude about a genuine compliment?" he asks. Roberta can hear the anger in his voice.

"Sorry." It's not a good time to antagonize him, especially when she remembers her snipe at him from last week. She will need him on side for a good review. Good reviews often translate into good sales. After her prolonged stay in Crete working on the translation, it would be nice to recoup some of her expenses.

Schubert pulls out a gold-clipped fountain pen and a small notebook from his back pocket. "Now set me straight, please. You translated some ancient papyrus rolls found in a cave in Crete?"

"Parchment, fortunately. We think the stories were probably copied from papyrus scrolls, and a good thing, too, because papyrus is so fragile and—"

"And it was a little boy who found them? He was foraging for firewood?"

"That's right."

"A Greek professor friend of yours then gave you access to them?"

"Dr. Paniota Andriopoulos, Chair of the Department of Archaeology at the University of Crete. I'd like to be sure she gets credit for giving me the chance to translate the manuscripts for an English audience. I'll spell her name for you, if you like."

"Yes, well, we must remember, dear Roberta, that the readers of *The Gazette* have an average educational level of Grade Nine. We don't expect them to absorb too many details. But you might tell me why she gave you this honour."

"I don't honestly know. Every Greek and Roman scholar in the world must have lusted after the chance to do the translations. I'd like to think my erudition was the deciding factor in the selection, but I'm sure everyone suspects it was my friendship with Paniota that gave me the edge."

"You claim that these ancient manuscripts were actually written by a woman?" He puts on his reading glasses.

"Not *claim*. The person who long ago copied the papyrus onto parchment made clear that the original stories were signed by a woman. Perhaps your Grade Nine readers won't be interested in her name, but it's Euripida. She identified herself as a cousin of Euripides."

Why did he bother putting on his glasses? He's not writing anything down.

"And why is all this important, dear?"

"Because until this small boy pulled the narratives into the light of day, we'd always seen the ancient world through the eyes of men. The Greek myths we read in school were male constructs: Ovid's or Homer's or Sophocles's view of how the universe unfolded."

Schubert yawns. "Your point?"

Calm, calm, she tells herself. "I guess my point is that all the heroes of myth — Jason, Perseus, and Theseus, to name only a few — can now be seen from a female perspective. Of course, there were female writers in ancient times, but most of their writing did not survive the bonfires of early Christianity. The patriarchs of the church made sure of that. Take Sappho, for example. We have only a few of her simple, eloquent poems left, though her contemporaries tell us she was greater than Homer. Better those early Christians should have burned Pope Leo." She stops. "Whoops, scratch that last bit, please, John."

Finally, he makes a few entries in his book and then puts it away. "Thank you, dear. Most interesting. And now, I suppose you want to get back to your fans. Isn't that the Provost heading to the mike?"

He turns away, giving Roberta a second to look over the pile of signed books on a table by the door where her publisher's representative is sitting with a cash box and a credit card processor. The stack has dwindled in size. Three hundred books, of which about half remain. So far then, considering a royalty of ten percent minus her agent's cut, she's probably making … not much.

"Figuring out the take?" Ed asks, coming up behind her. "Maybe our copyright lawyer at Plumtree, Pogson, and Peabody could give you input on e-book rights. At eight hundred dollars an hour, unfortunately. On second thought, forget it."

"I've been checking out the quadrangle," Charlie says, "and it's a nice evening. I may go out there and get away from the noise for a bit. Can you come, Mom?"

"Wait around, will you, until I say a few official words to the guests? I think Provost Witherspoon is about to introduce me."

At the podium, the Provost leads a round of applause for "one of the university's most noted scholars." Then, mopping his forehead, he says, "Over now to Dr. Greaves who will tell you all about this amazing discovery."

From the lectern, Roberta assesses her audience. Most of them, like her, have probably drunk two glasses of wine. So she will not tell them "all." She will keep it short.

"I want you to know about the little boy—Hector by name—who was responsible for the whole endeavour," she begins. "He found the manuscripts in a dark cave once dedicated to the goddess of childbirth. I'll always think of him as a midwife who brought a lovely new creation into the world." She tells about the unexpected pleasure of meeting Hector in Crete. And then, she speaks about how the parchment rolls got to the University of Crete and into the hands of Paniota Andriopoulos. Paniota's generosity must be acknowledged, even if Schubert doesn't give a damn. "Words cannot convey my gratitude for the trust she placed in me."

There is polite applause, probably as much for the brevity of her remarks as for the content. But the Q&A period drags on far longer than her talk. A pudgy little woman with wild white hair, who has been waving at her for a while, finally gets her chance to speak.

"Penelope Peckham." She blows out her cheeks and puffs into the mike.

"Good evening, Dr. Peckham. Let me just tell the audience that you're from Columbia University, and that you wrote an article on my book for the last issue of *The New York Times Book Review*. I know you have some reservations about my translation. Let's hear your views." *Best to take the wind out of her sails before she gets into the channel.*

"I'll put them succinctly. Greek women of the Classical period were chattels of their men. They were slaves, they were whores, they were wives. They were creatures confined to...." She drones on, in love with her parallel structure as she regurgitates the familiar creed of the old boys' network. "They had neither education, nor access to writing materials, nor—"

"So you're saying it's unlikely that a woman could have written the manuscripts?"

Roberta lets Dr. Peckham drone on for another three minutes of denial about the authorship of the translation, all the while noticing her audience's glances at the clock at the back of the Hall. Then it's time to intervene.

"I don't agree with you, of course, but I now have to wind up this part of the evening. My apologies. I want to give people a chance to get back to food, drink, and socializing." There is a cheer from someone in the back ranks, and a wave of laughter ensues. Roberta and her sons move into the quadrangle. As they exit, she notices the Peckham woman holding court with Schubert. He is tapping his teeth with his pen, seemingly no more interested than he was in his interview with her.

It is a warm Indian summer evening and a harvest moon shines down on the low stone wall on which they sit, Roberta between her sons. Over the chatter drifting from the hall, they hear the sound of a choir rehearsing in the chapel.

"We're proud of you, Mom," Charlie says and puts his arm around her shoulder. "It's going to be a winner."

"You never know," Roberta says. "Launches of a book are like a marriage."

"I think you're about to extend that metaphor, Ma," Ed says. "Feel free. We're listening."

"Thanks for the encouragement, my boy." She touches their knees with her hands and speaks softly into the night. "Launches and marriages are like the Titanic's maiden voyage. No one is thinking about 'the grey shape with the paleolithic face' waiting in the shadows."

"Got it," Charlie says. "E. J. Pratt, right?"

"Right. They're memorable words, and I've been thinking about them this evening." She clears her throat and resumes. "The iceberg *may* drift into my path, who knows? There's the possibility of malicious reviews — like Dr. Peckham's — or poor sales and dwindling royalties. Over such a fate, I have no control."

"Okay, Ma, got that part of it," Ed says. "But you've forgotten the marriage bit, haven't you?"

"Well, it should be obvious. At the beginning of a marriage, the sky seems clear and the surface calm. But who knows whether the relationship will hit an iceberg? You've got to be a careful navigator."

"Nothing to worry about with you and Dad, is there?" Charlie asks.

"No. I always try to keep my eye on the deep water that surrounds us."

It is time then to pick up James. His office is not far from Strachan Hall, and Roberta hopes the noise of the reception has not put him off his work. His door is slightly ajar, and when they enter, he doesn't hear them as they move up behind him. He's at his computer, intent on whatever he's doing, certainly not his scholarly article, for the screen is filled with bar graphs.

"What's that you're working on, Dad?" Ed asks.

James hits the exit tab, then swings around in his chair. "Oh, it's you. Finished so soon? How did it go?"

They fill him in as they walk to the car. Then Charlie plays a CD of Stan Rogers for the half-hour ride home, and Roberta unwinds, her head on James's shoulder. It is only later, as she switches off the night light and climbs into bed beside her husband that she thinks: Funny that James didn't answer Ed's question.

5.

IT'S TWO WEEKS SINCE ROBERTA'S LAUNCH, and she is in her workroom preparing the next day's lecture for her Classics in Translation class. The phone rings. Damn, damn, why now when she has got to get this stuff off her mind and get down to marking essays she has put aside for too long? She looks down at the number.

"Hi, Mother. What's up?"

Her mother's voice seems tight as if she's holding back tears. "Elsie Tindall's husband died yesterday morning. He'd gone to the IGA to get some cans of mushroom soup so that she could make a tuna casserole, and he fell in a heap at the cashier's counter."

"Sorry to hear that. It must have been a shock for Mrs. Tindall. But he was an old man, wasn't he? With serious heart problems?"

"Yes, yes, but one thing upsets her more than the way he died."

Roberta turns the page she's reading from *Women's Work: The First 20,000 Years.* "Get on with it, Mother."

"She can't forget her last words to Bill as he went out to the car. 'Don't slam the door' was what she said. And now she keeps asking me, 'Why didn't I tell him I loved him? That I couldn't get on without him?' I don't know what to say to her."

"Tell her it's only in literature that people get the send-offs right. As in 'Goodnight, sweet prince: / And flights of angels sing thee to thy rest.' Or sometimes, if we know a person's going to die, we have space to get our lips around the right phrases. Otherwise, it's bound to be something along the lines of poor Mrs. Tindall's last words."

"Perhaps we were lucky to have a day to say goodbye to your father. His heart attack was sudden, but he was able to understand us right to the end, though he couldn't speak. But even so, I think I passed up an opportunity to say a few things." There's a puzzling note of what — anger? — in this last comment.

Roberta finds her own voice getting tight. "I remember holding his hand and telling him he couldn't just die and leave me." She had been only eighteen. "I didn't think I could face life without him. And then I met James."

"And it's happily ever after, dear?"

Well not exactly, Roberta says to herself as she mutters an affirmative and they hang up. But James *has* seemed happier lately, though he hasn't talked much in the last day or two. He's in his study now with his CD turned up loud. It's Stravinsky's *The Nightingale*. The music stops suddenly, and in a few minutes he knocks on the door.

"Off to Trin now. I'm hoping to beat the rush-hour traffic and have an hour or two in the library before my lecture." He's wearing his bike helmet and his backpack is over one shoulder. "Catch," he says, throwing the CD at her. "You like *The Nightingale*. I do, too, but I'm always a bit skeptical about the power of beauty to vanquish death. Nice idea, though. I wanted to hear it one more time."

"Thanks." She puts the CD into her computer. "I'll play it while I'm typing up these notes. You'd better get moving. It's four o'clock."

But he hovers, moving over to her desk and touching her shoulder. "How about a hug?"

"Happy to oblige." She stands up and puts her arms around him. The backpack gets in the way, and he throws it to the floor. She puts her face against his soft cashmere sweater, feels his lean body against her breasts. "Are you okay now, James? Happy?"

"Not exactly happy, but better than I was." He picks up the backpack, hoists it onto his shoulder. "Goodbye, love." He pauses at the door, looks back and says, "Bye, love," again.

She hears him go slowly, step by step, down the stairs. At the foot of the stairs, he calls again, "Bye."

"See you later," she answers. "Best get moving. Time marches."

As the front door bangs shut, she thinks about the hug and the repeated goodbyes. Not his usual exit mode, but nice.

She works away for the next two hours. Charlie comes back from his chef-training course, yells, "Hi," and then Ed is next, home earlier from his law office than usual. "We're making grilled cheese sandwiches for supper, Mom," Charlie calls from the bottom of the stairs. "And we'll let you know when they're ready."

So at six o'clock, they are seated at the breakfast-room table enjoying sandwiches and Caesars when the doorbell rings. Ed answers. He comes back in a minute, his face pale. "There's a cop on the porch asking for you."

Roberta goes to the door. She sees a tall young man in uniform. Even in the dimness of early evening, she can see sweat gleaming on his face. He takes off his cap and runs his fingers around its brim.

"You're Mrs. Greaves?"

"Yes. What's wrong?"

"There's been an accident. Involving your husband. I'm sorry to say it's serious."

"A serious accident? Involving James?" She is totally at a loss. "What has happened?"

"Your husband has passed. I'm sorry."

"Passed? Passed what? What do you mean?" As Roberta says this, she realizes that her sons are standing close behind her. Charlie takes her hand.

"Passed away. Your husband is deceased. I'm sorry."

"Dead? No. No. He's at Trinity College giving a lecture. What are you talking about?"

Ed speaks. "I think we need to sit down, Ma. Let's all go into the living room."

Roberta sits on the sofa wedged between her sons. The policeman perches on the edge of the chair opposite. He runs a crumpled handkerchief over his cheeks. "According to witness reports, your husband was riding his bicycle along Bloor Street, keeping to his lane—"

"Stop, stop, please," she says. "Skip all that. Just tell me what happened." She can feel her heart banging against her chest.

"Like I say, he was in his lane, heading east, obeying the rules of the road apparently, and then he turned his bike right into the path of a van. The driver had no chance to stop. We'll have to investigate, but at the moment, it seems like an unfortunate error in judgment. No alcohol or drugs involved, as far as we know."

"So ... he's ... dead." She slumps forward and Ed steadies her.

"Yes, I'm so sorry for your loss, Mrs. Greaves. We've taken him to the morgue. He had paper ID with next of kin listed, but we need someone—preferably a close relative—to come with me and my partner and make a definite identification of the—"

"Charlie and I'll go, Ma," Ed says. "You stay here."

An image of Edvard Munch's *The Scream* fills her brain, but her sons are there — and the cop — and she tries to hold herself together. "I've got to go, too. Whatever has happened and whatever I'm forced to see, I've got to be there and deal with it."

The policeman who delivered the news and his partner sit in the front of the cruiser, Roberta and her sons squeeze into the back, and they're off, the siren clearing the road ahead of them. Her neighbourhood has grown dark; the shadows of the big trees cast a pall over the street lights. It seems like midnight, though it's only seven o'clock. Roberta takes deep breaths, tries to prepare herself. She can't make head or tail out of what the policemen are saying to her. But Ed is scribbling notes, recording it all. Charlie has draped his long wool scarf around her shoulders. There is comfort from their warm bodies, their breath. May the trip never end.

But far too soon they are at the morgue on Grenville Street, a place Roberta has only read about in the papers — when there is some grisly death or unidentified corpse. It is an ugly two-storey concrete building, dimly lit. What a place for James to come to. She remembers his words in her study, something about wanting to believe that beauty can vanquish death. Not a chance in this place.

They follow the policemen through the smudged glass doors into a murky corridor and down black-tiled steps to a basement room where they are met by a sober-faced man in a white coat. There is a stainless steel table on which Roberta sees the outline of a body covered by a green cloth. Suddenly, she knows that her sons must not see whatever is under that sheet.

She looks up at their faces. Ed's is pale grey, and Charlie's, bright red. "Wait outside, boys. I have to do this on my own. I'll be with you in a few minutes, and that's when I'll really need your help."

"Let me know when you're ready to view the deceased," the morgue attendant says in a low voice as Charlie and Ed move toward the door. "We've cleaned him as good as we could, but it'll be bad. Take your time."

Roberta waits until the boys have closed the door behind them. The room is as cold as the pit of Dante's Hell. And the stink. A sick mix of blood, feces, and ... mouthwash? She steadies herself against the edge of the gurney. "Now," she says.

The officers move a few feet away, and the man pulls back the sheet. Over the banging in her head, she hears him mumble again about "cleaning him up" as best they could. She takes a deep breath and forces herself to look down. It's not James in front of her. It's a head, yes, but an unrecognizable head beneath its disgorged eyes and the pit where a nose once was. Holding her hand over her mouth, she tries to swallow the bile that rises from her throat. She looks at the bits of plastic helmet smashed into the face. Nothing there that she recognizes. Hard even to tell what colour the hair is beneath the gouts of blood.

"Any distinguishing features you might remember?" the attendant asks.

Nothing. She can remember nothing. Except. Except. "Was there a backpack?"

He goes into a tiny room nearby and returns with a plastic bag, pulls a backpack from it, and passes it to her. It's sodden with blood, but she steels herself to draw back its flap and extricate the papers within. There, wet and sticky, are the lecture notes. The naked light bulb over the gurney shines on the title, still legible: "Lists in Dickens's Novels."

"Yes," she says. "It's James."

6.

THE FOLLOWING DAY, THE POLICE decide to call James's death "an unfortunate accident," and Roberta goes ahead with the funeral arrangements. Charlie and Ed ask, like a Greek chorus, "Was it suicide?" Or alternately, "It was suicide, wasn't it?"

"I don't know," she says. But she does know. She goes over and over in her mind the way James lingered in her study on that last afternoon, how he hugged her and mentioned he'd wanted to play the Stravinksy "one more time." She had enjoyed that hug, thinking he was getting over his depression at last. Other days, he would just slam down the stairs and yell goodbye as he went out the front door. "Turned his bike into the path of a van," had he? Well, that being a fact, it was no "unfortunate error of judgment," as the officer at the front door had stated.

There has got to be a note somewhere, she says to herself. And she must now force herself to look for it. From the back of the kitchen counter, she takes a half-empty bottle of limoncello, pours herself a small glassful, and feels its oily-sweet sharpness slip down her throat. Then she moves up the stairs to look in James's study. She hasn't been in his room since his death, and as she pushes the door wide open, she sidesteps the familiar piles of old journals on the floor, sees the books piled, as always, helter-skelter on chairs, and breathes in the musty disarray she was always asking him to tidy up. What did the mess matter, anyway? It was his affair. She should have kept her mouth shut.

On his printer is his favourite deodorant stick, its top uncapped, exposing the smooth green head. She picks it up and inhales its sharp mint fragrance. Suddenly, she is weeping, the tears spilling down her face, her throat raw.

As she reaches for the box of Kleenex beside the computer, she notices a letter on top of the stack of Dickens's novels he always kept to the left of his printer. Her name is handwritten on the envelope and inside is a card that a photographer friend gave him.

Afraid to open the card for a moment, she looks at the photo on the front: A sunset view of a placid lake with a canoe beached beside a dock. For a few seconds, she can't bring herself to look inside. She knows that the message will not match the tranquility of the picture. She takes several deep breaths, then flips to the note, penned in James's large, flamboyant script.

Dear Roberta:

I've got myself into a mess. You'll find out about it soon enough. I don't feel up to staying around to sort it out. You'll deal with it. You've always been able to cope.

I tried to be someone else all the years of my adult life. I tried to be like that perfect father you were always talking about. I tried to be like those noble, upright, solid heroes in my favourite Victorian novels. But I'm no Sydney Carton.

Remember Yeats's line, "Things fall apart; the centre cannot hold"? My centre is broken. I want to die. I don't know when the moment will come, but I imagine it will be just like heading into a jump on a fine October morning.

Whatever you and Charlie and Ed think of me, and I know you may hate me with good reason for what

*I've done and for what I'm going to do, remember I
loved you all.*

> *James*

She puts the letter away in her purse in their bedroom. Now
her teeth are chattering, and her whole body feels damp and
cold. Stumbling into the bathroom, she tears off her clothes,
turns the tap to hot, crawls into the tub, and lies on her back
in the stifling warmth. She pumps up the volume on the radio
she keeps on the shelf over the tub. Some erudite discussion on
the CBC about Heidegger: She cannot wrap her mind around
it. But if the boys are listening, they will not be able to hear
her sobs.

Over the next few hours, she cannot stop rereading the letter.
The fourth or fifth time, through, she notes its careful spelling
and punctuation: the possessive form of "Yeats" done correctly,
the double quotation marks around the line of verse. That may
be just the norm for an English professor. Or, looking at it another way, it may not be the letter of a moment's creation. He
may have thought about it, kept it all inside his head through
several revisions, and then sat down and put it on paper. She
finds herself wavering between sorrow and indignation. Desperation she can understand. Deliberation is something else.

It's way past midnight, and she cannot sleep. She gets out
of bed, turns on the light, takes the letter from her purse, and
reads it again. The door is open, and she's got the thing in her
hand when Ed appears in pyjamas and bare feet.

"What are you doing, Ma? What are you reading?" He
moves closer. "You've been crying. And that's Dad's handwriting, isn't it?"

"I thought you were asleep—"

"Asleep? I can't sleep. What's going on? We've got a right
to know."

Silently, she passes the letter to him. He reads it, his left hand
clawing at his hair. He emits a moan, more like a howl, that

brings Charlie running. It is his turn now to read. He breaks into sobs, and she puts her arms around him. For a moment, he leans against her. Then he backs away, wrapped in his own sorrow or anger, she cannot tell which. "I knew it," he says. "And you knew it, too, Mom. Why didn't you call us as soon as you found the letter? Do you think we're kids or something?"

"How could I tell you that your father was a coward? Because that's what people who commit suicide are. They're cowards." Her voice grows louder. She can't hold back now. "He's left us to bear the guilt of his death, to think about what we should have done, how we should have helped him. I wanted to protect you from that for a few hours at least."

"Okay," Ed says. "But I'm with Charlie. We're not babies. So you could've let us in on it sooner." He takes the letter back from his brother, and looks through it again. "'I've got myself into a mess.' I think that's the important line. We had our suspicions, didn't we?"

"Suspicions?" she asks. "What do you mean?"

"It didn't occur to you that Dad might have been up to something?"

"I thought he was getting over his depression. He seemed happier lately. He was always at his computer working away on—"

"Come on, Ma," Ed says. "You had to know he wasn't working on his Victorian stuff. Remember when we picked him up after the launch, and he was staring at a screen filled with bar graphs? Did you seriously think that had anything to do with Dickens or Trollope?"

"So? Lots of times when I'm working on a project, I take a break from the document and Google something completely inane. I did it all the time when I was writing my book. What are you getting at?"

"Leave it, Ed," Charlie says. "We've got to get through the funeral. Then we'll sort it out. One goddamn day at a time." He puts the letter on the dresser.

"Sorry, Ma. Let's all get to bed and try to sleep." Ed touches her shoulder. Charlie wraps his hand around hers. Then, they go back to their rooms, and Roberta gets into bed. She sleeps on the right-hand side, the habit of twenty-six years of marriage. She turns on the radio, hoping the Australian news on Radio International, always on CBC at this hour, will put her under. But after an hour, she is still awake.

There is a chemical solution to this, she thinks, getting up and going into the bathroom to retrieve the lorazepam tablets James took in the early days after Bucephalus's death. Where are the damn things? She spies them on the top shelf of the bathroom cabinet. She moves the stool close to the cabinet and climbs up. The little bottle is jammed to one side of the shelf, almost invisible for the wall of soap that surrounds it: Ivory, James's favourite. Where on earth did it all come from?

James must have bought all this soap in the last few weeks of his life. She remembers the night when he kissed her toes here in this intimate space, and she'd noticed his dry, rough, and scaly hands. Now that she sees the soap, she realizes that he'd been washing his hands, probably over and over and over, and she had never followed up on the reason why.

What did Ed mean when he said that his father might have been "up to something?" Was this handwashing some kind of symbolic cleansing? Or is she just being crazy? She stands by the sink, head and heart pounding. She swallows a lorazepam pill, not bothering to put it under her tongue as the instructions state. She dumps the rest of the contents of the bottle into the toilet.

Then, she takes the large bag she puts aside for charity collections, climbs up on the stool again, and sweeps the bars of soap — there must be forty or more — into it.

7.

JAMES'S FUNERAL TAKES PLACE in Trinity Chapel, a few steps from where he had his office. Roberta stands at the open door at the back with Ed and Charlie and her mother Sylvia, who has driven in from Summerton. She looks at the huge stained-glass window at the front through which the sunlight streams. There is a splendid pipe organ, and the organist is playing Stravinsky's fisherman's song from *The Nightingale*. It's the music James listened to on his last afternoon. The air is heavy with the scent of lilies.

Provost Witherspoon greets them. Roberta has asked him to conduct the service, and he's resplendent in a spotless surplice and a green stole. He holds a large prayer book open in his hand. They follow him and the casket down the long aisle to the front of the chapel and hear the familiar words: "I am the resurrection and the life, saith the Lord...."

The huge space is packed with students, colleagues, and friends. Roberta and her family seat themselves in one of the polished maple pews at the front of the chapel, and the pall-bearers place the casket at the bottom of the steps leading up to the chancel. Roberta has chosen *The Book of Common Prayer* because she likes the liturgy. She is not a believer. Immersed as she is in the Greek pantheon, she loves a good story, and she looks on the Christian narratives as good stories, some of them amazingly like the Greek myths. As she listens now to the words of the time-honoured service, she wishes that she could believe: "O death, where is thy sting? O grave, where is thy victory?" Beautiful. But meaningless. James's self-inflicted death has left a leaking fissure inside her that will never heal. And his resting place in the family plot in the churchyard at St. George's, in Summerton, will mark the end of his journey. Oh yes, Death is the victor.

The eulogies are given by two of James's colleagues and one of his favourite students, and the service is almost over when Roberta hears footsteps on the carpeted aisle and turns around to see Carl Talbot making his way to the lectern. Without apology and without notes, he recites "Crossing the Bar," one of the favourite old chestnuts from the Victorian Lit course that James taught for more than a decade. Carl has a pleasant bass voice, and years in the classroom have honed his delivery. Roberta listens, trying to be stoic, and she succeeds until the third stanza:

> Twilight and evening bell,
> And after that, the dark;
> And may there be no sadness of farewell,
> When I embark.

She thinks of James's decision to embark, carried out in the twilight hours as he biked along Bloor Street, and of her ride in the cruiser through the dark city to the morgue on Grenville Street. There should have been some "sadness of farewell," surely everyone deserves that, but James effectively shut her and the boys out. She struggles against the anger that invades her sorrow. Betrayal, that's what it was. She realizes that she is crying when Charlie hands her a crumpled tissue, and he and Ed move closer to her. She notices that the Provost, who is seated facing the congregation, is crying too.

Afterwards, the crowd goes down the corridor and up four steps into Strachan Hall for the reception. Roberta has ordered plenty of wine and food, and dark-suited servers are ready with trays of filled glasses and canapés. James would have been impatient with all the schmoozing, as he called it. But she hopes a convivial atmosphere will deflect uncomfortable questions about his sudden death and keep speculation at bay.

People crowd around her. Her throat is dry and her head aches and she feels bruised. She does not really hear what they are saying. The clichés slide in and out of her consciousness.

There's a brief moment when she finds herself alone with her mother under the portrait of Bishop Strachan, and that's when Carl Talbot joins her.

He does not close in on her, as so many others have done, suffocating her in their embraces. He stands in front of her, shakes her hand, and holds it for a moment in a warm grasp. His solid presence is a comfort. "Rob," he says, "you'll be able to manage?" She's thankful he doesn't mention the words "unfortunate tragedy," which she's probably heard a hundred times in the past half-hour.

"Yes." She introduces Sylvia. "Mother has asked me to stay with her in Summerton for a few days next week, and then I hope I'll be able to pick up the pieces and start again. Is Claire here today? I haven't seen her."

"She's too sick, I'm afraid. The last bout of chemo did her in. But my father came." He turns around to the tall, stooped man hovering behind him. "Let me introduce you."

Carl's father extends a brown-spotted hand and offers condolences. As he speaks, Roberta notices his flushed face and realizes he has probably had too much to drink. Even so, she is not quite prepared for his next words, which seem to be a weird echo of her conversation with her mother on the day of James's death. "It must have been difficult when you didn't have a chance to care for your husband in his last moments and say goodbye to him properly."

"Dad," Carl says, "I don't think Roberta needs to hear that. Let it be."

Perhaps the old man is hard of hearing. At any rate, he continues to speak. "I have a beautiful daughter-in-law whom cancer has ravaged. She has lost her breasts."

"Dad, please—"

"Her face is bloated from the poisons they pump through her system. Her hair has fallen out. Yet my son loves his wife as much now as he did when she was whole and perfect. I have always loved Carl" — here he pauses and his voice breaks — "but I love him most of all when I see him wiping Claire's forehead and cleaning up her puke."

Carl turns red, but he puts his arm around his father's shoulders. "Thank you, Dad. I don't think Roberta needs to know all this now, though. Shall I get your coat and we'll go home?"

"Let me make my point, son." Mr. Talbot's voice is loud now. It attracts the attention of the groups nearby who stop their chattering to listen. But he goes on, heedless. "You will have guilt, my dear, because you were not there in your husband's last moments. It's a blessing when we can ease someone into death with love and care, as Carl has done for Claire. But it's not always possible. Remember to put guilt aside, and go forward." He turns to Carl. "I'll just speak to Dr. Greaves's sons, and then we'll go home."

"Sorry about that, Rob," Carl says, as his father moves off. "He makes me into a saint, and some day — when it's all over for Claire — I'll tell you..." He breaks off, wipes his eyes on the back of his hand. "And if you ever have anything to tell me, I'm here, you know. You have my phone number." He leans over, kisses her cheek, and turns in the direction of where his father is talking to Ed and Charlie.

"Silly old man," Roberta's mother says, a frown disturbing the perfection of her carefully applied makeup. "I need another drink after that little spiel." She takes a glass of wine from the server who is hovering nearby.

John Schubert comes up to Roberta next. He is dressed in an impeccable grey suit, and as usual, he gives her his appraising stare. For a moment, she thinks he is actually going to comment on her black suit. Fortunately, he does not. "Roberta dear, so sorry. It was so sudden, wasn't it? You know, I'm still trying to wrap my mind around the fact that a man like James, used to cycling all over Toronto, would have such a terrible accident. So strange. How are you holding up?"

"Fine, thank you. It's kind of you to come." She tries to turn away, but he's still talking.

"Did you like my review of *The Cretan Manuscripts?*"

She's forgotten all about it, and the fact must show on her face, for he says, "Well, I know you've had a lot on your mind, dear. I said I liked the book, except for Euripida's take on the Pygmalion story, which I've always found perfect in its original form. I thought—"

"I'm sorry, John. At the moment, I'm simply not up to holding a literary discussion with you. Perhaps when things settle down we can talk."

"Of course. So I'll say bye-bye now and let you get on with it." He moves off in the direction of a server who is passing canapés on a silver tray.

"Your tone was a trifle rude, wasn't it, Roberta?" her mother says. "He seemed to me to be a pleasant man. I think he was just trying to offer a diversion with that mention of his review."

"Maybe, but I can't listen to his blather just now." Roberta hears her voice breaking. "Oh God, Mother, I'm cracking up." She looks over to the exit sign. "Just hold the fort, will you, while I go to the washroom?"

As she heads up the three steps that lead to the back corridor and the toilets, she sees Ed and Charlie just behind her. "We'll wait here for you, Mom," Charlie says. "And when you come out, I think we should head home. We've all had enough for one day."

It is past five o'clock when Roberta, Charlie, and Ed get back home. As they open the front door, they have to step around the pile of mail left on the vestibule floor. Ed picks it up and turns the envelopes over rapidly. "Quite a few condolence letters here, Ma, and a couple of business envelopes, bills by the look of them, that you'll have to contend with," he says. "But let's forget about it for now. 'Sufficient unto the day is the evil thereof.'"

"I hope you haven't got religion, bro," Charlie says. "I don't think I could handle a born-again right now."

"What's up, Ed? What do you mean by 'evil'? Is there something in that pile I should know about?"

"Maybe," he says. "But right now? Do you want to delve into all this right now?"

"No. I'll go through it all tomorrow." She needs space. When the boys have gone off to work and school in the morning, she'll have a look at what's there. She has arranged for a leave from Trinity for the rest of the fall semester. A retired prof who once taught her Classics in Translation course has agreed to take over the classes. That should be enough time to deal with the basics of whatever she has to confront.

Right now, two aspirins, a scalding bath, her flannelette pyjamas, and a hot water bottle are what she needs. Then into the arms of Morpheus. But Morpheus can take human form. If she falls into sleep, will James return in her dreams? What will he say to her? And how will she reply?

She stumbles up the stairs.

8.

IN THE MORNING, after a sleepless night, Roberta takes the mail to her study and spends several hours answering letters from friends who have sent condolences. She pushes herself at the task, tries to avoid the clichés that inevitably surface. But at the back of her mind, she thinks about the three business envelopes at the bottom of the pile and the way Ed spoke of them. Finally, they confront her. Probably only receipts, but she pours herself a glass of white wine, and settles in to deal with them — if any "dealing" is necessary.

The first envelope she opens is the contractor's bill for the eavestroughs and kitchen cabinets: fifteen thousand dollars. The invoice says, "Final Notice." How could that be? James paid for these two months ago. It had been his turn to take care of expenses. She opens the second envelope. "Takedown and clean-up of diseased mature Norway maple, including city arborist's report," and an invoice for just under five thousand dollars. And the third bill is for the new roof, another five thousand. But she has a distinct memory of writing a cheque to James for ten thousand dollars on the night that Carl and Claire came to dinner. That would have covered the tree and the roof. What has happened?

Three phone calls convince her that all these bills have, in fact, not been paid. Now she's ripping mad. Then she remembers the house taxes. She makes a call to the municipal office and finds out about the tax arrears of four thousand dollars.

"You must have received our notices," the male voice says.

Undoubtedly. But would she necessarily know? She lectures at Trinity every morning, and the postman comes at eleven. Which means that James could have picked the bills out of the mail before she got home. That is, if he was up to something, as Ed hinted at a few days ago.

She makes an appointment with the young man at the bank who is James's so-called "financial planner." Then she remembers that they probably will not tell her a thing without the death certificate. So, she makes a quick stop at the funeral home to pick it up, and then sets off in the direction of the bank. The two-kilometre walk takes her a quarter of an hour. She is so revved up by the time she arrives that when she looks into the mirror on the bank wall, she sees that her face is red from the wind and her long curly hair looks a bit like Medusa's snakes.

"Justin" has a name-tag around his neck. He wears round glasses on his round face, and his tiny office is papered with certificates testifying to his prowess. His desk and computer are the main pieces of furniture. After shaking her hand, he gestures to a chair and sits down facing her across an expanse of cheap veneer.

"So sorry to hear of your husband's passing," he says. "I read about it in the paper. We do need the formal certificate of passing, though, and a copy of the will before I can give out any information." She hands over the death certificate, and waits an interminable time for a teller to process her request to open her safety deposit box. By the time she has signed the register and retrieved the will from the box, she is ready to bite everyone within range.

Justin makes copies of the documents. "I see you're the beneficiary *and* the executor," he says, glancing at the will. "So we can probably go ahead without a probate. Now, how can I help you?"

Roberta smooths back the bangs that have fallen into her eyes. "I've received a number of unexpected bills today, and

I need to know generally about my husband's investments, though I'm aware you may not be able to tell me the whole story right now."

Justin turns to one side to look at his computer and taps away for a minute. But he does not seem really focused. Roberta has the feeling all this is just a formality, that he knows what's what without these manoeuvres. Long pause while he stares at the screen. Then he turns to face her. There are beads of sweat on his forehead.

"Your husband sold all his investments within the last two months."

She can feel her heart thumping against her chest. The room becomes a small box, and she is trapped inside, like a guinea pig in a pet shop cage. "So the proceeds went into his bank account?" Even as she says this, she knows how ridiculous she sounds.

"No."

"So, where...?"

"There's nothing left. Worse, I'm afraid. He took out a loan for fifty thousand dollars just two weeks ago." Justin pushes a box of tissues in her direction.

"You're his financial planner, I believe. Why didn't you...?" But she stops herself, realizing that it is wrong to blame this young man. "Never mind. Sorry. Just tell me, do you have any idea what he did with it all?"

"I only know that he told me he needed it for a new car."

"A new car? Did he give you any details?"

"Just that he'd always wanted to drive a Jaguar XJL, and he'd found one he really liked. Believe me, I did try to talk to him about GICs and conservative mutual funds, and I even mentioned Toyota Corollas, but it was his money, and I had no right to withhold it from him. And face it, I've always wanted a Jag myself, not that I'll ever be able to afford one. But I did understand his longing. We'd often talked about Jags before."

"Idiot!" For a moment, Roberta has no idea whether she means James or Justin. Then she sees Justin's stricken face. "Sorry, sorry, I'm upset, but that's no excuse."

"I failed, I guess...." Justin's voice trails off, and he takes back the Kleenex box and wipes his forehead with one of the tissues.

"Well, for sure he didn't buy a car — Toyota *or* Jaguar — with that money. So what do you think happened to it?"

Justin shakes his head.

Roberta gets up. Justin rushes to open the door for her.

"I think you walked here?" he asks. "Let me call you a cab now."

But all she wants is the wind in her face again. A ride in the back seat of a smelly cab would extinguish her.

Back at home, she pours another glass of wine, tries to take a sip or two, and finds there is such a pain in her upper chest that she can scarcely swallow. She spits into the sink and throws the rest down the drain. She paces, waiting for her sons to arrive home. She'll go mad if she has to keep the afternoon's debacle to herself for much longer. Each time she goes to the front door to look out to see if they're coming, she passes the family photo gallery on the wall in the hallway. There's a framed photo of James. It shows him — tall, slender, smiling — in his riding gear, his hand on Bucephalus's bridle.

The photo used to remind her of one of those old pictures of a gallant World War I pilot in his leather bomber jacket and jodhpurs, his long silk scarf trailing, standing by his Sopwith. But at this moment, at the end of this day of horrors, it seems phony, like a movie star's publicity still. She rips it from the wall and throws it into a green plastic bag that she hides in the back of the downstairs closet.

She's in the downstairs bathroom taking an aspirin when Charlie gets home from George Brown. "Hi, Mom," he calls. "How's it going? You okay?"

She hears him head for the kitchen. The fridge door opens, then shuts.

He is throwing his jacket over the hall banister as she emerges from the bathroom. "I had a pretty good day for a change," he tells her, "considering this past week." He launches into his account of cooking bannock in the open hearth at a local historic inn. It's all part of his Applied Food History course, and he loves it.

"Why don't I make us some? I'll use the oven, since we don't really need the hearth. Got any bear grease?" Not getting a response, he adds, "No lard, either, as far as I can tell. But not to worry, I'll just run down to Rabba and get some."

Finally, he notices her silence. "Why are we standing here? Something wrong?"

She tells him, tripping over the narrative, going back to scoop up some detail she has missed, at times almost incoherent as she tries to sort out the day's events.

He puts his arm around her while she's talking and steers her to the living room where they sit down on the sofa. He holds her cold hands in a warm clasp and listens, gnawing his lower lip.

"It's beyond me," is all he says, before taking out his cellphone. "Let's get Ed home early. Maybe he'll have an idea of what happened and what we should do."

Ed arrives within an hour. His face is pale, and he seems tired. His articling at the Bay Street law firm — with the ridiculous name Roberta cannot remember at the moment — is demanding, and for a moment, Roberta wishes she had stopped Charlie from phoning him. "Dad got into some mess, right?" he says as he puts his overcoat into the closet and comes into the living room.

Roberta tells the story again. This time around, she notices she has honed the narrative and is able to tell it with more dispatch and less emotion.

"You are remarkably calm about all this, Ma. I worried all the way home. I was so afraid I'd find you having a major spaz."

"I *am* in a major spaz. Charlie got the brunt of it. But right now, I need to understand what happened to all those savings he had. Do you have any idea, Ed?"

"I can guess. Online gambling. I knew something was up when I saw those graphs he had on his screen."

"What the hell is online gambling? I thought gambling always involved casinos and race tracks…"

"One of the guys who's articling with me is into the online stuff. There are hundreds of casinos on the Internet, he tells me. Some of them are even listed on the stock exchange. You just sit at your computer, pick out a casino or two or three or more, and download their software for free. Then you install the casino program onto your hard drive, register as a new player, and open your account. This guy at work is playing for fun. Apparently you can do that, no money involved, but he told me yesterday he may get into the real stuff."

"This is legal?"

"Well, more or less. Knowing Dad, I don't think he'd look into all the pros and cons. You can pay money into your account with Visa or some other form of cash transfer that you agree to. And if there are winnings—"

"I think we can skip that part of it," Charlie says.

"Yeah. Well, another thing is, they often have promotional offers for new players."

"What does that mean?" Roberta asks, though she has a good idea what will come next.

"They'll offer you eight hundred dollars, say, to get started with. To put on whatever game you're playing — blackjack, roulette, the slots — whatever. It's their way to hook you."

"So, all this time when I thought your father was working on his essay for the journal, he was really hooked into some goddamn crap game? How could I have been so stupid?" She tries to laugh, but the sound that comes from her mouth is more like a sob.

"You trusted him, Mom," Charlie says. "That's not being stupid."

"This isn't the time to discuss stupidity or trust issues," Ed says. "It's a time to get practical. So why don't we have a conference meeting — without the markers and flip charts. We'll crunch the figures and sort out what we're going to do next." He gets up. "How about the breakfast room where we've got good light and a solid table to work on?"

"Christ, Ed," Charlie says, "you sound like Warren Buffett." But Roberta is relieved to take some practical action.

She shows them the bills, and for an hour, the three of them look at the hopeless reality. There are thousands of dollars of bills to be paid, and there is nothing left in James's bank and investment accounts. The only sources of income left are her professor's salary and the dribbles from her book royalties. There is little left in her bank account, since she has paid her sons' tuition fees over the years, not to mention the horse hotel at Fair Hills.

"I think we may have to sell the house. I won't be able to swing the mortgage on my own. Your dad and I loved this place the minute we saw it, and for once, *I* took a gamble that we'd be able to pay it off. But it's hopeless."

"Now that I'm articling," Ed points out, "I can help out. You should have been charging me room and board for these past three months. I should have suggested it." He looks at Charlie and attempts a smile. "Warren Buffett would have drawn up a balance sheet long ago."

"And I'll be graduating at the end of the year," Charlie says. "I've already been thinking about jobs. Chef work doesn't pay much at the start, but there'll be something."

They look at her, their faces showing lines she has never noticed before. Charlie wipes the back of his hand over his eyes. Ed is tapping his pencil on the row of figures he's scribbled on a page. Roberta makes an instant resolve not to burden them with any more worries. There's got to be a solution out there somewhere. Whatever comes, she's got to see it through by herself.

"Know what?" she says. "I think I'll go up to Summerton for a few days. Your grandmother wants me to visit, and a change might help me cope better, see things from a different angle."

"Good idea, Mom," Charlie says. "Maybe Granny can lend you some money? But anyway, you'll suck in some fresh country air."

"Yeah," Ed adds. "It'll be the equivalent of getting out of the country. The bills can wait, and if they try to extradite you, my boss can take it to litigation."

Roberta finds herself laughing for the first time all day.

Charlie decides to go to the corner store for lard. "I'm going to adapt the bannock recipe for breakfast," he says as he puts on his jacket. "Got to get my mind off this mess." She hears the front door slam. She remembers his impossible Grade Five assignment on "The Space Age." He had put it aside and made peanut butter cookies.

Ed seems always in control. Roberta expects him to get a beer from the fridge and turn on the TV or go to his room to read a book or work on a case, but he lingers at the break-fast-room table. He licks his bottom lip and starts to speak, looking not at her but at the wall. "Got to tell you the truth, Ma. It wasn't a pal at the law firm that gave me the info on online gambling."

She can feel her face flush. "Ed," she says, twisting her hands, "you haven't got into this mess yourself, have you?"

"No way. It was Dad. Let's have a reprise of the night of your book launch. Remember we picked him up at his office and he had something on his computer screen that he didn't want us to see? The next day, he told me he was gambling online. I think I was pretty upset, but he made it seem like a joke, just something to fill in a few idle moments. So I didn't think much about it, until that night at the morgue."

"But how do you know so much about it if it was just a casual comment he made?"

"Trust me, Ma. I Googled to find out about what he was talking about. And right away, I found a site that gave me all the info on online gambling." He looks straight at her now. "You need never worry about me. I'm not going to get into Dad's messes."

Roberta is suddenly so tired she can scarcely think. "I need a hot bath now," she tells Ed. "I've had enough for one day."

The heat of the water numbs her for a half-hour, but then the angst returns. She goes to her purse and retrieves James's letter for the umpteenth time. She needs to read again the phrase that leapt into her mind when Ed was telling her about his father's confession: "I tried to be someone else all the years of my adult life. I tried to be like that perfect father you were always talking about."

Her father had been everything admirable in a man. When he had died, she had been bereft. And then she'd met James in one of her Trinity courses. Handsome, intelligent, loving, he'd seemed perfect — like her father. He hadn't even seemed to mind that she kept her father's name when they married. But perhaps, over time, he had been hurt or harboured a grudge he had never told her about. And was she to blame? Had she always measured him against her father, as he claimed?

When was it that she had begun to notice his flaw, the obsession with thrill-seeking? Perhaps at Carrick-a-Rede all those years ago. But she had prided herself on her ability to tolerate all the crazy things he had got into over the course of their married life: the rock climbing at Vulture Point, the marathon bike races, his snowboarding over crevasses at Whistler, the weekends with Bucephalus. Still, he had felt himself able to tell their son things he couldn't tell her. Had she shut him out, made it impossible for him to confess when he had needed her to listen?

Does she goddamn care?

No, she cannot forgive James for what he has put her through on this day particularly. Still, it is her own part in the fiasco that nags her as she tries to sleep.

9.

THE GO TRAIN FROM DOWNTOWN Toronto slips past the huge mall on Summerton's outskirts and stops at the station at the head of the village's main street. Roberta retrieves her bag from the luggage rack and steps down onto the platform. A cold wind snaps at her face.

Here on Victoria Street, Summerton looks much the same as it did when she was a child in this village north of Toronto. Of course, the nineteenth-century brick stores have been cleaned and the windows artfully "restored" with bits of stained glass made in Taiwan. New owners have replaced the old-timers from Roberta's day, and they have a whole new flock of customers.

Even now, in late October, Roberta sees a busload of retirees eating lunch in Thelma's Front Veranda (formerly Paterson's Dry Goods). They are undoubtedly enjoying Thelma's "home-baked pastries." The woman's an out-and-out fake. Early Monday morning, according to Roberta's mother, Thelma cruises the aisles of Loblaws in the mall, filling her shopping cart with pastry shells and cans of pie filling. But she does add some spices, and she puts it all together in her own kitchen. Charlie would be disgusted.

Roberta passes Olde World Antiques, which offers junk from local basements and attics. Beside it is Nora's Nimble Needle where several elderly women are buying stitchery kits, probably of the cute puppies featured in the shop window. Their husbands seem to have taken refuge next door in Finnegan's Pub where the barmaid serves Guinness in pottery steins painted with shamrocks. When Roberta was a child, the pub was the Chinese restaurant whose proprietor served sausages, mashed potatoes, and tinned peas. Daddy used to buy her favourite snack here: candied ginger in boxes with big pink chrysanthemums on the top. He'd make green tea, and the two of them would sit in the garden and eat a whole box in one go.

As Roberta passes the cenotaph, she hears a friendly voice. "Hi there, Roberta. Here to see your mother?"

It's Nora — she of the Nimble Needle. An attractive woman of her mother's age with a Roman nose, imposing eyebrows, and a tall, full-bosomed figure. "Put in a word with Sylvia, will you? She's a good knitter, and we could sure use some help getting ready for the Christmas bazaar."

Roberta knows that "we" refers to the women of the Eastern Star. Her father had been a Mason, as had all the business and professional men in the town, and the Eastern Star became its female branch. "I'll certainly ask her if she can help," she tells Nora, though she has a good idea of what her mother's answer will be.

"I know she spends most of her spare time at the Seniors Centre. Nothing wrong with dancing and playing bridge, mind you, but there are more important things in life. The bazaar is our big money raiser. It helps fund a lot of worthwhile projects in this town." As Nora speaks, she fingers a brooch pinned to the Persian lamb jacket with which she has faced early frosts for many years. There's some significance to this piece of jewellery, but at the moment, Roberta has forgotten what it's all about.

"Got to get back to the shop now," Nora says. "My daughters are a big help, but I like to keep an eye on things."

Roberta turns left into Osborne Road, a quiet street of venerable houses, big trees, and old churches. She passes Wesley United, a nineteenth-century brick edifice with an inspirational sign out front that she stops to read in the fading light of late afternoon: "GOD ANSWERS KNEE MAIL," is the message. Roberta sighs. *Oh God, if you are up there getting mail, don't you get sick of the stupid jokes?*

At the end of Osborne Road, she turns up the flagstone walk leading to the big stone house that was home until she married James. As she opens the front door, the scent of sage and onions wafts into the vestibule.

"Hello there, dear," her mother calls as she walks down the oak-panelled front hall, her arms open for a hug. Her mother, at seventy, reminds Roberta of Lauren Bacall at the end of her career. She has the same elegant outfits, drop-dead stare, beautiful long legs, and pageboy hairdo. All she lacks is the cigarette holder.

"You look fine, Roberta, but I've been worried. How are you coping?"

"In survival mode at the moment, Mother, but I'm okay." Roberta has always addressed her mother in this formal mode, though her father was always "Daddy." James used to laugh at her whenever she referred to her "Daddy."

"I cooked stuffed spareribs for you, dear. Let's sit right down now and eat. I thought you might want some of your favourite food."

The walnut table in the dining room is set with blue placemats, silver candlesticks, and blue-and-white dinner plates. Old furniture, good china, heirloom silver, and a solid dinner: It's what Roberta remembers as "home."

Roberta gives her mother an expurgated account of James's financial career. She doesn't mention online gambling, and simply says that he made some "bad investments."

"Like so many other people, Roberta. It's all part of this unfortunate recession. I'm so glad that I never got into the speculative stuff. Will you be able to manage?"

"Not at the moment, unless I can come up with something. I may have to downsize and Charlie and Ed may have to find their own accommodations." Roberta looks at the spareribs left on her plate. "Sorry, these were good, but I have no appetite.

I've been thinking ... could you put me up here for a week or so? I need a change of scene for a while."

"Of course, dear. Take as long as you need. And I've got a five-thousand dollar GIC coming due. I could let you have that, if it would help."

"Thanks, that's so kind." But Roberta knows she will not take the offer. Her mother has an independent life, but at seventy, she needs to face up to the monetary stresses of old age.

After dinner, she and her mother relax in front of the fireplace in the living room with their sherry and coffee. "I'll sit in Daddy's chair," Roberta says. It's a big comfortable recliner that has been reupholstered a couple of times since her father's death, but the wrought-iron floor lamp beside it, with its pleated silk shade, is just the same.

She tells her mother about Nora's request.

"Fat chance I'd do anything for that woman. Can you actually see me knitting toilet tank covers for their wretched Christmas bazaar?"

"Well, it wouldn't have to be toilet tanks. How about covers for their Depends packages? Come on, Mother, you could help out. Daddy was a Mason, and you could give them a few hours of your time. I don't know what you have against Nora."

"Plenty that I won't tell you about. Except to say she's one of the town's worst hypocrites. I suppose she was wearing her Widow's Brooch?"

"Well, her husband *is* dead, isn't he? What's wrong with the brooch, anyway?"

"As brooches go, nothing. It's how she got it that bothers me." Her mother pours herself another glass of Bristol Cream. Roberta tries not to count, but she's aware it's her third. Sylvia's voice is a bit slurred as she continues: "What does the Masonic rule book say anyway? Your father and I used to laugh about it." She thinks for a moment, then quotes from memory: "'The Widow's Brooch, crafted in sterling silver and gold plate and set with a .07 cubic zirconia, is to be conferred on all worthy

Masonic widows by the Masonic brothers.'" She gives a snort of laughter. "'Worthy Masonic widows'—that's a good one."

"Okay, so she was playing around. You've made your point." Roberta decides not to mention Nora's reference to her mother's evenings of dancing and bridge playing at the Seniors Centre. She begins to wonder if she'll be able to stand a week of the gossipmongering that seems to fuel Summerton's activities.

Across from Daddy's chair is the tall oak bookcase with glass-fronted shelves still filled with his medical texts except for the bottom shelf, which contains the mythology books he read to her when she was little. She gets up, goes over to the shelf, slides back the glass cover, and takes out a well-worn illustrated version of Edith Hamilton's *Mythology*.

"It's probably dusty," her mother says. "I haven't really done much with those books in quite a while. But I remember how you and your father would sit for hours while he read to you. You loved him so much. I think most little girls adore their daddies."

Roberta leafs through the book. "Oh boy, the memories this one brings back: 'The Adventures of Odysseus' was our favourite tale. I always imagined that Odysseus looked like Daddy. Perhaps he'd be more wind-beaten from his years on a sailing vessel, but he'd be essentially the same." Her father's image comes alive in her mind: tall with curly ash-blond hair, blue eyes, a dimple in his chin, and laugh lines around his mouth.

"I liked the last part the best," Roberta says. "I liked the idea of Penelope being faithful all those years while she waited for her husband to get back from the Trojan War." But she remembers being upset when she'd found out that Penelope scarcely recognized Odysseus after twenty years of separation. She had wanted them to fall into each other's arms, but Penelope had been wary at first.

"Married couples have ways of knowing each other," Daddy had assured her. "Homer told us that." He had smiled then at some private memory.

What were those ways? Robert had wondered. She had imagined it must be something they would recognize when they undressed. Did Odysseus have a birthmark on his bum? Or were one of Penelope's tits bigger than the other? Though she hadn't shared these speculations with Daddy, the possibilities had given her a buzz of excitement. And it had been somewhat of a disappointment when it turned out that Odysseus's accurate description of the marital bed had been the clincher for Penelope.

"I always found it strange that Daddy wasn't all that enthusiastic about Penelope."

"Really?"

"He used to say to me, 'Look, she wasted twenty years of her life doing nothing much, and when her husband returned, she didn't even recognize him. He was having adventures all those years, while she was just waiting around. '*Carpe diem*, Roberta,' he used to say to me. 'Seize life now and live it.'"

"Well, your father was a great one for living in the moment, especially at the end of his life." Before Roberta can comment on this sour-sounding remark, her mother continues, "And I've decided to live in the moment myself."

She reaches for the sherry bottle again, fills her glass, takes a quick gulp, and clears her throat. "Gearing up for confession time, dear. I've got a boyfriend. Neville's his name. We met at the Seniors Centre. He used to be an actor at Stratford, and he has a beautiful trained speaking voice." She gives an embarrassed laugh and looks down at the rug. "He may be moving in one of these days. The only problem is the smelly Rottweiler he owns. I'm afraid my attraction to him might be challenged by that four-legged impediment."

"For God's sake, Mother…"

"Well, what's wrong? I'm old enough, don't you think, to know what I'm doing?"

"Yes … but … I'm trying to wrap my mind around it. Here I am, sitting in Daddy's chair, and we're talking about the stories we used to love reading, about Penelope waiting all those years for Odysseus to return ... and you drop this bombshell on me."

"Well, haven't I been a good little Penelope? I've stuck it out for *more* than twenty years, haven't I! Or am I pathetic? Is that what's bothering you?"

"Not exactly. Oh, I can't sort it out."

"What's wrong with wanting some male companionship at this point in my life?" Her mother's voice has grown loud, and her face is flushed. "Are you worried about your inheritance or something?"

"Now that is an insult, Mother. It's a stupid remark, totally unworthy of you." Roberta gets up. "I think I'd better get to bed early. There's no point in continuing this conversation. Not now, anyway." She looks at her mother's stricken face and leans over to pat her knee. "I'm sorry to be difficult." She can't explain, can't say why this news about a *boyfriend* for God's sake, has seemed like one more blow.

Her bedroom is basically unchanged from her childhood. There's her maple bookcase opposite the bed, the tall bureau with the family pictures on top, the dressing table with the bench she sat on for her first try at lipstick. Her mother has made up the maple four-poster bed. Roberta crawls under the red-and-white quilt her great-grandmother sewed over seventy-five years before: A legacy of thousands of tiny stitches surviving multiple washings and three generations of use. The quilt smells faintly of the lavender sachets her mother stores in the linen cupboard. As she lies there, inhaling its fragrance, trying to put her mother's revelation to the back of her mind, she looks at the bookcase and remembers something she hid there so many years before. It couldn't still be there, could it?

She gets out of bed, goes to the second shelf where she reaches behind the Jane Austen novels in front. There, hidden from view but still familiar to her touch, is a tiny paperback. She pulls it out: Ovid's *Metamorphoses*. When she was thirteen or fourteen, she had taken this book from the bookcase in the living room and read the tale "Myrrha" to herself in bed. It had been her first foray into sex-themed literature and it had stunned her. She'd read it over and over, feeling dirty and excited at the same time. At night, she'd been unable to stop thinking about it and had often turned on her light to stare at its spine in her bookcase. Finally, she stashed it away hoping that it would be a case of "out of sight, out of mind."

10.

ROBERTA KNOWS THE STORY WELL now from a scholar's point of view, of course. Ovid is a major part of her Classics in Translation class at Trinity College. But the details still unsettle her as she rereads the plot. There's the young princess, Myrrha, whose father, King Cinyras, lines up an array of suitors for her to choose from. But Myrrha cannot love any of them. When Cinyras asks who she *could* love, she tells him, "Someone like you." Cinyras is touched by his daughter's answer, unaware of what Myrrha is really telling him.

Roberta turns the pages rapidly to the part that tormented her most. When the feast of Ceres is under way and the queen must remove herself from Cinyras's bed for nine nights, Myrrha, aided by her old nurse who acts as a go-between, creeps into her father's bed and indulges her passion for him. Roberta comes to the phrase that once perplexed her: "Cinyras filled her with his seed." She reads on. Since the affair takes place under cover of darkness, the king believes that the girl in bed with him is just an admirer, perhaps a lady-in-waiting, who has seized the opportunity to sleep with him. On the ninth night, curious to see her face, he lights a lamp and discovers the wretched truth. In his anguish, he seizes a dagger and attempts to attack Myrrha, but she escapes. Consumed by guilt, she prays to the gods for a solution to her grief, something that will remove her into some mindless limbo. They respond by turning her into a tree.

Roberta puts the book back into its hiding place, but she cannot sleep for thinking of the fascination the story once held for her. An idea slips into her mind. It's an absolutely crazy idea, but it stays with her nonetheless. "Most little girls adore their daddies." Her mother said that. Well then, if that is true, this idea, crazy as it is, could be the answer to her nightmare.

She could rewrite the Myrrha story as an erotic novel, couldn't she? Set it in modern times? Make the father figure not a king — that wouldn't work — but a crusader, perhaps a man like Barack Obama, on whom the hopes of a nation could rest. Or perhaps a lesser figure, a man who influences the people around him. Her own Daddy had been a crusader. A village doctor, he had fought for the rights of women to birth control information and hospital abortions.

She remembers how she'd gone into Budge's Pharmacy one day to get something or other and seen her father deep in conversation with Mr. Budge. "Look here," she heard him say, "probably every teenaged boy in Summerton is having sex in the front seat of his father's Studebaker. Get those condoms out from under the counter, damn it. Put them right out with the Listerine mouthwash and the Vitalis. I thought we'd agreed on that."

"I tried to oblige, Doc," Mr. Budge had said. "But the Eastern Star ladies gave me a lot of flack. Not to mention the IODE. I got to think of my business."

"You've got to think about what's right, man, and..." He'd seen her then and stopped in mid-sentence.

Later, as they drove home together in the Oldsmobile, she'd asked, "What's a condom, Daddy?"

He'd thought for a moment, as he manoeuvred around a couple of corners. Then he said, "It's a rubber cover that slips over a boy's penis and keeps him from impregnating the girl he's with."

"How would he get it on, Daddy?" Any penises she'd seen on statues in books seemed to be limp like rolls of playdough.

When they got home, he'd taken a prescription form and drawn an erect penis on it and explained how it got that way.

At that point, she had at last understood what Ovid meant when he wrote that King Cinyras had filled Myrrha "with his seed." And she had gone upstairs and reread the story with new insight.

"Most little girls adore their daddies." Her mother's words resonate in her mind. If it's true, there might be a huge female readership for an erotic novel based on "Myrrha." Of course, modern readers would be uncomfortable with the story's theme of incest, but she could make the Cinyras figure a stepfather rather than a father. It might be a way, perhaps a surefire way, to cover some of James's debts.

Roberta tosses and turns as she spins ideas. She hears the neighbours' car pull into the driveway next to her mother's house. Mrs. Baldwin and her "cousin" — the younger man who lives with her — are back, no doubt, from an evening of euchre at the Legion.

She remembers waking from sleep to the throb of her father's Oldsmobile turning into the driveway under her bedroom window. She had her arms around the teddy bear she still took to bed with her, even though she was twelve years old.

The ignition died, but instead of the sound of the driver's door opening, there was silence. She crawled down from her bed, went to the window, pulled back the curtains, and looked out. She could see her father's dark outline in the car. She watched while he took off his fedora and threw it on the seat, ran his fingers through his hair, laid his head against the steering wheel.

She had known then that someone had died. Who? He hadn't mentioned anyone being deadly sick. Must have been unexpected, one of those sudden midnight calls to a heart attack, a stroke, or a gunshot wound for which he could do nothing.

Still, he slumped in the driver's seat, while she danced from one foot to the other, wanting to go to him, but afraid. Afraid of the stickiness of the blood on his coat or the stink of vomit. Then, she heard her mother go down the stairs. Heard the screen door slam shut and watched her mother open the car door, reach in, and put her arm around her father's shoulders and draw him out.

Screen door opening and closing. Murmuring. Running water. Bang of the liquor cabinet door. She tiptoed to the head of the stairs, looked down through the banister where her father was sitting, glass in hand, opposite her mother, their knees touching. Roberta took a seat on the top step where she could see and hear.

"It was one of the Dorsey girls. Janeen. With her mother. They were sitting in the dark in the waiting room outside my office. I don't know how long they'd been there. I had no idea they needed me. Nora was wearing an apron, and Janeen was in her school tunic. They were both crying. It took me forever to get them calmed down before I could find out what was wrong. Finally, Nora blurted out that Janeen was pregnant. And she wanted me to do something about it."

"Oh Robert, she can't be more than fifteen years old."

"Just turned sixteen. And Nora said to me, 'If my husband finds out about this, he'd make her get married. I won't have it. The boy who did this is seventeen years old. You and I know about marriage. Kids are not ready for it.'"

"So you..."

"Right there on my office examining table. It was a fully formed foetus. Probably seventeen weeks. It had tiny fingers, like the claws of a chickadee. I rolled it up in bags and put it into the garbage...." Roberta could hear her father's voice breaking.

"Will Nora's husband find out?"

"I hope not. The girl will have to stay in bed for a day or two, but Nora intends to make up some sort of explanation. I told her to phone me right away if there was any bleeding."

Her father was hunched forward in his chair, staring down at the floor.

"You did the right thing, Robert. Think of what would have happened if you hadn't got involved."

Her father sighed then, set down his glass, and turned toward the staircase. Roberta got up from the top step and started to scamper back to her bedroom, but he must have seen her shadow against the wall.

"Wait, dear," he called to her. He trudged up the stairs, his footsteps dragging. "You must never tell anyone what you heard tonight. I killed a baby, but someday you'll understand why." He took her hand and held it. "Sometimes, you have to do things that are wrong in order to set the world right again." Then he turned away, back towards her mother who was coming up the stairs.

Her father's last words on that evening stay with Roberta as she drifts into sleep.

11.

ROBERTA GETS UP EARLY the next morning with the resolve to get back to Toronto as soon as possible and get started on Project Sleaze. It can't be that hard to write an erotic novel, she tells herself. I don't have to be back at Trinity until after the Christmas break. I've even been able to sign off on my obligations as a volunteer at the Christian Mission. But right now, I need to have my study, my computer, and my privacy.

She phones home and leaves a message for Ed and Charlie: "Plans have changed, boys. I'll be back sometime this afternoon." If they've made arrangements to have their girlfriends over in her absence, they'll be warned.

The smell of coffee and other good things — pancakes, maybe? — wafts up into the bedroom pulling her down the stairs into the large kitchen with its maple cupboards and big window. Perhaps the sunshine signals a good day, Roberta thinks, as she sits in a Windsor chair watching Mrs. Baldwin's mate use his finger and thumb to empty the contents of his nose onto the driveway next door.

Her mother sets blueberry French toast in front of her. It's always been Roberta's favourite breakfast. She even copied out the recipe once upon a time, but she has never made it. It's labour-intensive, involving an overnight soaking of the bread in eggs and milk, and fifty minutes in the oven in the morning. Who's got time for that? But as she asks herself this question, she remembers that James used to make it for special occasions: for their anniversaries, for the boys' birthdays, for Valentine's Day. It's one of the happy memories that keep surfacing, bringing on the tears and pushing back her anger over James's betrayal.

Her mother hands her a tissue from a box on the windowsill and sets a pitcher of maple syrup in front of her. "Have some syrup, dear, and indulge yourself with good things whenever you can."

And now, as she pours the maple syrup over the toast, she remembers that in Summerton, food is always the way of saying "sorry" or "cheer up." She thinks of the funeral-baked meats going up and down the street to neighbours after the death of loved ones, of the fifty cents her mother used to dole out to her when she'd had some childish sorrow, like a painful session with the orthodontist or a bad exam. "Go get yourself a banana split at Mr. Yu's," she'd say, and Roberta would go down to the Chinese restaurant and devour three flavours of ice cream with pineapple, strawberry, and chocolate toppings. The banana that supported it all remained on the plate. And she always came home feeling better.

"Delicious, Mother," she says now. "Just what I need. You shouldn't have gone to all this bother." She watches her mother's face light up with a smile. "But I'm glad you did."

"I wanted to do something special." Her mother pours the coffee. Even at this early hour, she's wearing a nice pair of tailored black pants and a bright red sweater.

There's a moment of silence. My turn, Roberta acknowledges. "It'll be a quiet Christmas this year, but I want you to come and have it with us. Why don't you bring ... Neville?" She hopes she's got the name right.

"What a lovely idea. Are you sure?"

"Perfectly. I'll even put up with the smelly Samoyed if necessary."

"Rottweiler. Not that it matters. Stink is stink."

Roberta is glad to have a moment of laughter with her

mother. They linger over their coffee, and then Roberta goes upstairs to pack.

Back in Toronto by mid-afternoon, Roberta goes straight to her study to make out an outline. She turns on the computer and gets down to work.

But after an hour, she stops and goes to her bookcase to get *Writer's Market* from the top shelf. She reads through the section on erotica, which has an article offering pointers on writing a bestselling novel that will appeal to readers "who enjoy vivid storytelling and sexual content." It urges writers "to seize your most vivid fantasy, your deepest dream, and set it free onto paper." There are several caveats: "No horror, rape, death, or mutilation." Inverted incest is not on the list. Well, that's something.

Then there is a list of magazines and book publishers that buy the crap. She decides to query George Korda at Mayhem who describes his audience as "daring, open-minded adults." Daring and open-minded she can handle, maybe — as long as they are not buying porn videos or ogling big-breasted girls in strip joints. Further thought: *Okay, I'm a hypocrite. I'm going to write a nasty little novel, and I'm being picky about the mindset of people who read it. And at the same time, I'm hoping for large sales because I need money. And to sink even more deeply into hypocrisy, I'm going to need a* nom de plume.

Back to the computer. She decides to set the Ovid story in New York in the sixties, make the father figure the crusading editor of a popular left-wing magazine, something like *Harper's*, but she will probably have to call it something else. Her agent, Marianne Blackman, can tell her about libel problems. And Myrrha will be his teenaged stepdaughter. She will give her a modern name. Mira, perhaps. The first chapter will have Mira looking out of their Greenwich Village apartment, waiting for her stepfather to come home. What will she call him? Hmm.

Babbo, maybe, or Papino, Italian names for a father figure. Papino will probably work. It will fit in nicely with Ovid's Roman ancestry, not that any of the people who'll read this sleaze will know or care.

And she will have to change the ending. Have Mira remorseful, yes, but maybe have her run away to the rain forest where, instead of turning into a tree, she could become a tree hugger.

So get down to it, she tells herself. She takes a half-hour to make a cup of coffee and then types four sentences and deletes them. The whole idea is just too much.

She needs someone to talk to. If James were here, she could tell him. It's the sort of wild and crazy leap over the cliff that would catch his fancy. But if James were around, she wouldn't have to do this, would she? She could phone Carl. He told her to call him. She picks up the phone, puts it down again. No, he's got enough on his plate looking after Claire.

Two cups of coffee later, she calls Marianne Blackman.

"You've got some reason for this crack-brained idea?" her agent asks.

"I need extra money. That's about all I want to tell you right now."

"I don't often handle mass-market stuff. That's one of the PC phrases for erotica — but what the hell. You could probably get a good advance, and I'd come in for my share of it too. Thing is, you're going to need an aka."

"A *what*?"

"You know, an alias, a ... what's the fancy term? Fill me in, you're the scholar."

"*Nom de plume*. I've thought about that. Of course, I'll have to keep it all under wraps." Now, the full horror of what she's doing comes home to Roberta. "One of the university's most prestigious scholars," wasn't that what the Provost had called her at her launch of *The Cretan Manuscripts*?

"Hey, are you still there, Roberta?"

"Sorry, you were saying?"

"You didn't read about that babe who got fired from her law firm for publishing an online erotic novel? But she didn't bother to cover her ass apparently. You don't want to lose your day job the way she did, but you'd probably be okay as long as you have a good what-do-you-call-it, and don't tell anyone what you're up to. I mean *anyone*. Especially those sons of yours. Let them have one too many beers in the pub and the whole thing could blow up in your face."

Roberta hates the way Marianne drags Charlie and Ed into this. Of course, she won't tell them, but not because she's worried that they'll be bragging about her erotic novel to their pals in a pub. She just doesn't want them to know anything at all about her plunge into the abyss.

"So get me the synopsis and the first thirty pages ASAP, and I'll contact Korda. You're right, I think we've got a good fit there, *and* he's coming to Toronto for a conference in a couple of months, so we could talk to him then. One on one. Or two on one, whatever you like." She pauses and laughs. "Bit of a double entendre there, I think. Anyway, go for it, girl."

Roberta hangs up and looks out the front window. The sunshine has died. ASAP, well that's a given, but how is she going to do it? In her academic writing, she always has a fund of facts and opinions roiling in her brain to draw upon. Maybe it will be easy enough to write about Mira's adolescent yearnings for Papino, but how is she going to write the sex stuff?

She puts on a warm jacket and heads out the front door for a walk in the neighbourhood, hoping that by moving her legs, she'll get her brain functioning as well. It's drizzling rain now, and she comes back to get an umbrella and put a long red slicker over her jacket. Off again, she decides to take a path along the creek through open fields. It's a local bike route, but there are few cyclists on it this fall afternoon. James never cycled this way. "Too boring," he said. He preferred the challenge of the traffic along four-lane Bloor Street.

And of course, the thought of James on his bicycle leads Roberta back to the horror of his broken body in the morgue and the aftermath. She comes to the one steep hill on the route. It rises on her right, and she decides to run up it. If she wears herself out, she may be able to get away from her thoughts.

At the top of the hill, she pauses, completely winded, and looks out at the rainy meadows below and the solitary cyclist weaving his way along the narrow paved path beside the creek. The leaves of the trees lining the creek have already turned from green to rusty brown, but there's not a splash of red or gold anywhere.

Rainy meadows; they are a metaphor for her. In another two months, snow will cover these fields, and there'll be another morose metaphor then. The rain is pelting down now, soaking her feet and one shoulder that the umbrella has not completely protected. She turns towards home.

It hasn't been a completely wasted afternoon. She thinks, at least I've got the "aka" Marianne was talking about. *Rainy Meadows — that will be my* nom de plume. *I'll spell it "Renee" and hope it goes over with hoi polloi. It's a good one — silly enough that no one will ever connect it with Roberta Greaves.*

"So, Renee Meadows," she says aloud, "all you have to do now is to write the damn book."

12.

IT'S EARLY NEXT MORNING, and Roberta needs caffeine. Charlie has ground some coffee beans, fortunately, and Roberta makes herself a pot of coffee. She tries reading the online erotic stuff first, but her head keeps drooping over the keyboard of her computer. The same phrases occur again and again. Several sites even seem to have the same online survey on the effectiveness of dildos in foreplay. She starts to wonder if there is any police surveillance of these sites and if her name will appear on someone's records.

She switches to articles that set out the rules for "creating" sexy stories. The writers of these have a tenuous grasp of diction. Someone called Suzy Possum, for example, doesn't know the difference between *complimentary* and *complementary*. And there's *flaunt* where the writer means *flout*. She's soon lost track of Suzy's "advice."

But at least she's found out that writers make a distinction between erotica and pornography. The former is apparently more subtle, employing the imagination. There has to be a plot along with the sex, it would seem, while pornography omits the plot. Well then, Ovid's story of Myrrha would certainly be classed as "erotica." She looks over her own story outline again. It looks more or less okay. Get to it.

More strong coffee while she centres the phrase CHAPTER ONE exactly one-third of the way down the screen. An auspicious beginning. Then she spends the next hour staring at the blankness that follows it. She feels she can handle the scenes that show Mira's crush on Papino, her anguish over it, and her rationalizations. But at the back of her mind, she knows that the nitty-gritty of the sex scenes — when she gets to them — will be too much for her. A wave of heat suffuses her cheeks. Too early for hot flashes, she acknowledges. This is pure embarrassment.

When she hears the front door open, she closes down her computer and goes to greet Charlie. Not much difference between me and James, she reflects. *Like him, I'm up to something I'm ashamed of, and I don't want my family to know about it.*

Two days later, Marianne phones her. "You've got a chapter or two ready, Roberta?"

"Call me Renee." And she tells her agent about her new name.

"Good start. But what have you written?"

"A few paragraphs, but I can't do the sex scenes. I just can't. I'm a classical scholar, and I just can't turn into a pornographer the way Clark Kent turns into Superman."

"Hey, forget pornography. This is erotica. The Blackman Agency does not handle porn. Get it?"

"Okay, okay. Sorry."

"And what makes your case so special? Didn't Dorothy Sayers have a double life? Noted scholar, acclaimed translator of *The Divine Comedy*, wasn't she?"

"I know, I know. But the Lord Peter Wimsey mysteries she came up with are a far cry from what Renee Meadows's trashy little novel will be. As I recall, Lord Peter and Harriet copulate only between the hours of midnight and seven in the morning — always fully clothed and always talking in complete sentences."

"Look, Renee baby, it's a role, so get into it. Know what I'd suggest? Go online. There's all that stuff on YouTube. I'll give you a few—"

"No."

"No?" There's a long pause. "Oookay. How about *The Happy Hooker*? You've read Xaviera Hollander's memoir, haven't you?"

"No."

Marianne's deep sigh wafts into Roberta's ear. "You've got one of those mom-and-pop convenience stores nearby?"

"There's one near the subway. I've never been in it, though."

"All the better. They won't know you. So go in there, go to the back where the magazines are, and look on the top shelf. That's where they keep all the horny stuff. Buy a bundle of the worst of them, bring them home, and read, read, read. You'll get ideas there."

Roberta can hear Marianne tapping her pencil against her teeth as she says all this. She pictures her small wiry body, the gnawed-off lipstick, and the bitten-down fingernails. There is a reason why Marianne is Toronto's most successful agent. She has a sharp eye for manuscripts that work — in every genre — and she never lets up.

"Have you any sales figures for *The Cretan Manuscripts*?" Roberta asks. "Any chance of it bailing me out?"

"Doing well, but it's an academic audience we're selling to. Paula Piper at Unicorn wants to talk to you about a popular translation for the unwashed. What do you think?"

"Great idea, but not now. I guess I've got to work on this other thing."

"So who's holding you back, Renee? Get with it. I know you'll have something for me by the weekend."

Yeah, sure. But she puts on her coat and considers how much money she will need. She has no idea how much this stuff will cost. Better take plenty. She heads out to the Korean convenience store, walking several blocks past the solid brick, middle-class houses that make up her neighbourhood. She wonders if any of the denizens of these places are — like her — embarking on a double life.

As she closes the door of the shop behind her, she pauses a moment to look around and orient herself. Then she hears a loud voice.

"Hello, Roberta. If you're looking for bargains, the bananas are on sale, and they look good."

Uh-oh. It's Mrs. Schubert, her next-door neighbour. She's a sweet old lady, rather deaf, so everything she says reverberates. Roberta notices the two store clerks glance in their direction.

"John tells me your new book about the manuscripts is such a success," she says. "Congratulations. I know he gave it a good boost in *The Gazette.*" She puts a package of hot-dog buns into her basket. "I'm so sorry I didn't get to James's funeral. My latest housecleaner has flown the coop, and I've had to deal with so much housework lately my back hurts. But John is looking around for someone new for me."

Roberta can picture her: late teens, yearning for a job, even housework, but unprepared for the fringe duties imposed by Schubert. Aloud she says, "Well, John was able to be at the funeral, and I appreciated that." *Liar, liar, pants on fire.*

While Mrs. Schubert is paying for her groceries, Roberta makes a pretence of studying the bananas. Finally, the old woman makes her exit, and she heads for the back of the store. There, she removes a dozen magazines from the top shelf and takes them to the cash register where she manages to stare down the pimply adolescent behind the counter who asks, "Don't you want the bananas?"

The magazines are in a pile on the counter, and she's just retrieving a folded plastic bag from her purse when she hears the door open and in walks Mrs. Schubert again. She's holding a sales slip.

"I just came back because you've charged me for two packages of buns. I only purchased one." As she says this, she looks at Roberta and the magazines that are still on the counter.

Mrs. Schubert makes no comment, but Roberta knows she's taken in the titles. And there's no way she could miss that top cover showing two women with their tongues in each other's mouths. She takes her refund and leaves for the second time, saying goodbye over her shoulder.

Roberta gets her purchases stashed away, but all the while she is thinking: What if Mrs. Schubert tells her son what I am doing? It's bizarre enough that I can certainly see her commenting to him. But if the book gets published, will he connect Renee Meadows with Roberta Greaves? Probably not.

Roberta moves towards the door of the shop, and just as she's closing it behind her, she hears the clerks laugh. She is painfully aware of how she must look to those kids. Middle-aged, respectable, wearing an ankle-length black coat, like a priest's soutane, and polished high-heeled leather boots, she's everyone's stereotype of the uptight WASP. Suddenly, she is as angry as she is embarrassed. She turns around, walks back in, *click click click* to the counter. She fishes into her bag and pulls out the first magazine her hand touches. When she looks at it, she sees its title, *Big Ones*.

"Just remembered I've read this already," she says to the youth with the rotten teeth. She slaps it down in front of him along with her eight-inch cash receipt. "I need a refund."

Back home, she catches a glimpse of herself in the hall mirror. Her cheeks are very red from the stresses of that excursion. And they get even redder as she ploughs through the sordid, poorly written stories that unfold in the magazines she's bought. Each of the wretched things can be summarized in three words: *bang, bang, bang.*

But by the end of the day, fuelled by six cups of coffee and a glass of white wine, she's written the first chapter of *Mira*. As she reads it over, she wonders how she could have actually put those words onto her screen. "Gross," she says out loud. It's a word she's borrowed from her Trinity students, and it's exactly right. Probably she could follow it up with one of the phrases her street kids enjoy using: "Yes, it's a piece of shit." But she's on a roll now. There's something weirdly exhilarating about breaking loose from the carefully argued content of her usual research papers. She's got the thing started, and it's going to be full steam ahead to the shitty conclusion.

CHAPTER ONE: WAITING FOR PAPINO

Mira stretches herself full length on the living-room rug of her stepfather's Greenwich Village apartment in Manhattan. Beside her, just above her eye level, his two Lab retrievers are having fun. Bud, the yellow one, is humping Queenie, the black one.

"Hey, cut it out," Mira says. "She's your daughter." She waves her book at them. But they ignore her. Bud keeps at it, making a strange kind of ongoing comment, halfway between whine and woof.

"*Woo, woo, woo, woo, woo, woo, woo, woo.*"

"*Huffa, huffa, huffa, huffa,*" from Queenie.

Mira puts down her book and watches. She is so close to them she can see Bud's long pink thing pushing into Queenie's bum. Yes, Bud is humping his very own daughter in the slanting light of a late September afternoon. But no one seems to care. Except perhaps Flossie, the housekeeper, who may have to wipe up some doggy mess afterwards.

There will be nothing in the papers to record the event. No headlines blasting from *The New York Times*: "Incest Scandal in Prominent Publisher's Pad." No dumb journalist rushing to gather the juicy details in order to write a novel. Maybe something like *Lolita*, the one she's just finished reading. All about a thirteen-year-old girl humping her stepfather. Or vice versa. Some good bits, but too many boring words, and not enough hot stuff. Animals can just go ahead and have their fun without words. It is so easy for animals.

Outside, in the street below, Mira hears shouts. She moves to the open window and looks down. A crowd of young women are waving placards. Some wear blue jeans and Indian cotton tops; some are in gypsy dresses and hand-knit shawls. She has seen these groupies outside the window a dozen times before. She is sick of their dumb placards: ROLL JOINTS NOT TANKS; DEAD DROP;

JOHNSON IS A MORRON; WAR — IT AIN'T PEACEFUL; SMOKE POT, NOT PEOPLE; LBJ IS A FASHIST PIG; and a new one, DO WE REALLY NEED A WARGASM? "God," Mira says.

A taxi pulls to the curb, and a tall, slender man with curly brown hair climbs out of the back seat. Papino, of course, just home from his day at *The New Socialist*. He is wearing that elegant Italian three-buttoned suit and the blue tie she'd picked out special for his birthday because it matches his eyes. She has only a glimpse, then loses sight of him as the crowd closes in. Kisses. Hugs. Screams. Placards and pens pushed in his face for autographs. A fat slut even flashes her boobs and pokes her sign at him: "MAKE LOVE NOT WAR." All of them loving Papi, just home from his day at work and the radio broadcast he'd told her about at breakfast.

She'd listened to it just before Bud and Queenie got to their afternoon's entertainment. When Papino spoke, when he talked about his interview with Hanoi Hannah in that lovely Boston accent she tries so hard to copy, she had felt her heart go bibbidi-bobbi-di-boo. Right now, she can smell armpits. She turns around to see Flossie standing just behind her, her hair a frizzy mess as usual. "Man, your stepdaddy sure is a hunk," she says, grinning at Mira.

Mira slams the window shut. "Go get his bottle of champagne ready."

"Shut your face, girl. You ain't payin' my wages."

But a minute later, Mira hears the fridge door slam, and then the pop of the cork. She backs away from the window, catches her reflection in the ornate gold-framed mirror above the mantel. Tall, with black hair and black eyes. Papi likes dark-haired women. Her dead mother, gone now for so many years Mira can barely remember her, had dark hair. No need to worry about Mama getting in the way now. She has Papi all to herself. Her Italian friend Gina from school calls her brother her "bambino." Gina told her the word means "baby." So she, Mira, has made up a little rhyme to sing when Papi comes through the door: "Dearest Papino, I'm your darling bambino." Then she'll give him a squeeze, and things may progress from there.

The dogs are no longer on the Persian rug. Now, they are standing at the door, ears perked, tails flashing back and forth.

Everyone, it seems, is waiting for Papino.

13.

ROBERTA LIES IN BED in the mornings until Charlie and Ed leave. She can't face the questions they might ask about how she's spending her time while she's on leave from Trinity. The minute the front door slams shut, she's got her computer turned on and she's in full flight across the keyboard. Things are easier at the end of the day. Then, her sons are often out with their girlfriends, or if they're at home, there's the television, or talk about their own work. In their absence, she's got rid of all the magazines, two by two, slipping them into the recycling box in the shopping area two blocks from the house. By the end of five weeks, she's finished the manuscript.

It's December now, two weeks since she's sent the damn thing to Marianne to forward to George Korda, and she's slopping around in her old blue flannel bathrobe when the front doorbell rings. It's the postman with a registered letter from the contractor to whom she owes fifteen thousand dollars. Tearing it open, she finds his threat to take legal action unless there is an initial down payment of five thousand within seven days.

Suddenly desperate for caffeine overload, she looks in the fridge. No ground coffee left, and she can't fuss about getting out the grinder. She pours some boiling water over Nescafé and sits down at the breakfast-room table. Perhaps she could put her principles aside — but hasn't she done that already? — and take her mother up on her offer of the GIC. Not that five thousand dollars would help much. Or maybe she should take a second mortgage on the house.... Damn it, the sleazy novel was supposed to solve these problems. But of course, she can't expect instant feedback from George Korda at Mayhem. These things usually take several months. Meantime, it seems, James's legacy is falling on her head.

The phone rings.

"Guess what? He says he wants to meet us."

"Who?" It would be pleasant if Marianne could slide into a conversation with an introductory word or two.

"Who do you think?"

The penny drops. "That's good. Just what I need to hear right now. So what's next?"

"He's coming to the Delta Chelsea at the end of the week. He's the keynote speaker at a conference of romance writers. And he wants to see us, probably has some thoughts on the manuscript. Suggests dinner on Saturday night."

"Oh my God. I'm not sure I can face George Korda now. Sorry. Can you handle it?"

"I could, but I don't think you should turn chicken at this point. I don't know what he wants, but you've got to pull yourself together and speak to the guy. A little oil, you know what I mean? I'll go with you, but I just can't tell him you don't want to see him. He must like the book or he wouldn't bother. Come on, Roberta. The worst is over. You've written it, and now you can suck it up and do what's necessary."

"You make me sound like a prostitute."

"So who needs the money?"

"Okay, okay. Where and when?"

Roberta meets Marianne in the lobby of the Delta Chelsea on Saturday evening. Marianne is wearing her well-made but frumpy brown suit, a worn camel-hair topcoat and a pair of low-heeled pumps, and Roberta finds this reassuring. Makes the evening seem like just another business interview. She herself has not gone to any special bother with her appearance. She's wearing a long bright red silk scarf, black pantsuit and patent boots, and a black coat. She hopes that no one in the lobby will find anything about her that might remotely link her to a writer of erotic fiction. In her mind's eye, she imagines Renee Meadows in a too-tight skirt, smudged blue eyeshadow, and bling.

She and Marianne have barely exchanged greetings when the elevator door nearby opens, and a short man in a short trench coat steps out, looks around, and walks over to them. He has long messy white hair scooped back in a ponytail.

"It's Korda," Marianne whispers. "He mentioned ponytail and I mentioned brown suit. Just keep your mouth shut and let me handle things, okay? I hear he's tough."

"Call me George," Korda says as he introduces himself and shakes hands. He doesn't fit Marianne's initial description of him. He has a jolly red face and a bit of a gut, and if it weren't for the ponytail, he'd be a dead ringer for Santa Claus. "Now, how about a drink at the bar here before we go to dinner at that fancy joint across the street?"

As he says this, he puts his hand on Roberta's elbow and steers her in the direction of the small, dimly lit room off the lobby. Marianne tags along after them, and for a moment, Roberta wonders if the evening is going to be just between her and Korda, with Marianne as an unnecessary accessory.

Roberta hopes to sit in a dark corner, but Korda leads them to a semicircular booth in the middle of the room and indicates that Roberta is to slide in first. He follows, so that he is in the middle, with Marianne on his right side.

The bar is noisy, so that it's impossible to exchange anything but pleasantries, and at first Roberta welcomes the din. If only the whole evening could be this way. But then she thinks, I've got to get it over with, so let's get on with it. She drains her glass of white wine and notices that Marianne has finished her pot of green tea.

Korda appears totally at ease and is taking his time over his martini.

"Shall we move on now to the restaurant where it will be easier to talk?" Marianne says.

Korda finishes his drink in two gulps. "Okay by me."

They are just sliding into their coats when a familiar figure passes their booth. It is John Schubert, resplendent in a long leather overcoat with a cashmere scarf looped artistically at his throat. He is holding a pair of gloves at Roberta's eye level, and she can see that they are brand new, stiff, and shiny as if they have just come from a box.

"Roberta, dear, what are you doing here?" His voice rises above the chatter. Then he looks at Korda. "And with the Emir of Erotica, no less?" He reaches across Marianne to shake hands with Korda. Then he takes a second look at the agent. "And the president of the Blackman Agency is here too. Looks like some important business is being transacted, *n'est-ce pas*? Or am I off base?"

"Just having a drink with friends, as you see," Marianne says. "Nothing serious."

"And what are *you* doing here, John?" Roberta asks.

"Wish I could say 'having a drink with friends.' But I've just come from upstairs where I had an interview with Lola Lancey. A bit like listening to Lady Gaga, but don't quote me on that one. Just be sure to read my upcoming review in *The Gazette*."

Korda leans forward. "You mean that Lola Lancey writes bad romance, is that what you're implying? She's one of my best writers, and I think I'm a good judge." He pauses and then adds, "*N'est-ce pas?*"

Oh, Korda, please, please keep your mouth shut. Schubert is already sniffing something out and any sarcastic commentary will only egg him on. But at the same time, Roberta admires the finesse with which the publisher has challenged Schubert. She likes the way he's put that tiny edge in his voice with the last phrase. And she has to concede that he's with-it enough to recognize Schubert's smartass reference to Lady Gaga's song, "Bad Romance." Charlie had filled her in on it, thank goodness. Otherwise, the whole interchange would have gone sailing right over her head.

"Oh, no offence intended, I assure you," Schubert is saying. He slaps his gloves against the tabletop. "So I'll just say bye-bye now, and let you get on with *whatever*." He gives an airy wave and moves in the direction of the lobby.

Korda helps Roberta with her coat, then does the same for Marianne. "Well, let's get on with *whatever*, like that son-of-a-bitch said." He looks at Roberta. "Sorry, maybe the guy is your best friend?"

"No, but he's Toronto's best critic and I respect that. There are book reviewers in this city that would find writers like the ones you publish beneath their radar." She doesn't mention that Schubert may very well get "inspiration" from Korda's writers for his goings-on with his mother's young housecleaner. Or cleaners. There's been a new one this last month.

"Oh, well then, excuse me. You're saying I should feel grateful to be called the 'Emir of Erotica'?"

The evening is going badly, but what did she expect? There's silence as the three of them jaywalk across the street to Angelo's. It's an expensive restaurant much favoured by overweight tourists who want "a good American steak." Its décor is nineteenth-century bordello, all swag and fringe and red velvet. It's the sort of non-trendy place that Schubert is sure to avoid, thank God. But Roberta knows the damage has already been done. Schubert is far from stupid, and perhaps all he needs now to put two and two together is to have his mother tell him about those magazines at the corner store.

Over the steaks — lamb chops for Roberta — they get down to business. Between mouthfuls, Marianne presses Korda on advances, e-books, reversion of rights, even translations. "My God," Roberta says, breaking in, "I can't stand it. Bad enough in English, but in Portuguese or Japanese...?"

Marianne tosses one of her shut-up-and-let-me-talk looks Roberta's way, but Korda takes her up on her comment. "You're ashamed of what you've written, right, Professor?"

"I'm afraid I'm a bit like a dog that gets off the leash, upsets a garbage pail, and gulps down a lot of stuff totally unlike its usual balanced diet of Kibble. At the moment, I've got severe indigestion — but that being said, Mr. Korda, I have no one but myself to blame for getting into the garbage pail." *Except James, of course, but Korda doesn't need to know all the ins and outs of that.* "Marianne may have told you I need money..."

"I know, I know. And *The Cretan Manuscripts*, brilliant as it is, necessarily has a limited readership."

"It's selling very well actually, and we're thinking of a popular translation that's sure to appeal to a broad market." As Marianne says this, she gives Roberta a nudge on her ankle, which Roberta translates as "watch out, dummy, or he's going to see how desperate we are and make the lowest possible bid."

Korda wipes bloody steak juice from his chin. "Look," he says, "I'm not out to stiff you on the deal. I know you'll probably have other offers. The book's a winner. I read it right through at one go. It plays right into the unspoken fantasies of my female readership, and like the compliment or not, Professor, you've written it well. Unfortunately, it can't be out for the Christmas sales, but if you go with me, I'll push it along and have it into Walmart and on Amazon by early April, latest. And, in the meantime, I can certainly see my way clear to offering you forty thousand as an advance. It's more than I'd normally offer, but I know a good sell when I read it. How's that?"

Marianne speaks up before Roberta can get a word in. "It seems reasonable." She presses her left arm into Roberta's side. Message received. There must be no "hallelujahs," no "my God, that's more than we ever dreamed of."

"I'll get the cheque in the mail Monday."

Roberta finds that she must say something. "One other thing I need to tell you, Mr. Korda."

"George, please." But there is no enthusiasm in the words.

"I need to have your commitment to keeping Renee Meadows entirely separate from my real persona. To be frank, I'm a bit afraid of what might happen if word got out. I have an established reputation in academe, you know."

"Got it, got it. You have my word that nothing will leak from Mayhem if I can help it. But I have a large staff, and I can't vet everything they'll say, can I? So I can't absolutely commit to absolute secrecy. I'll do my best, that's all I can promise." Korda pushes his plate away. "Now, anyone for dessert?"

Roberta and Marianne shake their heads.

"We'll call it a night, then." Korda signals the waiter for the bill. As he does so, Roberta notices the lines in his red face. The jolliness she noticed earlier has dissipated.

"Mr. Korda… George, you've treated us decently tonight. I want to apologize for…"

"For calling Mayhem a garbage pail?" There is anger here, and she can't do anything about it.

"Yes, for that, and for most of the other things I've said tonight."

Out on the street, they all shake hands. Korda's grasp is strong. He leans forward, his nose on a level with Roberta's. He's popped a Tic Tac into his mouth so that she's aware of the scent of peppermint instead of garlic. "You're forgiven," he says.

14.

ROBERTA STANDS IN LINE at the Toronto-Dominion Bank, waiting to deposit the advance cheque that has come to her from Mayhem. As the people move forward, one by one, she offers up a small prayer to whatever gods may be that the teller she has to deal with will not be Margot, the pleasant woman who often handles her business. Please, may it be the fat greasy-haired one who's new. But the man ahead of her in the lineup makes a quick transaction and she draws Margot.

"Wow," Margot says, her brown eyes staring at the cheque through her reading glasses. "This is a whopping big cheque." She looks at it again. "An advance for your work, is it? What's it about again?"

So Roberta gives her a quick summary of *The Cretan Manuscripts*, since Margot obviously knows nothing about Mayhem publications. Touch wood.

But then Margot says, "Sounds great. Hope I can remember the name of the publisher until I go into Chapters next time."

"Not to worry. Why don't I bring you a copy and autograph it for you? My gift for all the good service you've given me over the years."

Crisis averted. But how is she going to keep this sleazy secret? Has she just put herself deeper into trouble with this lie? Will Margot notice that Mayhem is not the publisher of *The Cretan Manuscripts?* God, she's got to start thinking ahead.

She should have been smart enough to have foreseen Margot's questions about the cheque and set up a new account in a bank downtown, near Trinity College maybe. Or used her bank card and the ATM.

Home again, she sits in her study and makes out the cheques to her creditors. She puts them into envelopes and delivers them to the post box on the corner. Mission accomplished, at least for the moment. With the most pressing debts now settled or at least partially paid off, perhaps she will have a time of respite until *Mira* appears in the bookstores in early April.

Pizza Nova brings supper to the door, everyone's favourite — thin-crust whole wheat with salami and olive toppings — and Charlie makes Caesars. He's wearing a pristine white bib apron, and since Roberta saw him last night, he's had his long hair shaved into a buzz cut.

"Liz has been giving me some grief about the hair for months," he tells her and Ed. Liz is a favourite teacher in his Applied Food History class at George Brown. "We were cooking Catharine Parr Traill's brown cakes in the hearth today, and she made me cover my head in a bonnet — I'm not kidding, something the Traill woman herself might have got decked out in — so for a mere fifteen dollars I've solved that little problem. I should have done it long ago." He strikes a pose, one hand on hip, the other touching the back of his well-shaped head. "Like it?"

"Wait until you get sick of it and try to grow it out," Ed says. "I'll get the name of that Bloor Street hairstylist my eight-hundred-dollar-an-hour boss is always going on about."

"I miss your darling curls," Roberta says.

Charlie makes gagging noises and they laugh. He sets the Caesars on the breakfast-room table. "I put in lots of Clamato," he says. "So, I think that with the pizza we've covered most of Canada's Food Guide: grain products, milk and alternatives, vegetables, and meat. Balanced nutrition with no sweat. Though really, Mom, I don't know about the salami. If you're serious about low cholesterol, better scrape it off. "

"Don't forget the vodka," Ed says, "listed under spiritual products and alternatives." They all laugh again. Ed has thrown his tie and suit jacket over the back of his chair, and for a moment, Roberta relaxes with them.

"Where's Dad's picture with Bucephalus?" Ed asks, out of the blue, as he clears off the table and brings in the cornmeal bread that Charlie made when he got home from class earlier in the day.

"I threw it into a garbage bag. It's at the back of the downstairs closet."

"Come on, Ma. I know you're mad at the guy, but wasn't that a bit extreme? He was our father after all."

"It's there in the closet if you want to fish it out," Roberta says. "But I haven't got to the point where I want it in the hall where I have to look at it every time I come in or go out."

"If we get those bills paid, do you think you'll ever be able to forgive Dad?"

"It's the secrecy, Ed. It's the fact that he never told me what he was up to. Of course, the bills are bad. Of course, they weigh on my mind night and day. But..." She stops, thinking of the way she is digging herself deeper and deeper into a morass of lies and evasions.

Ed brings a cheque out of his pocket, waves it in the air, and sets it down near her plate. She forces herself to look. It's made out to her for twelve hundred dollars. "I got paid today," he says, "and this is my contribution to those bills. There will be twelve hundred coming every two weeks now. I think if you phone the creditors and explain that you'll be sending them money regularly in instalments, we can put 'paid' to all this in a couple of years. So right now, we can start to put the whole mess behind us, forgive Dad, and go on...." His voice trails off, and he slumps back in his chair, his dessert untouched.

Roberta shoves the cheque back. Her voice rises. "I don't need it."

"Of course you need it, Ma," Ed says. He throws the piece of paper at her. "Didn't you just say the bills weigh on your mind? Stop treating me like a baby."

"Go easy, Ed," Charlie says. "Shit, we don't need all this anger."

What is she to do? She can't tell them what she's done, she can't, that's all there is to it. She takes the cheque and tears it into pieces. Some of them drift onto the floor.

"Christ almighty," Ed says. "This is crazy." He gets up from the table. "You hate Dad, I guess I can understand that much. But why you won't let me help with things, that's beyond me." He walks out of the room, kicking at the bits of paper as he leaves. Roberta hears him running up the stairs, and then he slams his bedroom door.

There is a long silence. Charlie pours maple syrup over his cornbread, but he doesn't seem to notice that it's about to flood over the edge of his plate. Roberta reaches out and touches his arm. Only then does he set the pitcher down.

"Ed's mad, and I don't blame him. I'm trying to understand why you won't accept help," he says. Long pause. He pushes his plate of cornbread away. "In fact, I've been wondering what's up with you lately." He clears his throat, and his face turns red. "I hope this doesn't sound as if I'm spying on you, Mom, but what's with that stuff you had hidden in your study? I went in there yesterday to use your computer and there they were, two magazines tucked under the edge of the rug. I noticed them as I was moving your chair back from the desk."

Oh my God, I thought I'd put them all in the recycling bin. Time for another lie. Or evasion. She says aloud, "Research."

"For what, Mom? What's a classics professor got to do with that crap? If you're depressed and that stuff is helping you at some basic level, tell me, please."

"I can't tell you more. I'm sorry."

"I guess I'm with Ed now," he says. "I don't understand all this. It seems like this whole family is falling apart, and there doesn't seem to be a bloody thing I can do about it." He grabs the plates off the table and bangs them into the sink.

Roberta goes to her study and sits staring at her computer. She has worked without a break on *Mira* for over a month. It's been sold to Mayhem, and now there is nothing to do except endure the fallout, which is already burying them all like volcanic ash. She hears Charlie slamming pots around in the kitchen. Later, she smells tomato sauce. *If only I could deal with things in such a straightforward way*, she thinks. No sounds from Ed's room. She goes down the hall and knocks on his door.

"Not now," he says. Then adds, "We can talk later."

Back in her study, she ponders. Maybe she should tell her sons what's what. It might make things better. Or worse. *Could* it be worse? She realizes she has to speak to someone she can trust, someone who won't judge her. She remembers Carl's words. "You've got my number. Give me a call if you need me." She can't tell him the whole story over the phone. But maybe they could have a drink somewhere, if he can find time with all his worries about Claire. She finds his number in her address book and calls him.

He recognizes her voice immediately. "Rob," he says, "I was just going to call *you*. Claire died yesterday." His voice stalls for a moment. "There won't be a funeral or a memorial service or anything, she didn't want it. At the end, she just wanted to die and be free...."

"Anything I can do, Carl? Please."

"Yes," he says. "I need some help. Can you give me an afternoon one day soon?"

15.

"DOWN HERE ON THE LEFT," Roberta says to the taxi driver. "Where the tamaracks are."

"Tamarinds? Here in Canada?" her East Indian driver says, smiling at her in his rearview mirror. "Wife uses in cooking. Very tasty."

"Good with pork," Roberta acknowledges. They're at Carl's house now. No time for a lesson on "Trees in Canada 101."

"Here we are. Don't bother turning into the driveway. I can get out right here."

Carl lives in a pretty fifties bungalow on a large lot in the west end of Toronto. Roberta remembers the spectacular beds of lilies, but now in December, the flowers are hilled up, the lawn is bare, and the tall yellow tamaracks provide the only semblance of life.

Carl has obviously been on the lookout for her because no sooner does the taxi stop in front of his driveway, than he's down the flagstone walk to greet her. In a minute, they're in the living room. "Sit here," he says, pointing to a Mission oak chair made comfortable with large, dark-red leather cushions. He has lighted a log in his fireplace, and he sits opposite her, a low, polished oak coffee table separating them. The furniture is like Carl: solid and handsome.

"I hope you like gin and tonic," he says, pointing to a large glass pitcher. "Let's fortify ourselves." He pours from the jug and pushes a square cut-glass tumbler over to her.

"I'm so glad you asked me over," Roberta says. "Not sure why you wanted me though. But as you can see, I've worn my jeans and flat boots and I've got my rubber gloves, so if it's housecleaning, I'm prepared. But if you just want to talk to me about Claire, that's fine too."

"I'm not ready to talk yet. Still have to process a few things in my own mind. But I do need you to help me sort out some of her stuff. But we'll get down to the nuts and bolts soon enough." He takes a few sips of his drink. "First, I want to hear how *you*'ve been doing. I know you had something on your mind when you phoned, and I cut you off with my own problems."

She tells him the whole story in as few sentences as possible, gulping down the gin to give her courage.

Carl twists his hands together. "Poor, poor James."

"I can't help wondering what I might have done to help him. Why did he feel he couldn't tell me what was going on? He told Ed. Why not me? I keep thinking I should have been more sympathetic, I could have maybe.... Oh hell, I'm in a dark place I can't climb out of." She pulls out a tissue and wipes her streaming eyes.

"It's the guilt, isn't it? The legacy all suicides give to those who are left behind." A pause while Carl picks up his drink again. "And the anger."

"Oh yes, that too: The pile of debts, the secrets I've had to keep from my sons, the shame of that book, that stupid book...."

Carl reaches across the table to pick up her glass and refill it. "Let me get some chips from the kitchen to go with that," he says. "I think it's a time for ingesting as much sodium and saturated fats as we can."

"We." That's the word he used. It means he's with me, whatever happens.

He brings a huge bowl of all the forbidden snacks in her low-cholesterol diet: potato chips, nachos, and Cheezies. "Dig in," he says as he puts the bowl close to her reach.

"What should I do, Carl?"

"About telling your sons about the book?"

She nods.

"Let's consider. You could continue not saying anything. Or you could tell Ed that you'll take his cheque after all, then squirrel it away in a separate account and give it back to him later. Or..." He pauses. "Or tell them the truth now."

She looks at his square jaw and direct blue-eyed gaze.

"You're right. I'll get on it soon." She feels relief. For a moment, she just wants to lean over and remove the tiny bit of nacho that's caught in the wire of Carl's braces.

"Young people can sometimes be more censorious than our generation," he is saying. "Especially if they're dealing with what they perceive as the aberrations of people our age. What would be A-okay for them, they simply won't tolerate from us. So be prepared. But you're doing the right thing. We both know that."

"And you, Carl, what do you think — what do you really think — about my dirty solution to a dirty problem?"

"You did what you had to do. Perhaps you might have acted differently if you'd had more time to sort things out. But it's done now." He stands up and stretches a hand across the table, helping her to her feet. "You know, Rob, I asked you here today because you're someone I trust. Doesn't that answer the question you just asked me?"

She smiles at him. "So, tell me, what do you want me to do?"

"I need you to help me go through Claire's clothes."

"Let's get started then. Where do you want me to begin?"

"The closet in our bedroom, please. I've left out garbage bags. Just dump it all into those, and I'll drive us to St. Vincent de Paul when we're ready." He picks up the bowl of chips and sighs. "We'll take these with us. I'll work in the bedroom with you if you don't mind. Claire kept all her personal correspondence, Visa bills, bank books, and tax info in the top drawer of the dresser. I haven't been able to open that drawer and deal with it. But with you there, I hope to be braver."

The bedroom door is closed. As Carl pushes it open, Roberta sees a large room with good oak floors and maple furniture. There's a peculiar smell though. Vomit and antiseptic, that's what is.

He must have seen her sniffing. "Would it help if I opened a window?"

"A minute or two of fresh air might be good." How on earth could Carl have stood the stink of the place?

He seems to read her thoughts. "We didn't sleep together," he says, looking down at the bed. "Not at the end. She just wanted to be alone. So I moved across the hall." He gestures to an open door across the hallway through which Roberta catches a glimpse of a narrow bed with a high slatted oak back and walls lined with books.

She opens the closet. It's musty. Obviously, the row of neatly arranged shirts, skirts, and pants has not been touched for weeks.

"She lived in sweatpants and tops for the last months of her life," Carl says. "Just too tired to bother putting together an outfit. I'd lay out a sweater, scarf, and matching skirt on the chair here, but she'd just leave it for me to put away again."

Claire was a frail little person, even before the cancer, and her clothes are diminutive and cutesy, puffy sleeves and swishy skirts, things a fourteen-year-old girl might wear. Roberta sweeps it all into bags. Then she notices a big box on a shelf above the other clothes. She opens it up. Inside is Claire's wedding dress in beautiful *peau de soie* — or "poo de soy," as they used to say in Summerton — and a long veil. She closes the box, but not before Carl notices.

"Don't worry," he says. "I know what it is. Just put it with the other stuff."

He's been sorting through letters in that top drawer he was so afraid of. Finally, he yanks the drawer out from the dresser and empties its contents on the bed. He stirs the pile of papers with his right hand. "I can't believe all the stuff she kept," he says. "There's a letter from her uncle telling her he's sending a Wettums doll for her seventh birthday. There's a report card from Grade Nine praising her progress in French. And all the love letters I wrote to her. Look at this, would you?"

He shows a card to Roberta. It's a reproduction of the Renoir painting of a pretty, dark-haired woman holding an opera glass as she looks down from a theatre box. "The dumb things I said when I was twenty-five." He reads the message inside. "'Every aria was yours.' I wrote that after I'd gone to see *La Traviata* with a buddy. It's my favourite opera, and all through it, I imagined myself singing those wonderful arias to Claire. And later, I did. I memorized the Italian for *'Libiamo ne' lieti calici,'* and sang it to her one night in a bar in Rapallo, and everyone around us joined in with the chorus."

"I'd forgotten what a good voice you have," Roberta says. "Do you remember singing 'Come into the Garden, Maud' when you were our TA in the Victorian Lit course at Trinity?"

"I guess I liked to show off in those days," Carl says, putting the card back into the drawer. "And the people I sang for then didn't even mean that much to me. So why didn't I sing to Claire when she was dying? Why couldn't I at least have put Verdi's CD on for her?"

"I know, I know, Carl. The guilt just piles up. I keep wondering myself why I didn't talk to James, I mean *really* talk. I loved him, but I could have told him that oftener. Paid more attention to him instead of drivelling on day after day, nagging him about getting out and about, oblivious to what he must have been suffering." They turn back to their tasks. Roberta fills eight large plastic bags with Claire's clothing. She takes the shoes from the rack and puts them in another bag. At last, the closet is empty. Only the musty smell remains.

"Big favour to ask now," Carl says. "Can you deal with the bathroom? She kept all her stuff in the cupboard to the left of the sink."

Roberta is almost afraid of what she'll find in the cupboard. Perhaps some squalid reminder of Claire's dying body? Or a half-empty bottle of birth-control pills? But the bathroom is spotless and smells of Javex. Obviously, Carl has done a thorough initial cleanup here.

As she stashes bottles of expensive perfume and lotion, all unopened, into bags, she remembers the bars of soap James stored on the top shelves of her own bathroom and wonders what Claire was thinking about with all these bottles. Was she trying to disguise the stink of her disease?

Carl is putting some letters into the shredder near the open door of the bedroom, and he sees her with a bottle of Armani's Emporio. "I'd tell you to take away whatever you want for yourself, but I don't think you wear perfume, do you?" Carl says.

"When did you notice that?" Roberta asks.

Carl doesn't reply, just turns back to the shredder.

"Claire had a lot of this stuff," Roberta says.

"People kept giving it to her, thinking it would cheer her up. But she stopped using it after her first rounds of chemo. You know, at the end of her life, I think she actually preferred the stink of chemicals to the scent of heliotrope." He bangs the lid of the shredder down and presses the start button. The whine of the motor spares her from coming up with a response.

On their way out to his car with the bags for St. Vincent de Paul, he stops for a moment in the living room and puts a bundle of papers down. "I'll deal with that later," he says, "when we come back."

In the hot and crowded aisles of the drop-off centre, they eventually find the IN counter and hand Claire's clothes and perfumes over to the elderly volunteer who's vetting the contributions. She opens the big box first, pulls out the wedding dress, and holds it up. Several shoppers stop in their tracks to stare. "This is so gorgeous," she says. "Someone will love it."

And then she looks at them and asks, "Are you sure now you don't want to keep it? For a daughter? Or a niece?"

Roberta glances at Carl. He's swiping a hand across his forehead as if he's about to faint from the heat. So she answers for him. "Please, just let someone enjoy it."

The drive home is mostly silent, punctuated only by Carl's intake of breath as the car beside him runs through a red light. Back in the living room, Roberta watches as he removes the Renoir card from the bundle and throws the remaining papers into the fireplace. There's a quick puff of flame and a burst of crackling.

"If I'd saved these for the shredder," he says, "I might have been tempted to save a lot more. This way, there's no time for second thoughts."

She stands close to him and takes his hand in hers, as they stare at the fire. "In one afternoon, I've thrown away the record of her life," he says.

"Except for the card."

"Yeah, happy times," he says, a sob choking in his throat.

"Oh Carl, it must be almost the worst part of what you've been through in these last days," she says. "I still haven't been able to get rid of James's favourite sweater. It's in my bottom drawer now."

He turns and hugs her. For a moment, she feels secure, purged.

Back home, she goes straight to the bottom drawer of her bedroom dresser and takes out James's sweater. It's a soft beige cashmere that brought out the gold highlights in his red hair. Got to get rid of it, she says to herself. She buries her nose in it, trying to remember his smell. It's there, the ever-so-faint minty aura of his deodorant and the soap he liked. As she breathes it in, she notices the small moth holes in the right sleeve.

She folds the sweater carefully, smoothing its softness with her right hand, returns it to the tissue paper it was wrapped in and lays it back in the drawer.

16.

CHARLIE OPENS AND SHUTS kitchen cupboard doors while he yells in a perfect French-Canadian accent, "*Pas du moutarde Dijon? Quelle catastrophe!*"

"*Pas DE,*" Ed says, from the breakfast room where he's reading *The Gazette*. Though his French accent is pure Anglo, his grammar is impeccable. Roberta wonders who would be more intelligible in a Québecois eatery.

She is cutting up apples and grating cheese, scraping the skin on her fingers in the process. She usually leaves the cooking to Charlie, and she'd really love to be sharing the newspaper with Ed, a glass of wine beside her. But since tonight is the night she is going to reveal all to her sons, she has decided to make an apple cheese crisp, hoping that everyone's favourite dessert will sweeten the news.

"What's up, Ma?" Ed asks, pushing a flap of his red hair out of his eyes.

"What do you mean, what's up?" Roberta asks.

"You're not usually in the kitchen with Charlie. That's his territory."

"Yeah, Mom, it's weird, you cooking," Charlie says. "And apple cheese crisp too. Totally out of character. So what's up?"

"Okay, okay, you know I'm up to something. So I'll tell you now." She whacks the last bits of cheese from the grater. "Come on into the breakfast room, Charlie, and we'll have it out."

When they're all seated around the table, she says, "I didn't accept your cheque, Ed, because I've already made enough money to start paying off your father's debts."

"Come on, Ma," Ed says. "You're not about to have us believe that royalties for *The Cretan Manuscripts* are that good. We know it's a niche market for that kind of literature."

"There are other niche markets," she says.

"Meaning?"

"I've got forty thousand dollars as an advance for writing a sleazy novel for a sleazy publishing house, Mayhem by name. I took an old story and adapted it to modern times."

"What exactly do you mean by 'sleazy'?" Ed asks, his lips in a tight line.

"A young girl seduces her stepfather. 'Be able to summarize your novel in fifty words,' I've heard writers say. Well, I've done it in six."

"Ovid, isn't it?" Ed says. "I remember something about it from those Trinity courses in Lit. There's a lot of really vile stuff on the Internet these days, but it's all about men violating women." He gives a laugh that sounds bitter. "So I guess this 'adaptation,' as you call it, gives bright and fresh insights."

"So now I know why you had those magazines hidden under your rug," Charlie says. "And why you told me they were for research. In a way, it's a bit of a relief to hear this. I thought you were missing Dad ... you know what I mean? I thought we were going to have to keep an eye on you. You know, first the magazines, then the male strippers down at the Fantasy Club on Dundas." His face is very red, but Roberta sees that he's trying to make a joke of it, and she loves him for his effort.

Ed shakes his head. "You think it's better that Ma was using the sleaze to furnish ideas for this filthy novel she's telling us about? You'd really prefer that to thinking that she was having it off by reading the stuff?" He turns to Roberta. "And now, having written this ... this *thing* ... have you even thought about us? About how the bespoke suits at my law firm will react if they hear about it? I could come in for a lot of flak, maybe even lose my job."

"Ed, you're being irrational. No one at your firm need know about this book. I've written it under a pseudonym, so I hope to keep the whole thing secret. I'm sorry, it was a crazy thing I did. But I guess my defence must be that I've been able to put a sizeable amount towards those debts your father piled up and left us to deal with."

"Yeah," Ed says. "Thirty pieces of silver for betrayal of—"

"Let it go, bro," Charlie says. "But remember the iceberg stuff you were talking about at your launch, Mom? Didn't you say that you've got to keep your eye on the deep water? Seems to me you may be sailing right into the path of disaster."

"Yeah," Ed says, taking a deep breath. "Straight into the iceberg."

They are all silent. Roberta bites her bottom lip. What can she say? Ed is right: The iceberg looms in her path.

"You know, Ma," Ed says. "You've been quick to condemn Dad for this mess of debt. Hasn't it occurred to you that you've done the exact same thing?"

"The exact same thing?"

"Yeah, you've gambled, just the way he did. At the moment, you seem to be winning. But the stakes are high. And I'll be surprised if you come out of all this a winner."

God yes, Ed is right. I've broken out of my safe and comfortable world and thrown everything away on a gamble. I always blamed James for thrill-seeking, for putting himself or the children at risk. And now I've done the same thing. I, Trinity's most respected scholar — at least that's what the Provost calls me — have possibly thrown my reputation away; that is, if the truth leaks out. And there's my own private shame to deal with; the guilt about that incest theme will haunt me forever.

"But at least I know now why you wouldn't take my cheque. So I guess I can't be mad at you about that any more. And if all this is another Titanic, you've got one good defence." Ed breaks off, gives a tug at his neck as if he were straightening his tabs and says in an imitation of one of his law firm's senior partners: "Your Honour, my client was simply updating an old story."

"Joke?" Charlie asks.

Ed nods, but no one laughs.

Roberta gets up from the table. "I'll still make the goddamn apple cheese crisp." Charlie rises, too, and puts his arms around her. Ed waits a few seconds, then does the same. Three comforting hugs in as many days. Maybe she'll get through it all.

The phone rings. "If it's for me," Roberta says, "just take the message. I don't feel up to talking to anyone just now."

Charlie answers. She sees him making a note on the telephone pad. "It's Provost Witherspoon," he says when he hangs up. "He knows you're on leave of absence and all that, but the Ethics Committee is having a major meeting tomorrow night and since you're Chair, he'd like you to be there."

"I'll phone him in the morning."

"What's this Ethics Committee all about anyway?" Ed asks.

"A student at another college has filed a grievance against one of the university's most venerable senior professors, accusing him of improper sexual advances towards her. She says he offered her the needed marks for an Oxford scholarship in return for sex. So Trinity is drawing up guidelines for professional behaviour."

"Covering its ass, that's what," Charlie says as he loads the dishwasher.

"What are you going to do, Ma?" Ed says. "I think, given what you've just dumped on us, you'd better stay home, send an email, and say you're resigning. You couldn't possibly serve on an Ethics Committee now. I mean, come on."

"I have to," Roberta says. "Don't you see? I've got to do what I normally do. Otherwise, people at Trin are going to wonder why I'm changing patterns. They'll think I've got something against these guidelines. And then when the book comes out, they might recognize the source of the plot and characters, and they might put two and two together...."

"Covering your ass, that's what you're doing," Charlie says.

"Yeah," Ed agrees. "A truly ethical stance."

"Okay, boys, say what you want. I deserve your cynicism." She takes a deep breath. "I just hoped your hug a few minutes ago showed that you'd forgiven me. But I guess it's not going to be that easy."

"You're serving on that bloody committee, Ma. It's hypocrisy on top of everything else. But I'm not going to say one more word about this shit." Ed picks up the newspaper on the breakfast-room ledge and starts reading. The only sounds Roberta hears now are the thump of the dishwasher door and the rattle of the pages of the paper.

17.

THE ETHICS COMMITTEE MEETS in the Provost's Lodge, the
elegant rooms at the end of the main corridor in Trinity
Colloege. When Roberta arrives, the other four members of
the committee are seated in what she thinks of as "the drawing room," and they are drinking Provost Witherspoon's
excellent sherry that he has served up in small crystal glasses.
It is such a refined world the Provost inhabits, courtesy of
Trinity's benefactors: book-lined mahogany shelves, Persian
rugs everywhere, and the Group of Seven's finest oil paintings
on whatever wall she turns to. She settles into a high-backed
armchair and catches a whiff of lemon oil from the small shiny
table beside her.

The only discordant note at the moment seems to come
from Joan Wishart, Trinity's Chaucer scholar, who is holding forth on her favourite topic: the declining standards of
today's students. She is at least fifty-five but prides herself on
dressing à la mode, as she calls it. This evening, she is in tight
jeans with a purple sweater that shows off her brown-spotted
cleavage.

"It's the stuff they read online, the porno sites they're viewing,
the violent video games," she's saying. "Pure evil. But I'll say
this for myself, I try to elevate the tone in my classes."

"Isn't that a bit difficult, Joan dear, given the nature of some
of those lines from *The Canterbury Tales*?" This question comes
from Doug Dunsmore, a shaggy-haired man whose tenacious

nature always reminds Roberta of a dog with a trapped animal in its mouth. He was one of James's friends. They shared the Victorian Lit courses between them with Doug concentrating on the "lesser Victorians."

"You're a fine one to make sniping comments. Why Lewis Carroll, paedophile *extraordinaire*, is on any university course *anywhere* is beyond me." As Joan says this, she holds out her sherry glass in her tiny beringed hand, and the Provost obliges with a second (perhaps third?) glass.

"How any professor *anywhere* could be so misinformed about Lewis Carroll is beyond *me*." Doug's prominent jaw tightens.

"Why don't we get started on tonight's topic?" Roberta asks, taking a glass of sherry and getting out her notebook. "We have to finalize the wording of these guidelines for resolving student grievances."

Joan wades right in. "We must take the stand that professors are *always* culpable in any sexual relationship with their students. The young person is *never* to blame."

"Is it that simple?" Geoff Teasdale asks. Geoff is a young lecturer in Comparative Religion. His slender figure with its nipped-in waist always reminds Roberta of the famous statue of the *kouros* in thethe Metropolitan Museum of Art.

"We can hardly ignore the Morris Shadwell case," Geoff continues.

The Provost speaks up. He is not at all like his name, being a bluff, hearty man with plump cheeks. "Ah yes, remind me. What was Shadwell's euphemism for paedophilia?"

Roberta fills him in. "'Intergenerational sex.' Not always a bad thing, according to him. I remember his comment that it can sometimes involve 'healthy self-awareness and delightful pleasure.' Those phrases got him into a lot of trouble."

"Got him fired from his teaching position, as I recall," Doug says. "So perhaps we should nail down a position that makes clear what we expect from our teaching staff here at Trinity. That way we can fend off trouble. None of us is likely to initiate 'intergenerational sex' if the rule book sets out our culpability in no uncertain terms."

"Cover our asses, you mean," Roberta says. The words have popped out before she can elevate her diction.

Doug laughs. Joan looks appalled. She fingers the little squares of shiny pink glass that seem to be glued to her neck. "I'm sure you're with me, Roberta, but really..."

"Okay, okay, sorry. But that's what we're doing. And now, if we can all agree on the need for ... clothing our nether regions, we can go ahead and work on the phrasing of the guidelines."

"Not so fast, please," Geoff Teasdale says. "Forget Morris Shadwell for just a minute. After all, some people might say that professors from his college are not quite up to University of Toronto standards. But how about one of our own? Didn't Robertson Davies defend Humbert Humbert? Didn't he point out that *Lolita* was all about, quote, 'the exploitation of a weak man by a corrupt child?'"

"Oh goodness me," the Provost says, mopping his forehead. "Surely not. It's been a while since I read it, but I didn't take that ... that message." He gulps his glass of sherry.

Roberta never believed in the cliché, *heart in my mouth,* until this moment. *Oh my God, corrupt child and weak adult, is that what* my *novel is really about?* While her thoughts are tumbling forth, she becomes aware that the Provost is speaking to her. "Sorry, you were saying?"

"I'm asking what *your* view of *Lolita* is."

"Well, I don't agree with Robertson Davies, as Geoff seems to," Roberta replies. "I'm with Lionel Trilling who said, I think, in one of his reviews or essays that Nabokov intended to show Humbert Humbert as an eloquent but self-deceived narrator who tries to con readers into condoning the violation of a child."

And what have *I* done? Roberta thinks with anguish. *Like Ovid, I've suggested the adult is blameless. Why did I not make it clear that Mira's stepfather should be held responsible?*

Joan Wishart looks at her watch. "So it seems, with the exception of Geoff perhaps, that we're in agreement about the responsibility of adults to young people. So, let's get on with the drafting of our guidelines."

More wrangling, but eventually they reach some sort of consensus. Roberta records the wording: "It is the moral responsibility of the professor to keep the teacher-student contract inviolate, whatever his or her sexual impulses might be."

"We must keep in mind at all times that the young person is never to blame." Joan's voice is shrill as she says this. The sherry is probably taking effect. "Put that in as well, Roberta."

"Joan dear," Doug Dunsmore says, "now you sound a bit as if you're Saint Paul laying down the law to the Corinthians."

"Let's just leave it as is," Roberta says. *Though what that sanctimonious twit Joan will say if she ever reads* Mira, *I don't really want to think about.*

"Not so fast. Back to Morris Shadwell, please," Geoff says, just as Joan has smacked her pen into her purse and is about to struggle to standing position from out of the Provost's comfortable sofa. "We haven't covered anything on classroom discussions about 'intergenerational sex.' Shadwell, as I understand it, got into trouble when he broached the subject in his class in response to a question about freedom of speech for journalists. That's what all the flak in the papers was about, not that I read much of it at the time."

"Think yourself too grand for the local media, is that it?" Joan says.

"Good thought, Geoff," Doug Dunsmore says, ignoring her. "So are we about to insert a clause in this so-called ethical guideline that limits our freedom of speech in the classroom?"

"What do you think, Joan? Should we cover our ass?" Geoff asks.

"Please," the Provost says, "let's try to keep this..."

Roberta speaks up. "There are tales from Ovid's *Metamorphoses* on my course curriculum. I mean the real tales, not those sanitized ones served up to nineteenth-century 'ladies,' and I refuse to consent to any written guideline that shuts down my right and my students' right to speak freely about them. The story of Myrrha, for example, whether it's about 'intergenerational sex' or paedophilia or whatever you—"

"That little slut," Joan says. "Pardon my language." She shakes her head as if she cannot believe that Ovid could conceive of such a character. One of her over-permed tendrils bounces out of its gelled niche.

My God, Roberta thinks, what possessed me to mention Myrrha? Now I am heading straight for the iceberg.

"But I thought you said earlier that the young person is *never* to blame." Doug's canine jaw parts in a grin that says, "Gotcha."

"Okay, so I was talking about real life, not literature. I'm not contradicting myself. You know, Roberta, Doug implied earlier that Chaucer was a wee bit naughty, but he's a turtle-dove compared with Ovid. I'm sure that at times you must have real reservations about teaching that kind of sick stuff."

It is nine-thirty now, and no one really wants to sit any longer. So they shelve the question of guidelines for class discussion for another meeting, another night.

18.

THE CHRISTMAS SEASON CONTINUES with its usual overkill from all sides. To have to listen to carols in every aisle of the grocery store, spend too much money on presents and then hours wrapping them, get knocked on the head with recipes for food and drink, confront the Christmas card list — well, it is all just too much. But at least it keeps Roberta from dwelling on the arrival of April with the appearance of *Mira* on every book rack in the city, probably even the pharmacies, if she can judge by the pulp fiction she sees every time she purchases her vitamin supplement.

Better to concentrate on the here and now. She puts a pile of wrapped presents under the tree, which Charlie has covered with decorated gingerbread men. The smell of the spruce boughs floods the living room.

In her memory, there is a long-ago room with a spruce tree in the corner and she is there, sitting on Daddy's knee, and he is reading her ... what?

And close on the heels of that memory is another one of another room, a bedroom filled with shadows, extreme pain in her right side, and one of the shadows is Daddy hovering at the foot of her bed. And she remembers feeling suddenly better, comforted.

Then came the ride in the back seat of the Oldsmobile down a long dark highway to what she now knows was Toronto. Nothing remains in her memory of the Hospital for Sick Children except the tubes in her ankle and that Daddy was there to hold her hand whenever the nurses changed them. She remembers the ugly orthopaedic oxfords she wore afterwards — she had to learn to walk again — and Daddy told her it would only be for a while and that he would buy her any shoes she wanted from Paterson's Dry Goods in Summerton.

And now, she was back to the room with the spruce tree, and it was Christmas, and she was just home from the hospital, sitting on the carpet surrounded by the smell of evergreen and a pile of teddy bears, puzzles, a miniature dollhouse, a doll's baby carriage, and a hundred other gifts. They were all in a heap under the Christmas tree, and it had taken her an hour to unwrap them.

"Everyone has sent you something, Roberta, to say 'glad you're well again,'" Mother said to her. "Now just be sure you keep the cards and put them with your gifts. We'll have to get busy with thank-you notes soon."

She started to cry. It was all too much. She imagined printing "R-O-B-E-R-T-A" on the bottom of a hundred sheets of note-paper. It would take a month at least.

And then Daddy crossed the room, picked her up, and carried her to his comfortable chair near the oak bookcase. He sat down, placed her on his lap, and handed her a small red tissue paper package. "Let's see what I bought for you, dear," he said. There were no bows to untie, no sticky tape to pry off. Just one rip and there it was: *Goldilocks and the Three Bears*, her very favourite book.

"Read it, Daddy," she said, and he obliged, making his voice deep for Father Bear, soft for Mother Bear, and squeaky for Baby Bear.

She laughed and laughed, safe in the wrap of his warm arms, as he read it over and over and over.

The doorbell rings. It is Mrs. Schubert. She is wearing a winter coat, but there is an inch or two of pink flannel nightgown showing, and her blue-veined legs seem bare beneath her heavy boots. Roberta pulls her into the warm vestibule.

"Sorry to bother you, Roberta. I have a big favour to ask, and I find it better to say it face to face than over the phone. Because then I can see your real reaction. So I just came right over though I know it's very early to be making a call."

"Well, if I can help you, I'm glad to."

"John is having a party at his condo on Friday. He wants me to go and he said, 'Bring Roberta along. She can drive you, and I'd be so glad if she'd come too.' He said maybe you'd like to bring a friend with you. So there it is. What do you think?"

Roberta looks at the old woman. She is probably about the same age as her mother Sylvia but far older in every way. Her small round glasses have slipped down her nose, and as she stands in the vestibule, Roberta can see, beneath the thinning white hair, the hearing aid, one plastic strand of which she has forgotten to tuck into her ear.

Well, I'm cornered, Roberta says to herself. But at the same time, she remembers what a good neighbour Mrs. Schubert has been over the years. "I haven't driven for ages, Mrs. Schubert. It always seems easier to take the subway. But I'll get the car out. I'm sure it will be glad to have some exercise. Or, on second thought, why don't I ask my pal Carl Talbot to drive us? You could clear that with John. If he said to bring a friend along, I'm sure he'd be okay with Carl."

"Oh dear, I'm sorry to have bothered you. Why don't I just take a taxi? Those subway steps are beyond me now."

"No, no. I insist. Let me do something for you, please."

Roberta remembers all the times she'd had a pile of papers to mark or an editor breathing down her neck. And her neighbour would say, "Send me the boys. I'll keep them happy." Charlie still has the necklace he and Mrs. Schubert made out of acorns they picked up in High Park. He used to wear it at Hallowe'en when he got dressed up as an Iroquois warrior.

Mrs. Schubert's eyes tear up. She wipes them with the edge of her hand-knitted scarf. "No worries then, as Charlie would say?"

"Absolutely no worries."

Roberta holds the vestibule door open for Mrs. Schubert, but her neighbour seems reluctant to leave. Her snow-covered boots are leaving a puddle on the tiles. She says, "Don't know quite how to phrase this, Roberta..." Then it all comes out in a rush. "I haven't mentioned to anyone about that day we met in the convenience store."

"Ah yes, those magazines."

"You see, John asked me if I'd seen you around, and I told a fib and said no. He's a lovely man, my son, but still he can make a mountain out of a molehill. I think it's his job. He's always searching for something he can print or 'leak' — I think that's his word."

"I appreciate your discretion, Mrs. Schubert."

"Yes, well ... I think I understand a little of what you're going through now without that good-looking husband of yours. You know, when my Edwin died, I missed him so much. I ... I ... got a copy of *Fanny Hill*. That was the naughty book then, 1968 it was, and I read it cover to cover over and over. I shouldn't be saying all this. In fact, it's probably a case of TMI, as John says. I do go on, he keeps telling me...." And with that, she is out the door, leaving Roberta to say "See you soon" to her back.

As Roberta goes into the kitchen to make a pot of coffee, she laughs out loud, mostly from a sense of relief. So, like Charlie, the old woman actually thinks she is getting some sort of a sexual buzz from those magazines. Well, at least John Schubert will not be able to *leak* that tidbit out of his stockpile of innuendos.

Still, he did see her with George Korda. Maybe it is too soon to laugh. The party would give him a perfect opportunity to pry further. Maybe that's what's behind this invitation to the condo. Maybe she had better get an excuse ready just in case. She could say that she was having a drink with Marianne, and they met Korda by chance. Marianne has a client who has published with him. "Forgotten her name," she'll say if Schubert forages for more info.

19.

SO SEVERAL DAYS LATER, Roberta finds herself in the front seat of Carl's car with Mrs. Schubert in the back, as they head to Schubert's condo on Bloor Street and Avenue Road. She is glad Carl volunteered to do the driving because really, as she told her neighbour, she prefers the subway to coping with city traffic. Besides, it is pleasant to have Carl along. As he manoeuvres into an underground parking space near the condo, he catches her glance and gives her a nod as if to say, "We'll get through this."

Mrs. Schubert is wearing patent-toe quilted pumps and it soon becomes obvious she is not going to be able to make it up the six steps from the parking area. One on each side of her, Roberta and Carl manage to hoist her up to elevator level.

"Sorry to be such a burden," she says. "It's these silly shoes. John gave them to me. I still have nice ankles, but he doesn't seem to realize my knees have gone."

Roberta takes another look at the shoes. She has seen them in the window of David's, the high-end shop she sometimes passes on the way to Trinity College. "They're Manolos, aren't they?"

"Possibly. All I know is John told me they cost him plenty. So I'll call them 'Payolas.'"

Schubert meets them at the door of his unit, his perfect teeth arranged in a smarmy smile. A few years back, as Roberta recalls, he had a mouthful of silver fillings.

"Mater, dear Roberta, and ... Carl, isn't it? I met you at the funeral, didn't I? So glad you can join us on a happy occasion. You're just in time for a personally conducted tour of my salon. No Christmas decorations, my dears, so *tacky*." He gestures with his cigarette holder towards the open space where a number of people have already gathered.

Roberta looks around. The walls are stark white. There is a huge oil of horizontal black stripes on a white background that seems to have attracted the notice of three bouffant-haired matrons. They are obviously smitten with it, judging from their *oohs* and *aahs*. "It's called *David and Goliath*," Schubert says. "Barnett Newman, of course. Cost a packet I can tell you."

"I call it *Zebra, Skinned*," Mrs. Schubert says.

"Oh, Mater, you are such a Philistine!" But his laugh seems genuine, even tender, and he gives her a quick hug. "And what do you think of my mobiles, Roberta?" He waves at a cluster of black-and-grey plastic ovals tied together by shiny wires.

"*Well!*" Roberta says heartily. Carl, who is standing just behind her, gives her a nudge.

"Now, do have a seat, and I'll ask the girl to get you drinks. Mater, do go and sit on that chair you're so fond of. I brought it up from the storage room especially for you. I know what you think of my Marcel Breuer suite."

Roberta heads over to a sofa of round upholstered pads linked by rods of steel. Unfortunately, when she seats herself, she comes down *between* the pads. She hisses at Carl, "I bet I'll have grooves on my butt." She watches as he lowers himself gingerly onto a piece of leather slung on weirdly angled steel supports that resemble the hind legs of a grasshopper.

"Not that I care, but the Barnett Newman must have cost more than a packet. How can he afford one on an editor's salary?" Carl asks.

"Probably a knock-off. It wouldn't take all that much talent, and he knows nobody's going to challenge him on it."

A beautiful girl with spiky bangs delivers two martinis. Roberta can see Mrs. Schubert far away in a corner of what is possibly the dining area, a space dominated by a sharp-edged glass table with steel legs. She is sitting on what actually looks like a comfortable Windsor oak chair, and Schubert is settling a plump cushion behind her back.

"You're a friend of John's, are you?" Roberta says to the girl, noting her designer white suit with black lapels, a perfect complement to the Barnett Newman.

"Hired for the occasion," the girl says, with a grimace and a shrug. "I'm really an actor, but you can't make a living in theatre these days. So I do my act here. This is my stage: I'm Galatea to John's Pygmalion. Excuse me, I have to take some fruit punch to *Mater*."

Roberta is barely into her third sip of martini when she sees a red-headed giantess closing in on her. It is Fran Franklin, who writes the "About Town" column for *Inside Toronto*. "Mind if I sit here?" she says and plunks her large satin-clad rear down beside Roberta. But she too misjudges the distance between pads and lands on the steel rods. She gives a squawk that causes several heads to turn. "I did the same thing," Roberta says.

"Who the hell is this Marcel Breuer anyway?" Carl says, smiling at Fran as Roberta introduces her. "No, please don't tell me. Let us just try to endure." He shifts his body to a different position on the leather thong of his chair.

Carl's back is to the rest of the room, and Roberta has no time to warn him that Schubert is just behind his chair.

"Marcel Breuer, you haven't heard of him?" Schubert stands between Carl on the chair and Roberta and Fran on the sofa and looks down on them. "Hungarian, key figure in the Bauhaus Movement, designed the Whitney Museum and..." He pauses to shake the ash from his Gitanes into the ashtray he holds in one hand before continuing: "...advocated the manufacture of furniture for the masses. But that was in 1932, my dears. A genuine Marcel Breuer these days — and I'm not talking about those cheesy reproductions — costs a king's ransom."

Roberta hates being talked down to and would get up if she

could, but she is afraid that she cannot make it with the martini glass in her hand. And there is not a table close to set it upon. Perhaps Marcel Breuer did not believe in useful surfaces?

"Furniture for the masses, eh?" Carl says. "Well, that's good. I'm glad to hear it. After working all day, they'd never have time to sit down anyway. They'd probably just go straight to bed and pieces like this chair I'm sitting on could stay inviolate."

"Not sure what you're going on about, Carl — I do have that name right, do I? — but never mind. What I really came over to talk about, Roberta dear, is George Korda. How *is* your friend George?"

Before Roberta has time to come up with her excuse, Fran Franklin leans forward. "The publisher of Mayhem? Really?" Roberta almost expects her to get out her notebook or switch on a tape recorder.

"None other," Schubert says. "There she was, Franny, having a glass of vino with the guy, right in the bar of the Delta Chelsea, all very cosy cosy — *tête à tête*. Except her agent, that frumpy woman, oh yes, Marianne Blackman, was there as well. Go figure."

"Well," Fran says. "This *is* news." She turns to Roberta, puts a large hand on her arm. "Since the agent was involved, I'd figure you have something going that George Korda might be interested in. Something the University Press would hold its nose over. Am I right? Don't tell me you're turning into a writer's version of Marcel Breuer, books for the masses, that sort of thing? I thought your specialty was Greek translation."

"Well, it's been done before," Schubert says. "Margaret Atwood is what you'd call an intellectual, *n'est-ce pas?* But dear Peggy's update on Penelope was a bestseller with the hoi polloi, wasn't it? I did like her calling Helen of Troy — what was it? — 'a septic bitch.' I gave it a boost in *The Gazette*, and it took off from there."

"I don't know about that, John," Fran says. "The masses, I suspect, would have no idea who Penelope and Odysseus were, and would care less. It sold well, I know, but hardly with the masses."

Well, they've got momentarily away from George Korda, so that's good. But now she sees them turn in her direction again. Uh-oh. Time for her little story about Marianne's client and the accidental meeting.

"Rob," Carl says out of the blue, looking at his watch. "My God, I forgot that I have to be someplace in an hour." He pokes his thumb into his lower jaw. "Broken crown, and my dentist is giving up part of a Saturday afternoon to its fate. I should leave right now. I'll drive you home and—"

"Just one sec, Carl, please. John and Fran asked me about George Korda. I think I told you that Marianne and I talked with him recently?" She turns back to her host and Fran. Keeps her voice casual. "Marianne and I were having drinks at the hotel. She was giving me one of her pitches about doing a popular rewrite of *The Cretan Manuscripts*. She was persuasive, as she always is, but I have to think about it. It would be a lot of work at the moment. Anyway, while we were talking, Korda came along. Marianne is an agent for one of his writers, so he joined us for a drink."

Carl looks at his watch again. "Sorry, Carl," she says, "I know you have to go right now. If you'll excuse us, John, I'll just see if your mother is ready." Roberta sets her martini glass on the floor and struggles off the Marcel Breuer pad. "Thanks so much. I've enjoyed looking at your extraordinary collection. Nice to see you, too, Fran. Sorry to rush off like this."

And she and Carl are away to the far corner of the huge room to collect Mrs. Schubert.

"I'm more than ready to go now," the old woman says. "Not a person has spoken to me except John in the half-hour we've been here. You get to a certain age and you're invisible."

As they gather up their coats from the closet in the hall, Roberta notices the beautiful "Galatea" pushing the Windsor chair behind a black-and-white screen that separates the dining area from what is probably the kitchen. She wonders what the girl's phrase about being "Galatea to John's Pygmalion" really involves.

Carl drops off Mrs. Schubert and then pulls into Roberta's driveway. He says, "I'd like to stay, but..."

"I know, I know. Your broken crown. Are you in terrible pain?" She laughs.

"I'll be fine once I can get home and rest my butt on a well-padded piece of furniture made by someone who doesn't want to torture you with a piece of leather that cuts your balls off. Excuse the language." He laughs too. One of the rubber bands pops off his braces, and he reaches into his mouth and puts it back on the metal hooks. Then he continues, "I must say, I admired the adjective with which you described that place. 'Extraordinary' was perfect."

"Carl, you were the brilliant one. Just at the right moment you saved me from a cross-examination I was dreading. Bless you."

"Well, I fear El Creepo will return to the subject sooner or later. And now that Fran Whatshername has been alerted.... Oh, Rob, I know the questioning will go on."

"Yes, it's probably inevitable. What to do? I'll have to deal with it as it happens. But you'd better take off now. I just saw Mrs. Schubert pulling up her kitchen blinds. It's best that she really thinks you're on your way to the dentist."

20.

SEVERAL GUESTS HAVE ASSEMBLED In Roberta's living room. She is so glad that Carl has accepted her invitation to Christmas dinner. Now, if only Daddy were here to join in the festivities. But instead of Daddy, there is Neville, her mother's new beau. He is tall and emaciated and has a white beard that could do with a pruning. With him is his Rottweiler, a large, fat animal, fierce-looking but friendly.

"Polonius by name," Neville says. "After Shakespeare's old windbag. You'll see what I mean, *heh heh*." Yeah, for sure, Roberta says to herself as she pushes up the living-room window in an attempt to air out the dog's farts.

Carl has come with his father. The old man has picked up a copy of *The New Yorker* from the coffee table, leaving Carl to make tentative conversation with Roberta's mother and Neville.

"You're an actor, Roberta tells me."

"Was. Mostly retired now. My biggest role latterly was Claudius two summers ago at Stratford. If I'd been thirty years younger, I might have done Hamlet. Know all the lines, could have walked right into the part." He launches into the "To be, or not to be" soliloquy, and Roberta retreats to the kitchen.

"Something wrong, Mom?" Charlie says. He is pouring red wine into the gravy to glaze it, or maybe deglaze it, Roberta can never remember which.

"'The undiscovered country, from whose bourn / No traveller returns....' I'm just not ready for that right now." She grabs the kitchen counter, takes a deep breath, and tries not to cry.

"We'll get through this, Mom, somehow. Consider that Neville doesn't know he's being a pain in the ass, and Granny can't tell him in front of everyone."

Ed is taking the prosecco from the fridge. "Let me get this into him," he says, "and maybe it'll shut him up. Things go better when everyone is slightly pissed." He pours the wine into champagne glasses, sets one aside for her, and takes the others on a silver tray into the living room.

"Told Granny about the novel?" Charlie asks.

"No, I'm going to wait. No sense spoiling this day any more than it's already been spoiled. I'll make a trip to Summerton in the new year and break the news."

Roberta and Charlie can hear Neville going on now about the pain in his right shoulder. "I've been having hot baths to ease the agony," he says. "And then someone told me that a cold pack works better. The other night, I couldn't sleep, so up I got and looked in the freezer for ice cubes, a package of frozen peas, or what have you. Nothing in the freezer but a Cornish hen."

"Gotta hear this one," Charlie says, setting down his wooden spoon and moving closer to the archway into the living room.

"So I took the Cornish hen into bed with me, and it really worked...."

"Wonder what that means?" Charlie whispers.

"And the next day, I ate it."

"Poor thing," they hear Carl say.

"Oh gross," Charlie says, snorting into his hand to keep down his laughter. "Really, Mom, that one is sicker, far far sicker, than anything you ever wrote."

The doorbell rings. Charlie runs to the stove and turns down the heat. "I'll get it."

Alone in the kitchen for a moment, Roberta hears Carl asking Neville about a recent jazz concert, and Neville's sonorous response is interrupted by the arrival of her sons' girlfriends.

As she moves into the hallway to greet them, she notices that James's picture is back on the wall in the family photo gallery. Either Charlie or Ed — probably Ed — must have put it in place this morning. She is happy about that. In the kitchen, she remembered how James had always loved to take charge of the Christmas turkey. It somehow seems appropriate that he is with them on this day.

Biff, Charlie's girlfriend, has purple hair and several holes in her earlobes for the planting of an assortment of small copper rings. Ed's friend Ashley is a pale spectre, long and languid, in a magenta dress with a straggly hem. Roberta has met Biff before — she plays the piano in a downtown restaurant — but Ashley is new on the scene.

"Wooo," Biff says, as Polonius farts and greets her with the thrust of his nose into her crotch. "I'm sure glad you gave me that cologne, Charlie." Her lavender scent covers most of the stench, and for this, Roberta is grateful. What's more, Biff has scarcely seated herself before she plunges right into the jazz discussion. "You heard Tommy Dorsey and Benny Goodman at the Palais Royale, Neville? Cool!" There is not a particle of irony in her voice. "And what do you think of Glenn Miller?"

"I try not to," Neville says, each vowel and consonant articulated.

"I'm with you. That guy sucks, big time."

Carl's dad has put down *The New Yorker*, and he takes a second glass of prosecco. Ashley, meanwhile, is assessing the furniture. She works in an antique store, as Ed told her a week ago.

"That's a lovely secretary," she says. "What's its provenance?"

Ed's allergies have been triggered by Biff's perfume. He sneezes and gropes for a tissue in his pocket. "If you mean who did it belong to, it was my great-grandfather's."

"What a beautiful pediment! Jacques and Hay, I'm sure. Probably carved by the master, Charles Rogers." Her pale face flushes with excitement. "Okay if I pull out this drawer?" she asks Roberta.

Not really waiting for Roberta's "sure," she opens it, uncovering a pile of old papers that spill onto the rug.

"Best not to snoop, dear." Roberta's mother speaks for the first time. "Remember Bluebeard's wife?"

Oh whatever gods there be, deliver me from family Christmases. But just as she is thinking this, Charlie creates a diversion by bringing in the turkey, burnished gold, on the Limoges platter that James purchased in an antique store in Summerton on one of their visits to her mother after Daddy's death. She remembers James's smile as he ran his fingers over the tiny pink roses and gilt edge. But that image erodes into the vision of him hunched over the keyboard of his computer, tapping away the family finances.

They all sit down at the dining-room table, and Ed goes into the kitchen and emerges with silver entrée dishes of buttery squash and whipped potatoes.

"Yum," Carl says.

Now comes the moment that Roberta has not planned for. Who is to carve? There's that empty space where James once presided. A moment of silence, and then Ed moves to the head of the table. "Time for '*Agimus tibi*,' Ma," he says gently, positioning himself in front of the turkey and picking up the carving set.

She starts bravely. "*Agimus tibi gratias, Deus omnipotens...*" and then she can get no further. Her tears flow, and everyone is witness. Not a chance of anyone pretending not to notice.

"Christmases can be difficult, Dr. Greaves," Carl's father says. "We understand, don't we, Carl?"

"My wife Claire died recently," Carl explains to the guests. He takes a handkerchief from his suit pocket and wipes his nose. "I'm having a hard time not to cry, too."

Charlie fills everyone's glasses with Pinot Grigio, and Ed shifts the focus by asking, "Dark meat or white? Dressing?"

Unlike Carl, however, Roberta is not at this moment mourning a lost spouse. It's Daddy she's thinking of. Of her first trip home from Trinity College at Thanksgiving time, and how she'd tried out the Latin grace she'd learned.

Her father had just risen to carve the turkey. Knife and fork in hand, he had listened to her quavering voice as she stumbled over some of the words, not sure she was getting them right. Then he had smiled at her and said, "My darling daughter, what a lovely blessing."

By the time Ed has finished carving, she's got herself in hand. The scent of the turkey and its sage-and-onion stuffing has overcome the dog's farts. Neville picks up his knife, and says, "'Is this a dagger that I see before me?'" What a pain in the ass, to use Charlie's term. How could her mother possibly find him attractive? But then, Roberta realizes he's probably trying to get a laugh. Well, forgive him, she tells herself. He is doing his bit.

She realizes that Carl's dad is speaking to her. "My son tells me you're an authority on Ovid, Dr. Greaves?"

"Well, I've read the original text of *Metamorphoses* and every translation or adaptation right up to Ted Hughes's, so I guess I know Ovid well, though I'm more of an 'authority' on Euripida's Cretan manuscripts."

Neville looks positively pouty at being upstaged. He may know Shakespeare, but he hasn't a thing to say about Ovid. And this seems to please Carl's dad who's in full flight now. Neville couldn't get a word in if he tried.

"I hate 'Pygmalion,'" Mr. Talbot says. "Though I suppose if the story gets that much reaction from me, it must be good in its way. But the idea of that jerk not being able to love anyone but the perfect woman — and one of his own construct too — is revolting."

"Revolting hardly covers it," Biff says. "Some of my friends, twenty years old, are getting Botox injections. Maybe they don't know about Pygmalion — Pig Male is my own private name for him — but they sure get the male hype about the perfect woman."

"I'll always think of my son as the antithesis of Pygmalion." Mr. Talbot's voice rises. "He loved a real woman and he kept that love right to the end of her life through all the chemo treatments and the disfigurations and the hysterectomy and the mastectomy."

"Dad, Roberta's heard all this before." Carl looks at the group around the table. "I'm no Pygmalion, but I'm not the Archangel Carl either. So let's change the subject."

"Before we do," Roberta's mother says, "I'd just like to point out that some women are every bit as bad as Pygmalion. They construct a perfect male in their minds, and they pour out their love on this figment of their imaginations, this ... construct ... as you would call it, Mr. Talbot. I loved my late husband, but I was always aware that he had his faults." Her glance sweeps over to Roberta who tries to figure out why this comment seems directed at her. Is her mother holding some sort of grudge against her?

"You were very young when your father died?" Neville asks her.

"Eighteen. Just finished my first year at Trinity. It was an awful shock."

"Perhaps better, really. I know, I know, it sounds callous, but the early death of a parent enables one to keep one's illusions. My own mother died when she was ninety-five, and by that time, I was glad to see her go. She was an ongoing drain on my resources: physical, financial, and emotional. After her death, I felt free. I started having a life of my own. And I met Sylvia."

Neville smiles at Roberta's mother. She smiles back at him and reaches for his hand, apparently oblivious to the gravy in his beard.

"Remind yourselves to give me an overdose before I get to ninety-five," Roberta says to her sons.

There is a long silence that Ed breaks. "Carrot pudding next," he says. "With lots of rum sauce and whipped cream. Maybe by the time Charlie and I put it all together, we can get onto a more festive topic." He pushes his chair back with a thud.

Later, after everyone has finally left, and Ed and Charlie have gone out with the girls, Roberta tidies up. The day could have been worse. She smiles to herself, thinking of Carl's comment to Neville about his cannibalism of the Cornish hen.

As she is straightening the coats in the vestibule closet, she notices Carl's gloves on the closet shelf. He'd been so busy finding his father's scarf and helping him on with his galoshes that he'd forgotten them. They are brown sheepskin, well-worn, but hand-stitched and beautifully soft. She picks them up, puts her hands inside. They are so warm.

21.

PROVOST WITHERSPOON'S BULKY Gore-Tex-clad figure blocks the front door of the Lodge. Roberta sees him as she turns off Philosopher's Walk onto the sidewalk that fronts Trinity College. It's a frosty day, but sweat has misted his spectacles and drips from his double chin.

Just back from his jog, she surmises. Must be eight-thirty. She checks her watch. Right on: She will have time for coffee and a quick review of the material she is discussing with her class later in the morning.

"Professor Greaves!" The Provost jogs in place in front of her. "My dear, welcome back to teaching. I know you've kept up with your marking while you've been on leave, and for that we're grateful. But your students will be glad to see you in the classroom again." He wipes his chin with what looks like one of the napkins from High Table in Strachan Hall. "Their youthful enthusiasm reflects what we all feel for your exceptional accomplishments, my dear. Really — you've brought distinction to the college."

"Thank you."

"So glad I met you this morning." He waves the napkin and trots to the door of the Lodge.

Roberta grabs her mail from the Porter's Lodge and moves up the staircase past Seeley Hall to her office. As she takes off her jacket, she stands at the mullioned window, relaxing for a moment in the January sunshine flooding in from the quadrangle. She remembers the Provost's compliments and smiles. A student looks up from the sidewalk and waves. For a moment, all seems right in her world.

Her phone rings.

"Got a message from George Korda," her agent says. "Things are hopping. He's hoping to have the advance readers' copies ready early February to send to four of the top writers of erotica."

"Who are...? Not that I really want to know."

"Jade Morningstar, Ishtar, Plaisir Foncé, and..." Roberta can hear the rustle of paper. "Eronomous."

"Hmm. Eromenos, maybe?"

More rustling of paper. "Yeah, you're right. Mean something?"

"Eromenos is the Greek name for a young male paramour."

"Hey, same as Mira except for gender. Well, there you go. Let's hope we get good blurbs. Why do I get the impression that Plaisir Foncé will love it?"

"Oh Marianne, stop it, please. I can only think that all these writers are like me, all ashamed of what they're doing."

"Because they're using these fake names, right? Well, suck it up, Roberta. Every reader in the Universe of Erotica knows these people. If they give us good blurbs for the back cover, who cares? It's all about making a pile, isn't it? And think about it, this Eromenos guy slash gal might even be the alias of a classics professor like yours truly."

Marianne is laughing as she hangs up.

On her Trinity desk, Roberta sees a copy of *The Cretan Manuscripts*. She picks it up and looks at the back cover. Four wonderful blurbs there, all from people she respects, including the host of a popular BBC program on ancient myth. And now she is stuck with Eromenos *et al.*

No time to dwell on it though. At the moment, she's got to get ready for her return to the classroom. Her lesson plan is in place. She just needs to check out the facts about the parentage of a sea nymph in one of the stories she will be discussing with her students. She pulls down a volume from the book-lined walls of her office. Whoa. Just as she feared. Daughter of Doris and her brother, Nereus. You cannot get away from incest in ancient literature. I just can't handle it today, she thinks. Her students have all read their translations of Ovid. So they will know the Pygmalion story. She runs through alternative lesson plans. Maybe I can segue into Euripida's take on the Pygmalion myth, or something.

Meantime, she remembers she has made a nine o'clock appointment with a student named Bryan Schmidt. She takes his essay from the middle drawer of her desk where she has stashed it ready for the interview, along with a book she is going to push under his nose. Right on time, there is a knock at the door and Bryan comes in. He walks with a bit of a swagger.

"So, there's a problem?" he asks. "Something about my essay, you said?"

"Plagiarism. From the Latin *plagiarius*."

He stares at her. "So?"

"It means 'kidnapper.'" She sets the essay entitled, "Sexual Segregation in Classical Athens" before him. She reads aloud a sentence from page four: "'The Athenian lady's greatest task was to manage the heterosexual gang of slaves which swarmed in every wealthy mansion.'" She pauses.

"So?" But his face has turned scarlet.

"This sentence is one you've kidnapped almost verbatim from William Stearns Davis's book, *A Day in Old Athens*." Roberta points to the book that sits next to his red-marked essay. She flips it open, turns to Chapter Seven, and points to the plagiarized passage. "Of course, Davis knows it's 'heterogeneous' not 'heterosexual.' But I can't find a footnote, a parenthetical reference, or a bibliographic entry anywhere that acknowledges your source."

"So?" And then he gives a huge sigh. "What are you going to do?"

"Well, I have two choices. I could report this to the powers that be and you could lose your year and end up with a transcript with 'Academic Dishonesty' stamped on it." She pauses. "Or I could issue a warning and hope you'll never do such a stupid thing again. After all, I did spend a good part of our first class in September warning against cheating."

Bryan's forehead breaks out in a sweat. "Man, oh man."

"So go forth now, and the next time you're tempted to kidnap someone else's research, remember this interview. Acknowledge your source. It's that simple."

As he leaves, head down, muttering "Thank you, thank you," Roberta thinks of the days when she would have driven a stake into Bryan's heart and left him to bleed. Until today, she has stood strong against academic dishonesty. She does everything in her power to avoid the possibility of plagiarism. She changes the essay topics each year, looks over her students' thesis statements, gives advice on their outlines and first drafts, teaches them the way to give simple acknowledgements in parentheses instead of coping with old-fashioned footnotes.

But now, she finds herself incapable of taking a high moral tone. She thinks of all those magazines from which she cribbed ideas for the dirty details of Mira's story. Is she likely to include an Author's Note for the back page? Something along the lines of "Heartfelt appreciation to the writers of *French Girls, Lolita Mag, Transsex, and GangBang* for supplying ideas for the sleaze that inspired this book." Yeah, sure.

Time for class now. She dons her academic gown, a tradition of stuffy old Trinity that she has always liked — right from the days when it covered her pyjamas in the dining hall at breakfast — and heads off to Room 101 for her Classics in Translation group.

Halfway down the hall, she meets Trinity's Chaucer scholar, Joan Wishart. Her dyed black curls have been carefully gelled, and she is actually wearing red tights, perhaps to evoke the Wife of Bath.

"Welcome back, Roberta."

"Thanks, I'm—"

"I just found out from that wretched Muna Mehta that you gave her eighty on her first essay, and now she's down my neck because she got sixty-five on her Chaucer essay. You really do fling marks about. We've got to keep standards up. It's shocking the way they've declined since I was a student."

"I can't talk for long now, Joan. Sorry. I've got a class. But I'm wondering ... have you kept your own undergraduate essays from the Golden Age?"

Joan puffs out her little bosom and smiles, nodding. "My average, as I recall, was an overall eighty-five."

"Well, take a look at them sometime. They'll give you a dose of reality. I read aloud my own seventeen-year-old views on 'Christianity in the Light of the Nuclear Age' to a group of dinner guests recently, and we laughed ourselves silly. And my dear old prof had given me an eighty-one for my adolescent idiocies."

She steps around Joan and moves on. As she walks through the door of her classroom, she notices that her students are all in place, obviously waiting for her, though she is not a second late. The buzz of conversation stops, there is a scraping of chairs, and the crash of a lecture board onto the floor, and suddenly, they are all on their feet applauding.

"Way to go," says a tall lad at the front of the room.

"What's it all about?" Roberta knows she must have a stupid look on her face. Have they heard her put-down of Wishart?

"Welcome back, and congrats on *The Cretan Manuscripts*. We haven't had a chance to say this before."

And now they're all chanting, "Way to go. Way to go."

"What a pleasant surprise," Roberta says, making a small bow. "Thank you."

She sits down behind her desk on the raised dais, opens her lesson plan book, and with a nod and a smile indicates that it's time to get serious.

She has noted that all the students have their copies of Ted Hughes's *Tales from Ovid* and undoubtedly have even read the sea nymph story in preparation for class. They are a keen bunch notwithstanding Joan Wishart's dismissive comments about declining academic standards.

"We'll come back to Doris, Nereus, and their daughter at another lecture," Roberta says. "I think that since this is my first lesson with you this term, we should talk about the role of translator. We'll often be reading the same story in several different translations, and we may notice some very divergent takes on the same narrative. So I'll start with the question. What's the translator's role?"

Muna Mehta, Joan's favourite student, speaks up. She is prepping for a Rhodes scholarship, and Roberta feels she'll probably be successful, barring a disaster with her Chaucer exam. "I think the ideal translator keeps as close as possible to the wording of the original."

"No, no." The comment comes from Jason, the young man who led the earlier round of applause. "The important thing is to get people reading the stuff. So it's not word for word what the original text says, so what?"

"Then," Roberta asks the class, "if you say that the translator's role is one of adapting the text to draw in a wider audience, how far are you prepared to go?"

"My brother's in a special ed class at Western Tech," another boy says. "He's reading a graphic novel version of *Romeo and Juliet*. It's Shakespeare's story, but it's not Shakespeare's words. My brother loves it. So what's wrong with that?" Roberta remembers that this student seldom comments, and his face is red now with the strain of speaking up.

Suddenly, the lesson that seemed "safe" has taken on dangerous overtones. But Roberta finds herself unable to resist the opportunity to look into the abyss.

"Would a graphic novel of, say, the story of Procne and Philomela, be a good way of introducing a wide audience to Ovid?"

Now there is silence. Then Muna says, "It's one of the sickest stories in literature. Do we *want* the great unwashed reading about brutal rape and cannibalism? Or that disgusting story about Myrrha lusting after her father?" She makes gagging noises. "If the bozos out there have to wade through a literal translation in a book with a boring cover, they probably won't bother. And that's okay with me."

"Yeah," Jason agrees. "This Classics in Translation class at Trinity is one thing. But the general public reading this stuff without you in charge, Professor Greaves, to steer them ... well, I wouldn't carry adaptation *that* far. But I think you're off base, Muna, calling people names just because they don't have our advantages."

There is a buzz now as the students get off track on the subject of Muna's elitism, and Roberta makes no effort to steer them back on topic. She should make a comment, of course, but her own worries take over. What a morning she has had. First Joan Wishart lecturing her on her failure to maintain standards, then her class seeing her as some sort of Dalai Lama figure who shows young people The Way. And it is only a few weeks until that wretched novel comes out. Maybe it will just die quietly, the way most third-rate novels do. But already in her mind she is fast-forwarding to the local Rexall Pharma Plus where, every time she goes to buy hairspray or toothpaste, she may have to look at it on the racks alongside the latest Danielle Steele epic. And it is so much worse than anything Steele ever came up with. And what if it takes off in a big way? Someone is sure to make the link with Ovid's nasty little tale. And then what?

22.

GETTING BACK TO HER morning classes at Trinity has also meant Roberta's return to her volunteer work at the Christian Mission on Major Street later in the day. It is almost two o'clock now, and she makes a point of always being on time. But as she hurries past the University Bookstore on College Street, she pauses briefly to drop a toonie into the cap of the red-faced old man who sits on a pillow of filthy newspapers on the sidewalk in front of the store.

"God bless," he says, and she moves on, cursing to herself. *With all the taxes we pay, surely there must be enough funds to provide something better for the poor than sitting on cold pavement dependent on the patronage of so-called do-gooders like me.*

That is why she is "teaching" (not quite the right word, she knows) poetry to a group of street people in the YES program. The government has shelled out a measly ninety thousand dollars for the endeavour, and along with many donations from the Mission supporters, Youth Employment Services does its darndest to get kids off the street and into the workplace. Most of them are sixteen going on thirty-five. They have little formal education, and Roberta's attempts at creativity are supposed to help their "communication skills," as the official pitch goes.

It is her fourth Wednesday afternoon with them, and she is not exactly looking forward to what comes next. But she is amazed that they come at all to these workshops. Probably it is a way to keep warm or safe. But maybe, just maybe, it's a secret longing for something better. Whatever the case, she wants it to work, and she has been worried that they may think she abandoned the project. Her first three "sessions" — as she inwardly calls them — were before James's death, and she doesn't know whether the kids were ever given an explanation for her absence or not.

As she reaches the building, she takes a deep breath of cold air and opens the front door. Immediately, the stink of over-cooked cabbage and stale cigarette smoke assails her. Down the stairs she marches to a basement room where twelve kids sit on an assortment of mismatched plastic chairs around an Arborite table.

"Hey guys, it's Roberta," Big Chris calls out. "Surprise, surprise." He smiles, revealing the gap where a front tooth is missing. He has a sandwich in his large, chapped hand. "Welcome back. Someone upstairs told us a while back that your husband died. Too bad. Sorry about that." He passes a Styrofoam plate of sandwiches over to her. "Have one of these. Roast beef and some kind of sweet-and-sour stuff that's real good."

"Chutney, probably. Charlie, he's my son, said he was going to send over beef and chutney on pita bread."

"He's a cook or something?"

"Yes, he's just graduated from George Brown College, and he's in his first job at a restaurant down on Queen Street, not far from here. The Fig Leaf, it's called. He's going to send over food every Wednesday when we have our poetry workshops."

Bat, a little guy with a shaved head, puts his half-eaten sandwich back on the plate. "We gotta pay for it? Is that what you're saying?" He rubs a nasty-looking bruise over his left eye.

"No, no," Roberta says. "Charlie's treat." And fearing that this will sound like charity, she adds, "It's all about promotion, you know? You like the sandwiches, you tell everyone about The Fig Leaf."

Yeah, yeah, they all say. They see through her subterfuge without difficulty.

But Big Chris has a suggestion. "Hey, if Charlie is giving us this good stuff to eat each week, least I can do is go down and pick it up. Wednesday, one-thirty on the nose. Right, Roberta?"

"Nice of you, Chris," she says. "Good idea. I'll tell Charlie to look for you."

She sits down at the head of the table, relieved that no further explanation about James's death seems necessary. "Okay, let's get to work. Today, we're doing concrete poetry."

"Shit," Hester says. "I hope it's not going to be like those fucking high-glues." Her dog, Scrappy, who sits beside her, head on her lap, looks up, recognizing anger. Roberta has to confess to herself that she likes Scrappy better than his owner. With a bath and a brushing, he would be a clone of the black-and-white pet collie in her favourite Renoir painting, *Madame Georges Charpentier and Her Children*. But even with a bath and a brushing, Hester would still remind her of the grim-faced figure in Picasso's *Woman with a Crow*.

"Okay, so maybe the haikus were a mistake, but I hope you can forget them and move on. These concrete poems are a bit of a challenge, but I think you'll catch on. Then, you can try writing one of your own."

She passes around several of ee cummings's poems and one by George Gabor. "What the fuck is this?" Bat asks.

"Hey, should we of brought our jackhammers?" Big Chris's question gets a laugh, and Roberta is grateful for his intervention.

"Trying to make us look stupid, is that what you're doing?" Hester asks, scraping her chair back and tugging on Scrappy's leash.

But just at that moment, Moose, a small boy with a large nose and stick-out ears, speaks up. "Hey, man," he says. "I know what this one is all about." He is pointing at Gabor's "The Critical Putt." "This is the shape of a golf ball bouncing along. Right?"

"You got it. Good for you," Roberta says, smiling.

"But what's this word 'Palmer' there for?"

Roberta explains who Arnold Palmer is, that he once had a horde of followers called "Arnie's Army," and there is laughter from the group. She notices that Hester has pulled her chair back to the table.

Soon, they have decoded the rest of the poems, and now they decide to give in and humour her.

They get absorbed in designing their own concrete poems, and in twenty minutes, they are ready to exchange their offerings with each other. There is a good deal of laughter, some rude comments, but soon everyone acknowledges that Hester's poem is the best. Though the girl is determined not to be pleased, she can't help showing it in the way her face grows red and in her repetitions of "Oh piss off, piss off."

"Good work, Hester," Roberta says. And it is.

DREAMS
b   k   r
a   e

HOPE
                    fades

_____

a child's life . . . e . n . d . s . . .

"I like that long line she's drawn," Bat says. "Makes it look like the kid's buried already under the ground. Heather's got everybody's fuckin' life into one poem." There are murmurs of agreement.

Well, Roberta reflects, that lesson certainly worked better than the haiku one. "I'll leave coloured pencils and paper here on the table," she says, "and for next class you can get your poems in presentable form, and we'll put them all up on the walls for display." She decides to stop on this positive note and let the kids disperse to their favourite spots in time for the rush hour traffic and a chance at some spare change.

With a long subway ride ahead of her, she visits the washroom tucked down at the end of a dirty hallway leading from the basement room. It is cleaner than she expected, and someone has affixed a handwritten notice above the toilet:

If you sprinkle when you tinkle,
Be a sweetie, wipe the seatee.

Ah, the power of poetry, she reflects, though when she thinks about it, she remembers reading the same lines in a novel by Carol Shields. *Unless,* was it? Is the quoting of doggerel from a novel whose writer has kidnapped some graffiti from a toilet somewhere double plagiarism? *Oh, the things you worry about, Roberta.*

She climbs the stairs back into the main area where volunteers are setting up tables for the evening meal for the drop-ins. She hears a familiar voice and sees that Hester has waylaid a stout, grey-haired staff counsellor named Annie and is yelling at her, "Oh, go fuck yourself. And then write a high-glue about it. You probably won't even need seventeen syllables."

When Hester sees Roberta, she hurries off, Scrappy close behind her.

"What's up, Annie?" Roberta says.

"Oh, that girl. Sometimes, I think she's beyond help."

"Perhaps. But less than an hour ago, she was describing haikus with her favourite four-letter word. And now she's using her knowledge of their structure to swear at you. Come on now, Annie, isn't that a leap?"

Annie laughs. "Sure is. I'm so grateful that it won't take seventeen syllables to fuck myself."

"Yeah, let's put a positive spin on things. Would you believe that when I was here earlier in the fall, she didn't even know what a syllable was?"

"I'm happy you can see the light. But I get discouraged," Annie says, shaking her head. "I've worked as a counsellor here for twenty-five years, and I feel sometimes that the world is sick. Sick, sick. Hester came in here two weeks ago, her arms all covered in bruises, and when I got her alone in my office, she told me — in a string of four-letter curses, of course — that her mother's boyfriend had attempted to rape her. She managed to beat him off with a few kicks in strategic places. I'll spare you the details. Said that her mom was in the kitchen when it happened, could hear her yelling, and did nothing. Scared, maybe. Though I won't make excuses for the woman. And the creep evidently said afterwards that Hester led him on." Annie sighs, brushing her hair back from her forehead. "How can I clean up that filth?"

Roberta tells Annie about Hester's poem. "It's a small creative miracle, you know. Lugubrious, but brilliant in its way. Perhaps she'll find something within herself to be proud of. If she can find self-esteem, she'll be able to move on to a better world."

"Yeah," Annie says. "We can hope. But let's not hold our breath."

As Roberta emerges into the waning afternoon sunlight, she catches a glimpse of a feathery tail disappearing into the dirty alley to her right. Scrappy. That means Hester is hanging around. Sure enough, she is about six feet down the alley, flattened against the Mission wall beside a stack of discarded wooden boxes. Shooting up, maybe?

Roberta takes a few steps into the alley. "Hester, anything I can do?"

"Bugger off."

Okay. There are times when she feels that way herself. She turns back to the sidewalk and almost bumps into Big Chris.

"Hi, Roberta. Everything okay?" he says.

"Hester's upset about something."

"Yeah, I seen her there in the alley. I'll stay with her a while. Bad things happening at her place, you wouldn't believe...." He punches one mittened hand into the other and shakes his head. "I heard what she said to you just now, but she doesn't, like, mean it the way it sounds."

"I know, Chris. And thanks. I just hope you can help her sort it out. Goodbye now."

Roberta decides to walk up to the Bloor subway instead of taking the Spadina streetcar. She needs to be alone with her thoughts for a few minutes. Hester lives in a foreign world. Roberta does not speak her language. But she can imagine, oh yes, she can imagine the horror of rape. What she cannot see, does not want to see, is Hester's mother standing there, listening to the would-be rapist blame Hester for "leading" him on. "Scared," Annie said. Well, maybe. But what kind of mother would let her daughter be abused in such a horrific way? No wonder Hester wrote that poem about broken dreams and a child's death.

She strides on, heaving her heavy briefcase from one hand to the other. She is almost to Bloor Street when another thought seeps into her mind like oozing slime.

If only she had remembered the abyss Hester inhabits, surely she would not have chosen to write that sick story that's coming out soon, the sleaze that lets men like Hester's rapist believe it's the girl who bears the guilt. What can such a piece of filth do except make the whole fuckin' world worse?

23.

ROBERTA GETS OFF THE GO TRAIN at the Summerton station. She jumps over a slushy pile of snow near the tracks in order to connect with Victoria Street, the village's main thoroughfare. Apart from an old man picking up a free *Toronto Weekly* paper from a box at the station, there seems to be no one about on this sunny Saturday morning. She makes a left turn onto Osborne Road and heads for her mother's house.

Roberta took the first train from Toronto's Union Station and it's now only nine-thirty. Her mother will probably still be lingering over her morning coffee, and Roberta hopes to break the news to her about *Mira*, do the necessary handholding and get back by late afternoon to the city and the stack of late January essays she has to mark.

It is not going to be easy to give her mother the news. She has put it off too long. She should have done it on Christmas Day as Charlie hinted. She'd had several moments alone with her mother upstairs while she was putting her mink coat on the bed and Neville was in the living room with her sons. That would have been perfect timing. No way her mother would have been able to say much with Christmas dinner pending and everyone on their best behaviour.

She walks past the stone bulk of Wesley United Church, noting the fancy moving sign that they've installed in the last couple of months on the lawn near the front door. "SWALLOW YOUR PRIDE" one flashing message advises. The next flashes, "IT

WON'T COST YOU ANY CALORIES." Not much different from Greek mythology, Roberta reflects, with its constant warnings of the punishments the gods mete out to people with hubris.

"Hey, Roberta," someone calls. "Like our new signage?" She looks towards the small parking lot at the side of the church. The pastor, a young man with a receding hairline, waves.

"Startling," Roberta says, waving back. She strides on, hoping not to have to engage in further discussion.

The flagstone walk in front of her mother's house, as well as the steps leading up to the front porch, have been neatly shovelled. She pauses for a second at the oak door with the lion's head knocker. Then she tries the handle. People seldom lock doors in Summerton. Sure enough, it's unlocked, so she pushes it open calling "Mother?" as she enters. The downstairs seems empty; no one is in the kitchen though the automatic coffee maker has kicked in, done its work, and the coffee stands fragrant and ready. She comes back to the foot of the stairs. "Mother?"

She hears a scuffle from Sylvia's bedroom as she starts up-stairs. By the time she gets to the landing, she hears a *thump* as if someone is trying to get out of bed. Could her mother be sick? She takes the second half of the stairs at a run.

The bedroom door is wide open and a man, stark naked, is stumbling towards it as if to shut it. Roberta takes another look. "Neville!"

He makes a pitiful attempt to cover his crotch. She glimpses a caved-in chest covered with a thatch of sweat-soaked, straggly hair. There's a familiar chlorine-like smell. Is it semen? Then from the bed itself comes her mother's voice: "Roberta!" She sits up, the sheets pulled up to her bare shoulders.

Oh my God. Roberta is down the stairs in a flash, out the front door, and down the porch steps. She's just hit the flag-stone walk when her mother calls to her. She looks back to see Sylvia, barefoot but covered now in a terry-cloth robe, standing at the open oak door.

"Please, please come back!" she calls.

But Roberta can think only of getting away, as far away as she can. But where is she to go? The next train to the city doesn't leave until noon. What's she to do? She turns back, calls, "I'm going downtown for a while. Be back in an hour."

It will give that asshole Neville time to get lost.

Back on Victoria Street, she thinks of where to go for coffee. Not Thelma's Front Verandah where Thelma would have a dozen questions about why she's here and why she's not having coffee with her mother. There's the small store next door to Thelma's where the proprietor, an East Indian newcomer to the town, sells dried fruit, nuts, spices, and pasta. There are a couple of tables in the back, Roberta remembers, where you can get coffee and scones.

Not that she could swallow a scone, but coffee would be good. "Darsh" introduces himself and brings her an espresso. She's just downed it when the door of the shop opens and in comes Nora Dorsey of Nora's Nimble Needle, carrying a thermos. Roberta hears her asking Darsh for coffee to go. Then Roberta sees her glance to the back of the store. Oh boy, she thinks, now I'm in for some heavy-duty questioning. *Damn, I should have bought a newspaper to hide behind.*

"Roberta," Nora says, "why are you here? I saw you heading for Osborne Road half an hour ago. Thought you'd be having coffee with your mother."

"She doesn't do espresso, and that's what I needed. Up too late these nights marking damn essays. I wanted the jolt."

"Translation needed here: You walked in on her and Neville, right?"

"You know, Nora, this town could very well function as headquarters for either the CIA or CSIS."

"Come on, Roberta. You don't need to be a professional spy to know what's going on. Everyone knows. Though the two of them try to keep it hidden. Every Saturday morning in this new year, Neville has left that dog of his in his apartment and walked up Osborne Road at about eight o'clock. Maybe, everyone's saying, they're just having a morning cup of coffee. But we all know that at Neville's age, you can only get it up in the early morning." She laughs. "They're not fooling anybody."

Roberta looks into her empty cup. No way will she let herself get involved in this conversation.

"You know," Nora goes on, "I don't see the attraction myself. Now that father of yours, he was something else. A good man in every way. Though goodness knows, he had..." Her voice trails off. "I won't forget how he helped me once in a crisis...." She breaks off again, taps her thermos with a manicured fingernail. "In comparison, Neville is a nitwit."

"I'm really not interested in this discussion, Nora."

"Well, it's obvious you're not going to rat on your mother and I understand that."

Nora turns away. Roberta watches her go. She's a strong-boned, solid woman, same age as Sylvia, but with none of her mother's elegance. Still, Roberta thinks, she is a presence. *I wouldn't want to mess with her.*

She looks at her watch. She's been here for more than half an hour. A saunter back up Osborne Road and she'll be with her mother again, *sans* Neville, she devoutly hopes.

When she arrives, there's no sign of Don Juan. Her mother is sitting in the kitchen, fully dressed in a pretty loose pink shirt and black pants. She looks ... well, younger. There's a becoming flush on her cheeks. She turns away from Roberta and goes to the sink. "I'll make us some fresh coffee."

"No coffee, Mother. We just need to talk."

"Okay, Roberta, I know you're upset. People of your generation can be terribly censorious. While you're all in favour of sex for yourselves, you just can't believe that people my age can have sexual desires too."

It's all sounding a bit like what Carl told me about Charlie and Ed's generation, Roberta remembers. *Am I wrong to condemn Mother for her natural desires?*

"Damn it, I see you and that man in bed, in the very bed where you and Daddy were...." She breaks off, remembering Sunday mornings when they all slept in late unless her father had an emergency at the hospital. She'd come down the hall from her own bedroom and climb in between her mother and father, relishing the warmth of their bodies on each side of her. She'd always have a book with her, and Daddy would read her a few pages while her mother dozed.

"You and he were together in that bed for all those years. And then I come home and find you've taken Neville right into Daddy's space. I'm trying to convince myself that I don't care what you're up to, but for God's sake, why does it have to be in that bed? Why not go to Neville's place?"

"Your father's been dead all these years, Roberta. I've slept by myself in that lonely room for so long. Surely you can't blame me for wanting a warm body beside me, someone to love, someone who loves me?"

"I'm trying not to blame you. I just can't process things at the moment. I remember eavesdropping on you and Daddy when I was a kid. You always seemed in harmony. That night he came home from aborting Janeen Dorsey's baby, remember? I watched you and Daddy through the banister. You and he sat opposite each other, knees touching, and he told you the whole sad tale and you said — I remember every word — 'You did the right thing, Robert.' You always backed him in every good thing he fought for in this benighted little town. I guess I've always assumed your love for each other was everlasting."

"Oh yes, I backed him. I was for ever the perfect little woman behind his noble crusades."

"You sound bitter, Mother. What's up?"

"Something I've kept from you all these years."

"What, for God's sake?"

"I haven't told you because you probably wouldn't have believed me. You always adored your father, but you don't know...." Her mother pushes her chair back from the table. The legs screech against the pine floor.

Roberta has never seen her mother this angry before. It's disconcerting.

"Don't know what? Get to your point, *please*."

"Your ... *Daddy* ... betrayed ... me." Then her mother is speaking so quickly Roberta can barely keep up with the sense of it all. "That heart attack that carried him off. He was with Nora Dorsey. Screwing her. That's what finished him."

"Nora Dorsey? Mother, please."

But her mother goes on. "I'd gone for a day of shopping in Toronto. But I got everything finished by noon, so I took an early train back. No sooner had I walked in the front door than there was Dorsey, running down the stairs, a bath towel wrapped around her fat rear, screeching about Robert being dead. And sure enough, there he was, in that marital bed you're going on about, only he wasn't dead. I had to call the ambulance while that bitch got herself dressed and—"

"Please, please, no more." Roberta struggles to keep her voice steady. A dog can howl out its pain, but what's a human to do?

"Your oh-so-perfect Daddy. Don't you think I've got sick of hearing that all these years? How do you think I felt having to keep it from you while you stood at his hospital bed saying, 'Don't leave me, Daddy'? I didn't want to shatter your faith. And I've kept it all quiet ever since. Maybe I could get some small credit for that?"

Her mother's words spill out, but Roberta can no longer process them. She can think of nothing but the double betrayal: James and Daddy. The men she loved.

Suddenly she knows she has to get away. "I'm so tired, Mother. So tired." She stumbles up the staircase and falls upon her childhood bed. She's so cold, so cold. She buries herself in her grandmother's quilt, pulling it up over her head, and curling her legs up and into her chest.

Daddy. James. Daddy. The names pound in her head.

Sleep. Sleep. That is what she needs. "Sleep that knits up the ravelled sleeve of care."

It's about an hour later when Roberta gets up. She comes downstairs to find her mother still in the kitchen, a bottle of Chardonnay on the table in front of her. "Pour one for yourself," her mother says.

Roberta takes a glass from the cupboard and sits down opposite Sylvia.

There's a minute of silence and then her mother says, "Believe me, I tried to keep you from knowing. And I've succeeded all these years. But I'm wondering... Why did you come up here today anyway, out of the blue?"

"I had some news for you. Something I should have mentioned before." And Roberta tells her mother about *Mira*. It seems anticlimactic now.

"I was worried about what you might think of it. And I kept thinking about what Daddy might have said about it. But it doesn't seem to matter now. I just feel empty, as if everything I believed in and everyone I trusted...." Roberta starts to cry.

"Oh, my dear," her mother says, reaching across the table to touch Roberta's arm. There's a long silence. Then she says in a quiet voice, "Your father was right in so many things. I admired him for so many years." Her face is pale, every line showing in the glare from the big window. "But finding him with Nora ... that finished my love for him. I've been so angry at him all these years, but I'm moving on. I've got Neville now. I'm making a fresh beginning, and I'm asking you to understand my needs. That's all."

She collects the wineglasses and sets them on the counter by the sink. She turns the water on full blast. Roberta moves into the hallway and puts on her coat and gloves. Then she goes back into the kitchen. Her mother is still standing over the sink, her back to Roberta as she looks out the window. Roberta turns towards the front door. There seems to be nothing more either of them can say.

24.

ROBERTA AND CARL HAVE SETTLED into banquettes at their favourite restaurant, the Hot Spot, where they have a fish-eye view of Front Street through the huge windows. They have gotten into the habit of meeting at the restaurant every other week. A bright mural of a sunny Mediterranean village covers the back wall, and a tall shelf of blue bottles partially blocks the view of the goings-on of the young lovers at the next table.

"One of the pluses of this place," Carl is saying, "is that they assume you can read the chalkboard. It's nice to be able to order the house white and the pork chops without having to listen to the epic tale called *Tonight's Specials*."

"You really don't want to hear about the Aspromonte Oxtail Gyoza?" Roberta asks. "Or the Ionian Piquillos?"

Carl laughs. He's wearing a dark red shirt that sets off his grey hair and wind-burned cheeks. "So, tell me about the meeting with your mother."

Roberta gives the story. She's gone over the wretched day so often in her mind that her narrative spills out now without pause. When the waiter brings their drinks, she interrupts herself to take a sip. "That's it, Carl. Sorry for the rant."

"I guess it's bound to be a shock for all offspring to find out that their parents have a sex life. But I know there's more to it than that. It's all about betrayal, isn't it? Your father's betrayal of your trust in him? But he didn't know you'd find out. He didn't set out to hurt you. Or your mother. I think it's important to remember that."

"Maybe not. But now that I know, I don't know what to do next. I'm wallowing in a morass. And I've been thinking, too, about James."

Carl sips his wine. Roberta is aware that he's listening, not judging. It's comforting. She takes several gulps from her own glass. "The buzz I'm getting from the wine encourages me to plunge into the next chapter of my saga," she says.

"Go right ahead."

"I'm remembering his note. The last note. I still have the exact words in my head: 'I tried to be someone else all the years of my adult life. I tried to be that father you were always talking about. I tried to be like those noble, upright, solid heroes in my favourite Victorian novels. But I'm no Sydney Carton.'"

Roberta stops, tries to get a grip on where she's going with this conversation. Then she says, "For the first eighteen years of my life, my father was everything to me. He was Captain Nemo, D'Artagnan, and Sydney Carton all rolled into one tall, handsome, perfect man who loved me too, who thought everything *I* did was perfect." She waits, uncertain where to go next.

"And then he died suddenly," Carl prompts.

"Yes. Only, as I told you, I didn't know until this week it was a new form of *coitus interruptus*. I always thought he'd had a heart attack at his office. That's what Mother told me all those years ago. For a while, there was a huge chasm. Then I met James. And I guess because I had this highly positive image of an adult male, I projected it all onto him. And he didn't always measure up. How could he? But still, I want to believe that we were happy together at least until the last year of his life when he had that damn riding accident and everything disintegrated."

"And something's bothering you now? I mean, beyond what you've told me so far?"

She doesn't answer. Carl looks at a point above her head and waits.

"Did *I* betray James? By expecting him to be perfect, to be like Daddy? Only Daddy wasn't perfect." She starts to cry.

Carl hands her his handkerchief, a carefully ironed square of immaculate linen.

"Oh Carl, you're so lucky you're not like me. You have nothing to reproach yourself for. You were the perfect husband through all those wretched last days of Claire's illness." But as she says this, she knows she's put a foot wrong. Carl's eyes close for a minute. His tongue slides over his lips.

"That's the story Dad tells, but he's dead wrong. At the end, I pitied Claire, perfectly aware that pity is despicable because it makes you a superior being and the person you pity, inferior. But I couldn't manage anything *but* pity. I tried, oh I tried to love Claire as an equal, to go hand in hand with her to the end of her life, but really, I couldn't get the stench out of my nostrils."

He breaks off, twists his hands together as if he's washing them. For a second, she thinks of James.

"The stench, Carl?"

"All those poisons from the chemo on her skin and her breath and in her urine. I could smell them in the bathroom even after she flushed the toilet. And then there were those ugly radiation burns, red patches all over her buttocks, her throat, her chest." He drains his glass and sets it down with a thud on the varnished surface of the table. "I wanted to do better, I wanted to help her. But I failed. I'm living with that failure, just as James tried to."

"Come on, Carl, I remember how you nurtured her that evening you came to dinner, how you wrapped your jacket around her to keep her warm. I remember how she seemed to lean on you, to look to you for comfort."

"You know, Rob, I think that was just a bit of theatre, part of an act we put on for people. She resented me mostly, resented the fact that I was staying in the sunshine while she was going down into the darkness. In the last months of her life, I think she looked forward to death. It all became clear to me on Valentine's Day last year. I'd bought her a box of After Eight mint chocolates. I couldn't give her flowers. Too evocative of what was to come. Her cancer had metastasized into her colon and her kidneys, and though she was just back from chemo, we both knew there was no hope. The doctor gave her five months, though her suffering went on much longer.

"I took the chocolates into her room. We hadn't slept together for weeks. I got some white tissue paper at the drugstore and I wrapped them up with a red bow. And the girl behind the counter knew what we were going through and she gave me some big red adhesive hearts, and I stuck those on. I sat down on the edge of the bed and handed the package to her. I tried, I tried, to say something about loving her, about our happy times together. I asked her if she could remember those times and love me despite her misery.

"And oh, Rob, she took the chocolates and dropped them into the bucket where she'd just puked up the tea I'd brought her earlier. 'The only thing I love now is Death.' That's what she said to me. And her voice was cold and dry and she stared at me through those pale grey eyes and her head was bald and she'd lost her eyebrows and her eyelashes and for a minute I thought those words were coming through the mouth of a snake."

Roberta takes one of his hands in hers. It's cold. She wraps her own cold fingers around it.

"I hated her at that moment. Yes, I hated her. I went into the bathroom, turned on the taps full force, and cried. And while I was blubbering away, all I could see were the clumps of hair she'd left in the tub and the row of bloody Q-tips she'd left on the counter along with a bottle of milk of magnesia."

"Milk of magnesia?"

"She was always painting the sores inside her mouth with the stuff. She wanted me to see it all. In a way, she was trying to show me her suffering. And yet she wouldn't let me go to the hospital with her. I begged her to let me sit with her during those long hours of intravenous chemo, but she said no. I tried to understand it all, but I couldn't. Oh Robbie, when you talk about betrayal, you hit a nerve. I should have persevered. I should have tried harder...."

He breaks off and signals to the waiter for the cheque. "Let's go home now. I don't think we want a gooey dessert on top of all these grisly details. I've got a Peter Robinson mystery I bury myself in when things pile up. And you?"

"I feel so shivery now it's into a hot bath. I've got a P. D. James. And then a hot water bottle and oblivion."

He helps her into her coat and picks her gloves up off the floor.

They walk to the King Street subway station together. The wind is raw and cold, and the tall buildings hug the sidewalk, forcing the early evening hordes walking north and south to step carefully around each other. Roberta feels tired but less fraught than she was earlier in the evening. "You know," she says to Carl as they go down the subway stairs littered with paper cups and cigarette butts, "in a strange way, I think we may have helped each other out tonight. We've confessed our sins."

"Yeah, it's been a bit like the General Confession from *The Book of Common Prayer*."

"'We have done those things which we ought not to have done,'" they both say in unison. Then they laugh.

Roberta says, "It's all about getting beyond that stupid word *perfect*, isn't it?"

"A word I hate," Carl agrees.

"Have we been channelling 'Pygmalion'? Is that what we've been doing?"

"I sure as hell hope not," Carl says. "That goddamn story. It's affected our whole society, even people who wouldn't know the first thing about the details. Your son's girlfriend summed it up well at Christmastime, didn't she, when she talked about twenty-year-olds getting Botox injections? It's insidious. Look at all the divorces over nothing much, and the obsession with stars and what they're wearing and who they've got in bed with them...." He kicks at a Tim Horton's coffee cup that's rolling on the subway platform.

Their train rattles westward. A pretty young woman sitting across from them does a complete makeup job, starting with foundation, followed by a tube of concealer squeezed needlessly under her lovely eyes, then eyeshadow, mascara, and lipstick. Roberta and Carl watch in silence, saying nothing except "goodbye" when Roberta gets off at the Old Mill station.

Back home, she thinks over every detail of the evening's confessions. Hers. His. She remembers how she took his hand, how he called her "Robbie." It was nice, comforting somehow. And his comment about "Pygmalion" echoes her own views of Ovid's story. In its way, its theme is every bit as sick as the "Myrrha" story, just not as grisly in its details. She goes to the bookcase in her study and takes *The Cretan Manuscripts* from the top shelf. She wants to look again at the fresh reality Euripida brought to that stupid tale.

Yes, Roberta says to herself as she reads, Euripida understood the inevitable outcome of the Pygmalion-Galatea marriage. When Pygmalion's perfect ivory statue becomes a real woman and, in time, a mother with leaking breasts and a bawling infant to suckle, the sculptor turns against her, unable to endure her imperfections. Undaunted, Galatea finds new life in a nearby village, makes friends with a pleasant old woman and her husband, and eventually becomes a successful writer whose poems reflect the themes of the real world around her.

25.

ROBERTA DRESSES FOR WORK, putting on a new blue wool pantsuit and twisting a red silk scarf in place as a gesture to the day. Valentine's Day. Not a day she's looking forward to.

As she comes down the stairs and goes into the breakfast room, she sees a thick white folded sheet of paper on the table. On the front fold is a crayon drawing of what looks like a dark brown fedora with the crown crushed in the middle. Inside is a message in handwriting that alternates word by word between Ed's and Charlie's. She smiles. That must have taken them a while.

> *Hi, Mom*/Ma:
> *Does* this *image* make *you* nostalgic? *Guess* our *tastes* have *evolved* these *days*, but *our* primal *love* for *you* hasn't *changed* a *bit*.
> *Lots* of *love*,
>   *Charlie*/Ed

She studies the image. What on earth does it represent? Then she remembers. Of course, it's the Roman Ruin, one of her long-ago baking disasters.

She was just about to take the chocolate cake out of the oven. It was an easy recipe, taken from Peg Bracken's *The I Hate to*

Cook Book. It involved only one dish, that being the pan it was cooked in, and there was no beating of eggs or creaming of butter and sugar. All you had to do was put the ingredients in four corners of the pan and then mix them together with a big spoon. She could handle that. At least that's what she told herself every Valentine's Day.

As she took the cake out and set it on the granite countertop, it looked impressive, nicely risen above the edges of the pan. "Got it right this time," she says to Ed and Charlie who are standing next to her.

Charlie's nose barely reached the level of the counter. "Yum," he said.

But Ed, who was a good six inches taller, saw the phenomenon unfolding in front of him. "Uh-oh," he said, pointing to the cake's middle, which was rapidly caving in.

James joined them. He'd been in the breakfast room, finishing a glass of prosecco from the bottle he always opened on Valentine's Day. He placed his arms around his sons, and said, "Not to worry, it'll taste good. It always does."

To Roberta he said, "The Roman Ruin."

"Wow," Charlie said. "Now we can make lots of icing and fill up the centre."

"It'll have to cool for a while," Roberta said. "So why don't we walk over to the Village Café and have supper? Then we can ice it when we get back."

The restaurant was on Bloor Street, an easy walk from the house. It was a basic place, but the food was generally good and it was cheap, and on Valentine's Day and other state occasions, Joe, the owner, offered "bottomless Fanta" for the boys.

"Hi, folks," Joe said as they entered. "I guess you guys want the usual, right?" He did the cooking and the serving. No wonder his broad red face was always shiny with sweat.

"Right," they chorused.

"And hold the fries, at least for the old folks, right, boys?"

"Right."

It was a matter of minutes, and then Joe set their sandwiches, a new bottle of ketchup, and drinks in front of them. He wore a clean T-shirt that said, "Practise safe meals. Use a condiment." The sandwiches looked good as usual. Roberta and James usually had the peameal back bacon on rye, and Charlie and Ed had cheddar cheese with green tomato pickles on white. The bread was always thick and fresh. And Joe brought plates of fries for the boys, and one serving for the "old folks," which he set dead centre between Roberta and James. "Just in case you change your minds," he said.

When they got back home, the Roman Ruin was cool, and the boys got busy making a runny butter icing, trying to fill in the sunken middle but licking as much from the bowl as they put on the cake. The icing ran down the sides of the cake and made a round sticky circle on the plate so that the whole thing looked, yes, like a fedora with the top smashed in. Then, they all settled down at the breakfast-room table and devoured large pieces.

James brought out her Valentine's card then. It was the mushiest, most expensive Hallmark card he could buy from the Value Drug Mart. Roberta and James enjoyed their laugh over the poetry scrolled between the satin heart and the embossed garlands of purple roses.

James handed her a red marking pen. "Get busy," he said. "There's lots of bad lines here for you to scan."

And she obliged while James laughed and had another glass of prosecco.

"Now for your video, boys," he said, putting the Blockbuster tape of *Black Beauty* into the recorder. "Your mother and I are going to bed. Long day."

And he took the rest of the wine with them and they sat against the pillows listening to a CD of Robert Burns's love songs. Then he rolled towards her and sang, "*O my luve is like a red, red rose*" into her ear. By the second stanza, he could no longer sing, and she didn't hear him anyway, caught up as they were in the crescendo of their lovemaking.

Now, Roberta sets her sons' card on the dining-room buffet. She goes back to the breakfast room and searches in the cupboard for the recipe for the "Roman Ruin." Eventually, she finds the frail little paperback called *The I Hate to Cook Book*. There, on page 92, are the ingredients for "Cockeyed Cake" almost obliterated by greasy fingerprints across the page. Should she make it this afternoon when she gets home from work? No, she decides. James is gone, the boys have grown beyond the love for runny butter icing, and there's no Hallmark card to laugh at.

And now that she thinks about those Hallmark cards, she realizes that her scanning of the bad lines may have hurt James. He seemed to laugh, yes, as she marked out the lapses in metre and scoffed at the cheap rhymes. She remembers his bright eyes looking at her as she made fun of his annual gift. Were there unshed tears in those eyes? Did he see her little academic sneer as a put-down of his love?

Come back, James. Come back. I would do better, I would.

She walks to Trinity College from the Spadina station, wanting the exercise of an extra block. She strides along the south side of Bloor Street, breaking her pace only to step around a couple of bodies stretched out in filthy sleeping bags on the pavement. Across the road on the corner by the Medical Arts Building, she sees a familiar figure. It's Big Chris from the YES program. He's got a little stand in front of him, and he looks up from talking to someone who's buying something and waves at her.

She crosses at the light to see what's going on.

"Hey, Roberta! Wanna buy a poem?"

She steps in closer to get a look. "Hey, Chris! What's up?"

He gestures at his little stand on which are two stacks of paper stashed neatly in white stationery boxes. He's wearing his familiar scruffy ski jacket, but on each side of the front zipper, he's pinned a large red Valentine, cut from heavy paper. "Remember them poems we looked at last week? Well, I did them in colour on the computer at the Mission. So here's the fucking deal. You get to choose one or the other; I give you a personal inscription on the top. And all for a loonie or any donation you wanna make. A bargoon, eh?"

Roberta sees "Come live with me and be my love" in one box, and "How do I love thee? Let me count the ways" in the other. She likes the fact that he has two of the poems they studied in a session on "The World's Best-Known Love Poetry." And if he can make a few loonies from it, well, that makes her happy too.

"How about it, Roberta? You got a man in your life?"

"I did have one, my husband."

"Aw, fuck, I didn't mean to... Hey, I remember now, he died, didn't he? That's why you were away from the Mission for so long. So why'm I talking about selling you love poems, eh?" Big Chris reaches out his large hand wrapped in a ragged mitten and touches her sleeve. "Sorry, sorry."

"It's okay, Chris," she says. "I'm okay, really." She takes a deep breath. "And yes, there may be someone new in my life. I'm taking a chance here. But give me Elizabeth Barrett Browning's poem, and I'll tell you what to write on the top."

So she waits while he kneels behind the tiny folding table, takes off his mittens, and with a thick-nibbed pen, inscribes, "To Carl: I love thee freely" on the top of the poem in a script remarkably like the computer font.

"Hey, it's on the house," Big Chris says as Roberta offers a loonie. "See you next week."

"Thanks, Chris. Good luck with your enterprise. I really like the idea." She moves off, making room for a grey-haired woman with a gentle face who's been standing behind her. Does she have someone in her life to love? Or is she pretending too?

When Roberta is out of Big Chris's range, she considers putting the poem into a recycling bin, but at the last moment, without looking at it, she tucks it into her purse.

.

26.

JUST INSIDE THE FRONT DOOR of Trinity College, the Porter hails Roberta. "Professor Greaves, I've got something for you." On the counter in the Lodge is a huge bunch of white lilies, red roses, and little white blossoms, the name of which Roberta cannot remember.

"Got an admirer, looks like," the Porter says. "Sign here, please."

Bouquet in hand, she turns towards the door and almost bumps into Provost Witherspoon.

"Saw you coming up the front walk and just had to get over here," he says. "Have you seen this?" He thrusts a copy of *The Times Literary Supplement* so close to her face she cannot avoid seeing the picture of herself on the front cover with the words below in huge print: "Canada's most eminent classicist" and "Fiona Black reviews *The Cretan Manuscripts.*"

She's taken aback for a minute. "I had no idea—"

"Well done, my dear," the Provost says, beaming at her. "I know you'll be hearing more about it." He pumps her free hand and then pushes his copy of the *TLS* into it and says, "Must run now. The troops await my views on St. Paul among the Corinthians."

In her office, she sets the flowers on her desk. They're wrapped in a square of snow-white cloth and tied with a silk cord — clearly from an expensive florist. Could it be Carl? But why would he send her flowers? She opens the envelope attached to the cloth with a fancy silver pin and reads the card inside: "From the Faculty of English in recognition of the distinction brought to the College with your renowned translation of the Cretan manuscripts." Well, that's a nice tribute. But the cloying scent of the lilies chokes her. She opens a window to let in the cool morning breeze from the quadrangle.

She checks her office answering machine. Nothing there. What did she expect?

She'd better get the flowers into water, but she needs a pitcher or something. She goes next door to Joan Wishart's office, then changes her mind — no favours needed from that woman, thank you — and moves two doors down to Doug Dunsmore's office. There's a moment's pause, then Doug opens the door. His face is rather red, his tie is unknotted, and he's running his hand through a dishevelled mop of hair. On a chair near the bookcase, Geoff Teasdale, the young lecturer in Comparative Literature, sits. He's flipping through the pages of a book, but Roberta notes that it's upside down.

Have they been having an argument about something? "Sorry to disturb you," she says, "but I need some sort of container for those lovely flowers the English Department gave me."

Doug has an attractive brass-plated wastebasket that he scoops up from the floor, emptying its contents into a plastic bag hanging on his coat rack. "Will this do?"

"Perfect."

"And congratulations, Roberta. Have to tell you it was Wishart's idea about the flowers. Just so you know to make a big fuss when you see the woman, okay?"

Roberta takes the wastebasket along the hall to the washroom where she fills it with water. The flowers look pretty in it, but the scent of the lilies reminds her of funeral homes and funeral wreaths. Oh God, will she ever be able to put the last few months behind her and move on?

She sits at her desk and reads the TLS review. She has always been a fan of the publication with its long paragraphs and erudite style, its total indifference to what John Schubert would call "the masses." But this praise of her translation troubles her. Phrases like "mesmerizing new translation" and "exceptional accomplishment" grate. It's only a few weeks until *Mira* hits the bookstands. On the one hand, all this fame may protect her from discovery. On the other hand, if her double identity *is* discovered, the wreckage may be even worse than she has anticipated.

She looks at her watch. No time now for further speculation. The flowers having been taken care of and the review filed in the bottom drawer of her desk, she heads off for her morning lecture in Room 101.

Just outside the door, she hears a familiar voice loud over the buzz of the others in the room. "Hey, can anyone recommend a love poem that would turn up the heat tonight? I can't think of anything but that Ogden Nash thing, you know the one—"

She steps into the room, interrupting the laughter and catching the speaker by surprise. It's one of her favourite students, a slender young man wearing a torn academic gown over a T-shirt that says, "I'm a born-again Christian." His face flushes, suffusing for a moment the rash of acne on his chin.

"Thanks, Jason," she says, putting her books and lecture notes on her desk. "You've set the stage for my comments today. I thought I might tell you something about the origins of St. Valentine's Day before we move on to Ted Hughes's translation of Ovid.

"Stories have come down to us of two men called Valentine who lived under the rule of the Roman Emperor Claudius II and who were executed by him on the same day, February 14, in 269 A.D. So I think it's likely that there was really only one individual.

"Valentine was a bishop who performed marriage ceremonies for young men and women. When Claudius, attempting to free up recruits for the Roman army, banned engagements and marriages, Valentine ignored the edict and continued to marry people.

"Claudius imprisoned Valentine, of course, and sentenced him to death. In jail, he fell in love with a blind girl, the jailer's daughter. Just before his death, as he was put into the tumbrel to go to the place of execution, he handed her a love letter signed 'From Your Valentine.' It was the first handwriting she had ever seen because, as he gave the letter to her, he said a few words and miraculously restored her sight."

"You're kidding," Jason says.

"You can say that," Roberta asks, "wearing a T-shirt that indicates you're a believer?"

The class laughs, and Jason says, "Oh please, Professor Greaves, I got it in the bin at the Goodwill. What can you expect for a loonie?"

"Not belief, evidently. And of course, the story of St. Valentine is myth. But Northrop Frye, my favourite professor from my long-ago student days, defined myth as an important story that has shaped our culture. He himself, a former minister, always referred to the Christian stories as myths; that is, important stories. Know these stories, he would say, but make up your own minds about belief. And I think all of us believe in the power of love, so we may be ready to accept the St. Valentine story and its miracle." There is silence while they digest this. Then Roberta starts in on Ted Hughes's translation.

Noon hour finds her at High Table in Strachan Hall, an experience she usually enjoys, even though she sympathizes with the student rant in the latest issue of *Salterrae* that calls High Table elitist, patriarchal, and generally contemptible. The table is "high" because it's on a platform looking down on the undergraduate tables stretched out below. She'd be happier to have everyone on the same level, but she cannot imagine actually sitting at a student table, and she knows most of the students would be uncomfortable having to make conversation with their profs.

Today, as she cuts into the excellent roast beef, she nods across the table at Doug Dunsmore and Geoff Teasdale who are seated side by side. They're generally good company. They like to talk about their courses and the books they're reading.

"What a day," she says. "Do you hate Valentine's Day as much as I do?"

But the two men are not listening. They are laughing together, in fact giggling, in a decidedly idiotic way, and do not seem to register her presence. Her napkin drops to the floor. Diving between the heavy oak table legs to retrieve it, she notices Doug's shiny Florsheim loafer pressed against a well-scuffed boot. *So that's what the embarrassment this morning was all about. Well, good for them.* But really, Valentine's Day is starting to make her feel like some sort of pariah.

"Sorry to rush off, Roberta," Doug says, finally noticing her. "Geoff and I arrived here early, and we're going to take a quick trot around Queen's Park Circle before afternoon classes. We'd ask you to come with us, but you've got to eat, right?"

Roberta is left now to stare across the table at two empty chairs. She finishes a few mouthfuls of beef, and seeing Joan Wishart coming through the dining hall to High Table, she decides it's time to escape.

There are two messages on the answering machine when she gets home. For a moment, she's hopeful. Maybe Carl has phoned to ask her to go to the Hot Spot for dinner. Even if they are beside lovers, it will be pleasant to get out and away from this horrible loneliness. She presses "Play."

"Hi, Ma," the first message says. "I'm taking Ashley out tonight. A romantic interlude if you know what I mean. Don't worry if I'm home very late. Hope you got our Valentine this morning. Bye for now."

"Hi, Mom," Charlie's voice says in the second message. "We're totally booked here at The Fig Leaf. Not a table that hasn't been reserved. Our *prix fixe* menu features beef heart or pork tenderloin — get it? — with a gooey chocolate cup-cake for dessert. Revolting, but what can I do? I'll probably be back late. See you."

Roberta pours a glass of wine and stretches out on the sofa with a volume of William Trevor's stories. She can count on him to eschew the romantic. She dips into one about a husband who has run off with his wife's sister. The phone rings. Here it is, she thinks, leaping up. Carl at last.

"God, what a day," he says without preliminaries. "I had to pass out those stupid Valentine cards that the kids bought from the Student Council. It's a fundraiser. And there was so much giggling about who was going to get one and from whom. Know something? I hate copulating seventeen-year-olds who have no idea what love is all about. But I run on. How was your day?"

"I think my college students are already starting to get a bit disillusioned about love." She tells him of Jason's cynicism about the St. Valentine story.

"Good for him. I did *my* best to introduce a little cynicism into the day. I told the kids how it all started with Pan, brutish in appearance and brutal in his desires."

"You didn't!"

"Yes, I did. I mentioned how, on February 14, Pan would make a whip out of a strip of goatskin and beat any innocent maiden who came his way...."

"Thus ensuring her fertility. Oh Carl, wasn't that a bit ex-treme?"

"Probably. I expect I'll be summoned to the principal's office tomorrow. But before she gives me my walking papers, I'll show her the relevant passage from *The Golden Bough*." He clears his throat. "And tomorrow, I'll apologize to the class and make up for my sins by reading them a sonnet or two from the Bard: '*Love is not love / Which alters when it alteration finds*,' etc., that sort of stuff."

"What are you doing tonight?" Roberta asks. "Besides confessing your sins?"

"I've got a bottle of good Scotch I'm going to get into in a serious way." There's a long pause. Then he says, "Remember how I told you about Claire and our Valentine's Day a year ago? How she threw the box of chocolates I bought her into the basin she'd just puked into?"

"Yes, I remember."

"I can't get it out of my mind. I hate Valentine's Day." His voice breaks. "But I shouldn't have taken out my sorrow on the kids. And I'm sorry about us, Rob. I wanted to do something tonight, but…"

"I understand," Roberta says. "Let's just get this day over with, and I'll see you sometime soon."

She hangs up. I've been acting like one of those silly girls in Carl's class. Get used to being alone, she tells herself. There are worse fates. Like being outed as Renee Meadows, for example.

She's so cold now. What to do? Only the usual. She goes into the bathroom, fills the tub with scalding water and climbs in. An hour later, she wakes up. Her *New Yorker* magazine lies soaked in the tepid water. What time is it? Still only eight o'clock. She turns her hair dryer on the magazine and sets it over the shower rail to finish drying. Then she crawls into bed.

As she tries to get warm under the covers, she thinks, I don't hate Valentine's Day. *I just need a warm, loving body beside me.* And then she remembers that her mother said the very same thing to her a month ago.

She gets up, searches through a cardboard box in the clothes closet and extracts the old CD of Robert Burns's love songs. To the strains of *"O my luve is like a red, red rose,"* she thinks about James and falls asleep.

27.

A FEW WEEKS LATER, on her way down St. George Street
for her volunteer work with the street kids, Roberta pulls
out her BlackBerry and sees a message from Marianne. *Call
me.* She punches in Marianne's number.

"Oh, Roberta, I'd been hoping you'd call. Got a carton of
books here for you."

"Books?"

"Yeah, books. That's what we're here for, isn't it? So what
do I do with them, eh?"

"You mean the damn thing's out already?"

"Oh, get with it, Renee baby. Didn't George Korda say
early April? And it's end of March now, isn't it? So I've got
this box of free author's copies for you. Twenty-five of them.
George sent them special delivery this morning. So what do I
do with them?"

Well, she knows what her poets would say, but Marianne
doesn't deserve their four-letter words.

"Hello? Anyone at home?"

"Got a recycling box down there, Marianne?"

"Yeah, I get what you're saying. But it seems a shame. Are
you sure?"

"Sure."

Toss out a box of books, sure, that's the easy part. But it's
like the old story of the Dutch boy who tried to stop the flood
by putting his finger in the dyke. Soon, *Mira* will be on book-

shelves everywhere, and there won't be a goddamn thing she can do about it.

In fact, the Christian Mission may soon be the only safe haven she'll have. The kids in the YES program are always a challenge, but at least she won't have to fear awkward questions on *Mira* from them. She doubts that any of them would have money to spend on a book. She does sometimes see them carrying the free subway paper, *Toronto Weekly*, but they seem indifferent to the copies of *The Gazette* and *National Telegram* that the Mission provides, perhaps because they resent the way Annie, the staff counsellor, removes some of the pages carrying the most sensational news of the day.

As Roberta turns onto Major Street and comes through the front door of the Mission, Annie waves at her from the cubbyhole that passes for her office. "Nice of your son to provide that food every week," she says. "It's a big factor in getting the gang here on time, too. Big Chris was back with it at five to two on the dot, and by that time, they were all waiting for it down below."

"I'll tell Charlie," Roberta says, smiling.

She goes down the stairs to find the kids sitting around the Arborite table. Big Chris is just opening the box he has picked up from The Fig Leaf, and a scent of cheese and onion escapes in a puff.

"Smells good," Bat says. The bruises have gone from his face, and Roberta sees a nice-looking boy with good cheekbones and blue eyes. "But what the hell is it? Looks like a plank of plywood."

"Don't quote me," Roberta says. "Charlie's the cook, but I think it's flatbread."

Big Chris cuts it in squares with a knife from his pocket. Oh, Lord, am I supposed to report this? Roberta wonders, but the moment passes as Bat distributes the paper plates and napkins Charlie has provided.

They approach their treat cautiously, but after the first small tentative bites, they gulp it down. "Good stuff, good stuff," is Moose's comment. He's a skinny kid whose ears always seem too big for his face.

It *is* good, with walnuts and slices of baked — what? Pear? — added to the onions and cheese. Roberta is hungry. Possibly something to do with the sheer relief of having a momentary respite from what's to come now that her dirty little book has been let loose on the world.

"So, let's get down to poetry," she says as Moose gathers up the empty plates and dumps them in a garbage bag. "I'd like you to write a poem today that starts with the words 'I remember.' You can write about any event you can remember that's made a difference in your life for better or worse. The only catch is that you've got to have a metaphor somewhere in it."

"And what the fuck is that supposed to mean?" It's Hester's first comment of the afternoon. She's been crying about something, and her mascara has run down her cheeks. Her dog Scrappy is sitting close to her, as always, but he seems to know she's unhappy, and he's put his nose on her lap.

"Let's look at this poem and I think it'll be clear," Roberta says as she passes out some lines that she found recently in a journal she'd written years before, just after her father's death. "It's not a great poem," she tells the kids, "but I wrote it at a time when I felt desperate and I think you may find something in it you can relate to."

> *Reach high for hope!*
> *If you let hope go,*
> *The sky grows dark*
> *And the wild snow blows.*

"Okay, so let's look for words that show what happens if you don't hang on to hope," Roberta says. "My father died, and for a while I was desolate. I had little to sustain me. Then

I wrote this poem about reaching for hope and I started to feel better."

"You were a druggie, right?" Moose says.

Where the hell is this coming from? Roberta asks herself.

"Man, it's crazy. You're saying that life is bad when you don't have hope? Snow *gives* you hope. For a while anyways."

"You've lost me," Roberta says.

Big Chris takes over. "He means that crack makes you feel good."

"Crack? Why are you talking about crack?"

Laughs all around the table. Clearly she's out of it.

"Snow," Chris says. "Moose thinks that snow is a metaphor for cocaine."

"I haven't a fuckin' clue what you guys are talking about," Moose says. His face and his big ears have turned red. "Hell, snow *is* cocaine. So what's all this shit about metaphors?"

Roberta gives a sigh. It's hopeless. Hopeless. Maybe she should have foreseen this double-talk about snow. She *has* heard the term, now that she thinks about it. Where to go from here? "Maybe we should just get started on the 'I remember' poems and forget about metaphor. Yes, let's do that."

"Hold it a sec, Roberta," Big Chris says. He turns to Moose. "Let's put it this way. You're telling a bunch of kids about something real weird you did last night, and they say to you, 'That's a crock of shit.' What do they mean?"

Moose thinks for a moment. "They don't believe nothing I said to them."

"Right. They don't actually mean that there's a big container of stinky brown stuff. So, 'crock of shit' is a metaphor for a story that doesn't seem true. Get it?"

"Got it. Why didn't you explain it right the first time, Roberta?"

There's some brainstorming then — first-time sex, the day Dad topped himself, a foster home from hell, a picnic with Grandpa in High Park, and so on — and they get down to work.

All of them, except Hester. She's heading for the door, Scrappy behind her. It's a quiet exit, and Roberta waits until she can no longer hear the sound of her feet on the staircase. Then — since the group seems absorbed in their memories — she gets up, puts her purse over her shoulder, and leaves the room.

Annie calls to her from her office. "Out in the alley, if you're looking for Hester." She gestures at the dirty window, and Roberta sees the girl sitting on an upturned wooden crate, lighting up a cigarette, her dog beside her.

Roberta goes into the alley, finds a crate, and pulls it up beside Hester. For a minute, she thinks the girl will bolt, but she doesn't. She just stares at Roberta through tear-stained eyes.

"Sorry you didn't like the class," Roberta says. "Anything I can do?"

"It's not the fucking class that pissed me off."

"What has made you angry then?"

"They're all, like, remembering things. But I don't want to remember. Some things, better you should forget them."

"Yes, I know that. Lots of things in my life I'd like to forget. But sometimes, it helps if we can get them out of our heads in some way or another. In a poem maybe. Or a story. Or maybe just talking to Annie?"

"That bitch? Thinks she's a helluva lot better than me and lets me know it."

"Anyone else then you could talk to?"

No response. Roberta waits for several minutes, then decides to get back to the rest of the kids. Nothing she can do for Hester evidently. She pushes herself up off the crate. But as she moves away, Hester's voice stops her.

"Last night. I didn't have no money, see, people been cursing me all day. I even went out on that goddamn highway and tried cleaning windshields. All I had at ten o'clock was a dirty pail of water and an empty baseball cap with a couple quarters. I was hungry and Scrappy didn't have no food either so I did…" She puts her arms around her dog's middle and pulls him towards her.

"Did what, Hester?"

"Turned tricks."

"And something bad happened this time? That's what you don't want to remember?"

"I went along Front Street to that big grey building where this guy works. He always comes out into the parking lot after ten. He has this big black car with leather seats, and he parks it in a dark spot in the corner of the lot. If me or Lori-Lyn is there, he wants a blow job. Always quick and the bills are good."

Roberta waits. She doesn't want to hear any more, but she's not going to walk out on this child now.

"So I just stood in the shadows near the car and waited till he came out. When he was turning the key in his lock, he sees me. 'Get in,' he says. So I tied Scrappy to a bike rack and got into the back seat where he likes to do it. 'Make it quick,' he says.

"So I go, like, straight for his crotch. Trouble was, I couldn't get his fucking zipper down. It got caught on his gotchees. And I couldn't see in the dark how to get the fucking thing fixed. And my hands were shaking. He yelled at me, 'Damn you, damn you, if you tear my silk boxers, I'll knock you senseless!' I was scared. See, once he whacked Lori-Lyn and gave her two black eyes.

"And while I've got my head down trying to get the zipper open, I could hear this ripping noise. I'd tore his gotchees. I knew I was in for it." Hester stands up now, throws her cigarette butt into a puddle, and grabs Roberta's wrist. Her nails are dirty and broken and her grip is hard. Her breath is fetid with onion and cheese and cigarettes.

"He belts me one across the back of the head with his fucking BlackBerry." She turns her head so that Roberta can see the bloody abrasion at the base of her neck.

"Then he yells, 'Get out, get out,' and opens the door and pushes me onto the pavement. 'Go to hell,' he says. And he drives off with a screech, almost got Scrappy when he backed up. And that's it. No bills neither, so I had no food, just a mess on my head."

"The police should get involved in this. You're sixteen, right? Do you know anything about the guy? His name, for instance?"

"I don't want no cops in this. And I don't know his real name. Lori-Lyn and me, we call him 'The Skunk.'"

Oh my God. "Why do you call him 'The Skunk'?"

"It's his fucking name, see? He's got this big white strip in the middle of his hair, and he stinks like … like air freshener in a subway toilet."

"And he works in a big grey building on Front Street?"

"Yeah, didn't I say?"

Roberta has heard enough. She has a pretty clear idea who The Skunk is. She's always known John Schubert was a creep, but his indulgence in this sort of sexual exploitation has gone too far. *Oh my God, yes, I'm going to have to do something about this.*

"Look here, Hester. I can go to the police and tell them all this. They'll probably want to talk to you, but I can set it — "

"No cops, no cops. When Lori-Lyn showed them her black eyes, the fuckers said, 'You're a slut, whaddya expect?' No way I'm going to the cops. If you tell them, I'll … I'll … top myself."

She lets out a wail that ends in hiccups. "Who would care, except maybe Scrappy." She grabs his leash. "Come on, we're outta here."

"Wait. I have another idea." Roberta fishes in her purse, pulls out two fifty-dollar bills and shoves them towards Hester. "I'm giving you these. I want you to take them. But I need a promise from you."

Hester looks at the bills, then turns her head away so that Roberta has no idea what she's thinking. But at least she's not moving out of the alley. So she continues: "Here's the deal. The money's yours. But you've got to promise me that you won't do any more tricks or mention topping yourself. Meantime,

I'll talk to Annie about getting you into some safe place where you'll have a room to go to every night and where you can get a sandwich or something when you get home. She can maybe help you get a job too. I think even behind the counter at Mc-Donald's would be better than getting beaten up by skunks. Am I right?"

"Yeah. But I'm not promising nothing unless *you* promise me, no cops."

"No cops. It's a deal then." And she hands the money to Hester.

"Thanks." There is a long pause while the girl tucks the bills into a dirty little cloth purse that dangles from a cord around her neck. There's a smile now, not much of a one, but definitely a smile. "You're a good person, Roberta, and this ... talk we've had ... it's one nice fucking memory."

28.

AS ROBERTA WAITS WITH HER CAN of hairspray in the lineup at Pharma Plus, she notices what the man ahead of her is clutching: A copy of *Mira*, no less. He's a middle-aged man with stubby fingers and a dirty scarf thrown over a scruffy topcoat, and since the lineup is not moving — the cashier having gone off somewhere to get more change — he looks back at Roberta, sees her staring at his book and says, "Read this one?"

"Yes," she says. "Sickening."

"I Googled it," the man says, evidently proud of his computer savvy. "And wow, the reviews. It's apparently a new take on the *Lolita* thing. You know, I get sick of the guy always getting blamed. And with this one," he waves the book at her again, "it's the kid who's to blame. Heard what that cop said on the morning news today?"

"Mmm." *Oh God, where is the cashier?*

"And I agree, one hundred percent. If a girl dresses like a slut, she deserves to get raped. Right?"

"No."

"No? You gotta be kidding. But maybe you don't know what I'm getting at. In this here book, there's a kid called Mira. She gets into bed with her old man, well, her stepfather actually — believe it, totally nude — and he's turned on. That's what I mean. She's the slut, isn't she? She's asking for it. This Renee Meadows person gets it right for a change. So it's worth the fifteen bucks I'm shelling out for it."

Roberta stares at the floor, trying to shut out the man *and* the book. She tries not to think about the interview she has later this morning with John Schubert. What's he going to say to her? More questions about George Korda?

"Well, guess you don't wanna talk. Okay by me." The man turns his back on her , and then the cashier mercifully arrives and the lineup moves forward.

To get to the damn exit, she's got to pass the book rack and a pimply girl with spiky green hair who has picked up a copy of *Mira*. She's looking at the cover. It shows a young girl in a white bra and briefs about to climb into bed beside a much older man, his face barely visible in a dark room. Roberta doesn't know who designed it, but it certainly sums up what's inside.

Oh, just let me out of here, Roberta thinks. Even the fumes of traffic along Bloor Street West are preferable to the poison of this place. She looks at her watch. Time to catch the subway for her ten o'clock class at Trinity.

And all the way to the university, she steadies herself against a metal pole and looks down at the passengers reading in the seats in front of her. She's always been interested in what people read on the subway. This morning's choices range from text messages to the *Toronto Weekly* to Nora Roberts. But the encounter with the *Mira* reader has made her uneasy. What next? Will there be someone else this morning who will be reading it? The Spadina subway stop, her exit, comes as a relief.

Her Classics in Translation class is quiet, thank God. Not a mention of *Mira*. Perhaps it's the time of year. The students are much more serious and much more focused than they were a few weeks earlier. It's the worry over the final exams, Roberta suspects. She delivers her lecture on T. E. Lawrence's translation of *The Odyssey* in a silence punctuated only by the rattle of the radiator and the tapping of fingers on laptops.

As she asks for questions at the end of her lecture, she sees Jason Grubben's hand in the air. Uh, oh. Is the great axe about to fall?

"This guy's Lawrence of Arabia, right?"

"Right." She gives some details of Lawrence's biography. *Tap, tap, tap* on the laptops. Jason scribbles away in his notebook. Will this be on the exam? That's what they are probably thinking.

And now comes the part of her day she's been dreading. Up the stone stairway in front of her second-floor office, John Schubert is waiting for her on a bench. He's looking at his watch as she approaches. "You did say eleven o'clock, didn't you?"

"Yes, it's five after now. Sorry about that."

"You're forgiven, but if I'd known you were going to be late, I'd have smoked a Gitanes in the quadrangle."

Schubert is dressed in a beautiful double-breasted grey suit and he has a small leather satchel — on a woman, it would be a purse — over his shoulder. His black hair with the distinctive white stripe is carefully slicked back. The Skunk. Roberta hates the sight of him, especially now that she knows about his abuse of Hester. But she agreed to the interview a couple of weeks ago, before she heard the girl's story.

He takes a seat without waiting for an invitation and pulls out a digital voice recorder from his purse. He fiddles with it for a few seconds, then puts it away and gets out his leather notebook and fountain pen. "More comfortable with this, I confess."

"I'm with you there," Roberta says, trying to smooth down her anger. Exposure in *The Gazette* will probably promote sales of her translation. But more important, it will put focus on the good side of her writing life.

"As you know, I'm here to talk about *The Cretan Manuscripts.* You got this big-time review in the *TLS* — congrats on that, by the way — and I thought a major interview for *The*

Gazette might be in order." He looks at his watch again. "The photographer should be along by now. I *told* him eleven—"

There's a knock on the door, and the photographer comes in. In contrast to Schubert, he's wearing an open-necked shirt and jeans with holes in the knees. "Joe," Schubert says, his only effort at an introduction. "Now let's get to it. I'd like a shot of the professor behind her desk with her bookshelves as background."

"Bit of a cliché," Joe says. "How about in front of that nice leaded-glass window?"

"Behind the desk with the bookshelves," Schubert says, as if he were Norman Jewison directing Michael Caine. "Let's not waste time." He looks at Roberta. "Maybe you want to fix your hair a bit, dear. There's a teeny strand sticking up."

"This is how I am, and this is how I'll have to be," Roberta says. Behind Schubert, Joe gives her a wink.

He takes a dozen shots in rapid succession, then waves his hand and hoists his equipment onto his back. "Can't stand that cretin," Schubert says, as Joe shuts the door behind him, "but he's one of the burdens I bear on a daily basis.

"Now, let's get to the important stuff, the interview." He picks up his leather notebook and uncaps his pen. "What were the major problems you encountered with your translation?"

"Deciphering the script on the parchment, definitely. But really, I was lucky to have a parchment version because we think that the stories were originally written on papyrus, and that would have meant trying to piece together broken bits and pieces. But it seems someone copied it over on the parchment." Roberta goes on to describe the hours spent looking at the long scrolls in the Heraklion Archaeological Museum, magnifying glass in hand. As she talks, she remembers that her whole family had been with her in Heraklion for eight weeks. While she worked, James had spent his days in a neighbourhood taverna sipping *raki* and working on journal articles on Anthony Trollope, while the boys, who were teenagers then, had loved the hours of surfing and sunning on the beautiful beaches. Almost every evening they'd spent on Paniota Andriopoulos's terrace drinking the local wine — fresh orange juice for the kids — and eating pilaf. Those were happy days.

"You seem a teeny bit out of it today, Roberta." She snaps back to attention and tries to concentrate on the interview: questions on her university pedigree, the course content of her present-day classes, her concept of the role of a good translator, and on and on. She has to concede that Schubert knows his stuff.

At last, it's over. Schubert puts his notebook away. "Thanks for this."

"I'm impressed with the understanding you have of the problems translators face," Roberta says. But she cannot stop herself from adding, "You've come a distance since that backyard review you gave of my poetry book."

He's caught off guard for a moment. Then he laughs, only it's more of a sneer. "Well, perhaps that's because *The Cretan Manuscripts* is just not in the same league as your little poetry offering."

"I guess I asked for that."

"This *is* big league stuff, my dear. I liked the stories, *except* the 'Pygmalion' one. I'm a teeny bit *miffed* by what Euripida has done with that one. The original story is lovely. To me, it describes the perfection every artist should strive for. You know, in a way, I look on Ovid's Pygmalion as a sort of role model. I too seek perfection." Schubert has beautiful hands, and he flips his palms up whenever he makes a point.

"I guess there's nothing wrong in seeking perfection. But it seems to me that Pygmalion wants to sculpt a perfect ivory woman because there isn't a human one good enough for him. You think that's *lovely*? *Sick* might be a better word."

"I'm not here to argue, dear Roberta. You're the star of this show. *Moi*, I'm merely the humble conduit for your opinions." He waves his fountain pen at her and bares the teeth in what passes for a smile. Oh, the miracles of modern dentistry.

"And by the way," he continues, "you've rekindled my interest in Ovid. Not only have I reread 'Pygmalion' in one of those translations my Chapters card pays for, but I've segued into 'The Rape of Philomena' — now *that's* sick — and 'Myrrha' — well that one's even sicker. Oh, the depths to which humanity can sink. But fascinating, *n'est-ce pas?*"

"Glad to know I've contributed to your fund of sick knowledge, John." *Now how to get rid of him?* She looks at her watch.

"Oh, I see you're busy too, dear, so I'll take off." He moves to the door. "*Ciao.*"

Roberta watches him cross the quadrangle. Oh God, probably heading for the parking lot. And a big black car with leather seats? She tries to remember the kind of car she's seen in his mother's driveway. But face it, she's always had zero interest in cars. He *does* work in a big grey building farther downtown. But that description fits a thousand buildings. His hair with its white stripe could certainly earn him the name of "The Skunk." But perhaps hair had little to do with the name that Hester and her friend called their attacker. She said the person who hit them smelled bad. Well, today Schubert had a stale smell: cappuccino and cigarettes — correction, Gitanes — along with that dreadful cologne he's so fond of. So what? It's all what a lawyer might call "circumstantial evidence." Nothing to prove that he's the person the girl was talking about.

Roberta takes out an essay from the never-ending stack she keeps in a bottom drawer of her desk. She reads two pages but has no idea what she's reading. She cannot get Schubert out of her mind. *Was he telling me something when he mentioned Ovid? What was that all about? Or am I getting paranoid?*

More important: Should I have put my own fears aside and said something about his extracurricular activities? Am I so self-centred that I try to find excuses for not tackling him head-on about his abuse of a vulnerable child? I cannot fool myself. It was Schubert. I'm pretty sure of that. I've seen him in action in his mother's backyard. What was James's word? Groping the young housecleaner. But what am I going to do about his abuse of Hester?

She picks up her pen, sighs, and starts again on the essay.

29.

ROBERTA SPENDS THE REST of the day in her Trinity office, working through the pile of essays. Or hiding, if she wants to be honest. Outside her office, there's the noisy tide of students going by, but no one disturbs her. At five o'clock, she comes downstairs, passes the Porter's Lodge, and goes out the front door without having to talk to anyone.

By the time she gets home, it's after six o'clock, and Ed and Charlie have made grilled cheese sandwiches and are eating them in the breakfast room.

"Guess you've seen the book around town today?" Ed says. "I had to go into Chapters to get *Antique Furniture of Quebec* for Ashley's birthday, and there was *Mira*, right on the front table. Maybe it's not as bad as you thought, Ma, if it's featured in mainstream bookstores."

"And in every drugstore, Walmart, and subway toilet too, probably." Roberta tells them about her encounters at Pharma Plus.

"You're going to have to live with it, Mom," Charlie says, putting a sandwich on her plate. "We've just got to hope that nobody will figure out who Renee Meadows is, and there's no reason anyone should know, is there?"

"I'm worried about Mrs. Schubert's son. You know, the big-time book reviewer for *The Gazette*? He had an interview with me today, ostensibly about *The Cretan Manuscripts*. It seemed to go well enough, except that at the end of it, he made a point of telling me that he's reading Ovid. He even mentioned the 'Myrrha' story and told me how sick it was. Maybe it was all chit-chat — he does like to blather — but I think there could have been a bit of a threat there."

"Doesn't sound good to me," Ed says. "You're right to be worried. He's bound to hear about your version of the story, as it's his business to know about new releases, and he'll put it all together. From what you're saying, he's a creep, but probably a smart creep."

"Hey, bro, let Mom finish her supper without all the doomsday stuff." Charlie pours her a glass of white wine. "Drink up."

She takes a sip, then sets her glass down. "Sorry, even the wine doesn't soothe. I have another worry about Schubert. But before I get into it, Charlie, I just want to tell you that all the kids in my volunteer program seem pleased with your food. Annie, the counsellor, told me that it's a factor in getting them there on time for my classes. She says she doesn't have to round them up like a sheepdog anymore."

"I was a bit worried about the pears and walnuts — an oddball combination — but it was our lunch special for the food snobs who come to The Fig Leaf and I didn't have time to get anything else ready. I like Big Chris. He's reliable. I've also noticed how clean he is, and that must be one big problem living on the street. You know, I think I might be able to find him something to do at the restaurant that would pay him more than what he gets on the street. And it would be safer too. Maybe dishwasher or security or gofer. Anyway, I'll work on it. I'm getting quite palsy-walsy with Mr. Fig Leaf himself."

"So what's the other worry about Schubert?" Ed asks.

Roberta tells them Hester's sad story. "I'm not sure where I can go with what she's told me. I can't talk to the police, she made me promise."

"It'd be useless anyway," Ed says. "You haven't got that much proof, have you? And even if you had, you might not get far. Cops like to put people into compartments, and she'd fit into their 'slut' slot perfectly. What I know from their testimony in courts, it would be an open-and-shut case if it ever came to trial. She asked for it. She lay in wait for him, got into the back seat when he asked her to, so what's more to be said?" He sighs. "Face it, folks, we live in a fallen world."

"But she's only sixteen. And he's what? Fifty? What the hell, Ed? You're turning into a cynic, big-time." Charlie shakes his head.

"Well what could be proved? He'd deny everything. 'A big grey building' is not exactly compelling evidence of where he works. And the lot the car was in is just one of acres of public space given over to downtown parking."

"Man, doesn't the skunk description point to someone specific?"

"Come on, Charlie. I heard the term today from Mr. Peabody, no less. I was in his office getting my day's work laid out for me, and the phone rang. So he turns on his timer, even though he spent all of two minutes with the caller. But two minutes at eight hundred bucks an hour, well, he finds that significant.

"But I'm getting off topic. I hear him say ..." Here Ed swings into his Mr. Peabody impersonation. 'The firm of Plumtree, Pogson, and Peabody has no dealings with drug dealers or other forms of the common criminal.' Then he hangs up, waves his manicured paw at me and says, 'Our dealings are with elephants, not skunks!'"

"'Elephants' being a metaphor for big-time white-collar stuff?"

"You got it, my boy. Enron and Madoff? *They're* elephants."

"And 'skunks' are the lower orders. I see what you mean, bro." Charlie rubs his hand across his shaved head. Everyone is silent for a minute. Then Charlie bangs his fist on the table. "Got it!"

Roberta and Ed stare at him.

"What I mean, is this: We pretty well know that this Schubert prick *is* the skunk. I know, I know," he continues as Ed tries to break in, "there's nothing we can *prove* in a court of law. But we do know what's what and we can scare the guy."

"To what point?"

"Well, let's say Mom gives him a phone call, drops a few innuendos into the conversation just to let him know that she knows what he's been up to with Hester. That would work, wouldn't it?"

"Ah, I get you," Ed says. "A little blackmail." He leans back in his chair and looks at the ceiling for a minute or two. Then he sits up straight, smiling. "Good thinking, Charlie. It *could* work."

"I know it's a fallen world, bro, but I wasn't thinking about 'blackmail.' I was thinking about scaring him off any more sick encounters with vulnerable people. But now that you mention it—"

"Please, boys, fill me in, will you?"

"It's this way, Ma," Ed says. "Suppose Schubert *did* have something in mind when he made a big deal out of telling you he was reading Ovid. Suppose you talk to him soon — maybe phone him up and thank him for the interview or something — and he makes another reference to the 'Myrrha' story, says again that it's sick or something...."

"Then *you* say," Charlie adds, "something to the effect that there are so many sick things in this world. And then you pitch in with Hester's story about her encounter with some prick she calls The Skunk...."

"And there'll be a standoff without a word having to be spoken," Ed says. "He'll be so scared of *his* reputation being torn apart if you speak out, he'll know to keep his mouth shut about *your* reputation. Secrets will stay secret."

"You'll cover your ass, that's what, and he'll be able to cover his." Charlie gets up from the table and takes the wine bottle from the kitchen counter. "So let's drink to problems solved."

"To problems solved!" Roberta's sons clink glasses. And then they notice that she's not joining them.

"What's up?" they ask.

"I'll have to think about it," Roberta says. "If I could stop Schubert from victimizing girls like Hester, I'm for it. But blackmail — yes, you called it by its right name, Ed — is one step deeper into the abyss I've already fallen into..." She breaks off. "Thanks for trying to help. But I don't see blackmail as a problem-solver."

"You'll think about what we've said though, won't you?" Charlie asks.

She pushes her glass of wine aside and nods. Yes, she will certainly think about it.

30.

WHEN ROBERTA COMES DOWN to breakfast the next morning, the boys have already left for work. They've put the morning edition of *The Gazette* on the table beside a glass of freshly squeezed orange juice; Charlie's offering, she suspects.

She turns immediately to the "Entertainment" section. There it is, titled as always, "The Schubert Interview," this time with the subtitle, "Roberta Greaves talks to *The Gazette.*" She glances at the photo that Joe took — not bad — and plunges into the text: "Attractive Roberta Greaves, scholar, writer, and teacher ... *blah blah* ... surrounded by books in her Trinity College office ... *blah blah* ... mid-forties, but looking ten years younger ... impressive credentials ... chosen from a worldwide academic community to translate the most important ancient manuscripts to surface in the past half-century...."

The next paragraphs get down to a description of the finding of the scrolls by a small boy searching for firewood in a cave and how he gave them to his teacher who handed them over to the University of Crete. She reads on. "Greaves freely acknowledges that her friendship with Paniota Andriopoulos, Chair of the Department of Archaeology, may have influenced her appointment as translator, but there's not a scholar anywhere who would deny that the choice was a good one."

And then there are two columns about the contents of Euripida's stories, the translation process with its difficulties, and the worldwide accolades for Roberta's work. All generous, she has to admit.

Then she comes to the last paragraph: "But Roberta Greaves, in spite of her international acclaim and impeccable reputation, has always been a free spirit. She is not defined solely by her role in the world of academe. She has always had her own milieu. Her husband, with whom she lived happily for many years, was a racehorse owner who died suddenly. Lately, she seems to have rallied from that tragedy and moved on. I'll be interviewing Dr. Greaves at the Harbourfront Reading Series in May, and perhaps by then, her many fans will be able to hear about fresh projects she's been working on."

Shit.

The phone rings. It's Carl. "You've seen this morning's *Gazette,* Robbie?"

"Just read it."

"El Creepo is onto something, wouldn't you say?"

"I think so."

"What will you do?"

"I'm about to phone him and ask him to meet me somewhere after work. There are a few things I need to straighten out with him. I met George Korda once, for God's sake, and now he's babbling about my moving on to 'fresh projects.'"

"No, no, Robbie. Whatever you say, don't mention Korda. El Creepo would infer that there's good reason for your angst."

"Well, I've got to say something, but I'll think carefully how to word it. James was a 'racehorse owner,' was he? Schubert knows very well he was an academic, like me."

"He wants to set you up as having a double life. Too bad he introduces that bit of innuendo in the last paragraph. Some people I know don't bother reading the middle. They just glance over the beginning and jump to the end."

"Well, I guess I do have a double life. But he has one too." Roberta tells Carl about Schubert's assault on Hester. "The boys think that since I've got this insider's knowledge about him, I could use it to my advantage."

"To keep him quiet about you and Korda, you mean?" Roberta hears his microwave *ping*. "Just a sec." Roberta hears him open the door and slam it shut again with a loud bang. Then he's back on the phone, and his voice sounds strained, angry in fact. "Blackmail? Is that what you're telling me?"

"Don't worry. I have no intention of making my mess worse with that sort of stuff. But I've got to find out what he knows so that I can work things out. And I'm going to make sure he hears my suspicions about his assault on Hester. If I say nothing about anything, I'll just be a trapped mouse that he can toss in the air and play with before he moves in for the kill."

"Okay, Robbie, but please, please be careful." His voice is warmer now. It makes her happy.

"I think whatever is in that microwave is waiting for you, Carl. So go eat it and get into teaching mode. I've got to do the same. I'm so glad you called. Don't worry about me. I'll find a way to handle all this."

"I'll be thinking of you. Call me when you can."

She doesn't have to be at Trin until ten o'clock, and she puts off her call to Schubert while she gets into her high-heeled boots and dark-green pantsuit in honour of spring, though it's not until she's got it all together that she realizes she doesn't feel all that spring-like. She's too busy rehearsing her comments to Schubert to experience any of the so-called rebirth and renewal of the season. A final wrestle with some gel on her wavy hair, and she knows she's put off the call long enough. She's just coming down the stairs to the phone in the kitchen when the front doorbell rings.

It's The Skunk himself. He's dressed in his usual tailored Italian suit, but Roberta notices a bulge in his right pocket that distorts its perfect fit. "Dear Roberta," he says, inserting himself into the front vestibule as she opens the door, "it's way too early to be calling, but I had a teeny errand to run for

Mater and, well, I just *had* to drop by and see how you liked my interview." He treats her to his perfect smile. "Do feel free to rave on and on. I'm listening."

"Well, since you're here, John, why don't you come in for a minute — only a minute since I'm running a bit late — and we'll talk about it." She gestures towards the living room.

Schubert looks around at her comfortable Victorian furniture, most of it inherited from her grandparents. "Oh dear," he says as he moves in to scrutinize the Jacques and Hay secretary that was her grandfather's favourite piece. "How utterly..."

Roberta finds herself wishing for Ed's girlfriend Ashley. She too had been intrusive as she snooped around at Christmas, but her comments had at least been admiring.

Next it's the pictures that draw Schubert's scrutiny. "Good heavens," is his comment as he looks at her favourite, the 1910 de Foy Suzor-Coté oil on canvas of the habitant settler Esdras Cyr. Cyr is seated in a rocking chair, his eyes fixed slightly downward with a look of ineffable sadness. Roberta has often wondered what caused the old man's sorrow and marvels at the skill with which the painter captured the moment so perfectly. Now, she moves in front of the painting, feeling somehow that she must protect Esdras Cyr from Schubert's rude scrutiny.

"Please sit," she says, gesturing at a nearby chair. "I don't have all that long to talk."

Schubert takes the yellow silk pocket square from his suit and for a moment Roberta thinks he's going to flick it across the walnut arm of the chair. But he puts it back into his jacket pocket and sits down gingerly, perhaps worried about when she last vacuumed the dark-red velvet seat.

"Well, what did you think, my dear?"

"There was much of it I liked, John, much that was generous and insightful. But the last paragraph I found somewhat puzzling. One thing that bothered me: Surely you know that my husband James was a Trinity College professor with a special interest in Victorian literature."

"Ah, perhaps that explains this room and its furnishings and paintings. So ... quaint. So..."

"*Out of it*. That's probably the phrase you're searching for. But back to James, please. He was *not* a racehorse owner, though he did have a thoroughbred he loved to ride as a sport."

"Ah yes, well... But surely you have something to say about my comments on your new projects."

"I wasn't sure what you meant by that remark. I *may* get to a popular translation of *The Cretan Manuscripts*, but I certainly haven't committed myself to it yet."

"Dear Roberta, I know you have a rich and varied life. There's so much beneath that elegant, refined surface you present to the world. And I'm just discovering that *underbelly* — if I may call it that. Lola Lancey, remember her? Well, she and I made a deal this month: I would give her latest grubby little novel a generous review if she could extract some inside info from the editors at Mayhem. Well, dear Lola has come through with a really interesting speculation." And he draws from his right pocket the item Roberta noted earlier. *Mira*. "This is just a teeny something I wanted to check out with you. Now fess up. You *did* write it? You're Renee Meadows, *n'est-ce pas?*

"Yes."

"I knew it. The sentence on the back cover confirms my worst suspicions." He turns the book over and reads, "'A wicked, wanton, wonderful remake of age-old erotica,' a blurb by one Jade Morningstar — whoever she is. You'll fill me in, I hope, dear. But let's just take a break now if you'll permit, while I give myself a teeny pat on the back. I've done such amazing detective work. Feel free to call me Sherlock." He leans forward so that his face seems uncomfortably close, though a few feet of Persian carpet separate them.

"I don't imagine it was that hard to put together, John, and I'm not too surprised you figured it out. You saw me with George Korda, you still had it on your mind at your Christmas party, and then, at the interview at Trinity, you made a point of telling me you were reading Ovid. I had a pretty good idea that sooner or later you were going to spring it on me. So feel free to call *me* Nancy Drew."

He sits back in the chair and shoves the book back into his pocket. She can see his disappointment. No doubt he expected — indeed, came over this morning to enjoy first-hand — wild weeping and denials. Perhaps she's been the victor for round one. But she knows there's more to come.

"Now, I have a teeny dilemma here and I have to think how to handle it. I don't want to be a big meanie, but the hoi polloi have the right to know that you wrote this little gem of erotica. Yes, indeed. Here they have the big-time scholar who's translated an important archaeological moment for the world. They bow down and worship her. But for their own good, they must know that this goddess of academe is as lowdown as they are. So I think I must tell this frightful secret. Let everybody know that the high and the mighty are no better than—"

"Oh please. Stop it. I'm finding it hard to cast you as The Avenging Angel." Roberta waits for a moment to calm herself, but her anger rises up and takes over. "You, of all people. You, the big-time reviewer who translates the art world into simple language for hoi polloi. By the way, *hoi* is the definite article, so you don't need to say, *the*. And I'm not too surprised to find out that some of your big-time reviews are based on sordid little deals that you make with authors. But I digress. Perhaps the masses should know the down-and-dirty about you, too."

Schubert's face has turned pale. He puts his thumb in his mouth and takes it out again. "Dear Roberta, I haven't the faintest, teeniest idea what you're talking about."

"Then I'll remind you. I'm talking about your wretched assault of a young girl I know. She showed me the mess on the back of her head that you inflicted on her with a blunt weapon — your BlackBerry to be precise."

He takes out his handkerchief and dabs his forehead. "You have no proof." A simple declarative sentence for once in his life. Roberta knows she has nailed him.

"Oh yes, I think I have. The girl could identify you, your car, and the big grey building that houses *The Gazette* offices."

"Stop it. Stop it. I'll deny everything if you take your accusations beyond this room." He starts mopping his cheeks. "But let's not be hasty, dear. I think we can make a deal. Or put it this way, can we not have an understanding between two friends, an understanding to keep our secrets *secret*. Yes?"

Roberta does not answer.

"We *are* friends, Roberta?"

"No."

His thumb goes into his mouth again. Then, astonishingly, tears slip down his cheeks.

Roberta watches him, feeling like a snake eying a toad. She could almost pity him, were it not for that poor child in the alleyway, that lost soul with no one to love but her dog. Schubert deserves no pity.

He wipes his face again and takes a deep breath. He seems to be struggling for control. "To put it crudely then, let's say that I keep *your* dirty little secret … and you say nothing about—"

"Yours?" She stands up. "You'd better go, John."

"I need a promise."

"No promises."

He's in the vestibule now. "You bitch," he says, and then he's out the front door, slamming it behind him, fleeing like a prisoner from a lock-up. Roberta watches him run to his car in Mrs. Schubert's driveway — yes, it *is* a big black one, just as Hester said. He backs out in one smooth motion, and she can hear the roar of the engine seconds after he's disappeared from sight.

Roberta takes several deep breaths. Steadier now, she looks at her watch. Yes, she has just enough time. She goes up to her study, turns on her computer, and writes the necessary email.

To the Editor:

In the last paragraph of "The Schubert Interview" (April 6), your arts editor speculates about "fresh projects" I may be working on. He's right. I've taken a major leap from my academic world recently. I have written an erotic novel called *Mira* for the publishing company Mayhem, just out now under the pen name Renee Meadows. The story is an old one — Ovid wrote it first — and it evidently appals and titillates its audience as much today as it did two thousand years ago.

Yours truly,

Roberta Greaves

31.

I T'S AN UNSEASONABLY COLD APRIL MORNING, and Roberta pulls her cashmere scarf up around her chin as she exits from the subway. On the ride across the city, she read *The Gazette* and saw her letter on the editorial page, one day after she sent it. So the news is out. But the great axe may not fall for a day or two. Not everyone reads "Letters to the Editor" immediately.

From the subway exit at Bedford Road, she strides south on Devonshire, hoping to have time to check out a source in the Robarts Library before heading to her office. Her students have several study days before exams start, and she has to be available in case someone needs help.

But as she reaches Hoskin Avenue, she hears a commotion. Looking down the street, she sees twenty or more students on the sidewalk in front of Trin. Some of them are holding up placards. Something political maybe? Grumbles about the bombing of Tripoli? Squinting into the biting wind, she can make out some of the words on one of the signs: "SCHOLAR SCUTTLES TRINITY STANDARDS: SOMETHING SOMETHING." So the news she has dreaded is out. Damn it.

Now she has to make a decision. She can turn right, as she intended, and head for Robarts Library on St. George Street. Or do what she must do. She turns towards Trinity.

In sixty-five steps — she counts them, hoping to slow her heartbeat — she is in the midst of the protest. She looks around: Nobody here she could name though many of the young faces look familiar. At the bottom of the steps leading to the front door, a blonde girl in knee-high boots starts a chant: "PORNO PROF! PORNO PROF!" Soon, the rest of them are with her: "PORNO PROF! PORNO PROF!"

The crowd seems to thicken as more students in academic gowns emerge from the front door and join in the chanting. Roberta knows there's no way she can get into the building without being pushed about. She's able now to see the other signs. There's the inevitable pun: "GREAVES GRIEVES US." And the others say it all: "DON'T BLAME OVID FOR THE MIRA MESS," and, "SHAME, PROF GREAVES, SHAME." Now all she can think of is escape. Where? Up Philosopher's Walk? Cross Hoskin Avenue and head for the quiet of Hart House?

Panicked, she turns and finds herself pitching into the path of a tall, spindly young man who brandishes a tape recorder in her face.

"Jeff Lyons, from *The Varsity*. Care to comment on your letter in today's *Gazette*, Professor Greaves?"

"There's not much to say. The gist of it is there in the letter." She could probably get around him now if she moved quickly. No. She summons a dollop of courage from somewhere deep inside. *Stand your ground, Roberta.*

"Have you ever used your classroom as a platform for the discussion of paedophilia or kiddie porn?" A nicely loaded question.

"When I'm discussing Ovid's story 'Myrrha' with my students, naturally I have to deal with the theme of a young girl's sexual obsession with her father. But I think you mean, do I defend this theme as a lifestyle? Absolutely not."

The young reporter looks a bit at a loss now. He's still holding the recorder under her nose, but he frees one hand to take a peek at a notebook in the pocket of his windbreaker. "Perhaps you should know that one of the students here today says that if this book becomes a bestseller, it will deliver a devastating message to survivors of childhood abuse."

"Look," Roberta says to the boy, "I wrote the thing. I'm not defending my decision. The theme of incest is abhorrent to me, and especially the idea that incest may be instigated by a young woman. But I needed the money, not that that's any excuse. My dirty little novel may well become a bestseller. Perhaps not. But if it does, it will prove what H. L. Mencken says: 'No one ever went broke underestimating the taste of the American public.'"

"That's a good one. Can you spell the guy's name for me?"

Suddenly, Roberta finds herself in teacher mode again. She spells it twice, s-l-o-w-l-y. And then, she hears a shout from the front of the college. Turning, she sees Jason Grubben and just behind him, Muna Mehta, and yes, there's Bryan Schmidt with them, the kid who plagiarized parts of his essay.

They come down through the crowd to her. "Let's go, Professor," Jason says. "Take my arm, will you?" Muna's on her right side now, so close that the sleeves of their coats brush against each other. And Bryan places himself in front of them.

"What's this about?" Roberta asks.

"We're going to get you through the crowd and inside the building," Jason says. "Just hang on."

The students seem momentarily confounded. Perhaps they are hoping for some physical violence. They stop chanting, and in that brief pause, Roberta feels herself pulled forward by Jason and Muna. Bryan charges in front of them, spreading his arms wide and yelling, "Get the fuck out of our way!"

The front doors of the college have apparently been locked, but for now the Porter and a caretaker open them to let Roberta and her saviours inside. Thank God, Roberta thinks, that the Porter has always been friendly to me. Once inside the building, she is struck by the quiet. She turns to her protectors. "Thank you. You've been kind to me and I really appreciate it."

"I think your Translations class is solidly behind you," Jason says. "Most of them, anyway. And we do know the difference between erotica and porn, in spite of what those morons are shouting."

"Yeah," Bryan adds, "even me." He reaches out to shake her hand. "I remember you let me off when you could have turned me in over that kidnapping stuff." He blushes. "Sorry. I know I don't remember the right word."

"And I'm with you, too, Professor Greaves," Muna says. "Even though I think that Ovid story is one of the sickest. But you've always been fair. Not like some profs I could mention."

They stand there looking awkward, and Roberta says, "I felt a bit like one of the warriors inside the Trojan Horse back there. And I imagine you three were scared too. You showed courage. Thanks again."

They laugh now, and Jason says, "I expect the war isn't over yet. Lots of enemies out there still. Good luck, Professor." Then, the three of them head out the back door into the quadrangle.

Doug Dunsmore and Geoff Teasdale emerge from the Porter's Lodge. They are wearing their academic gowns and carrying metre sticks. "Our weaponry," Doug says. "The Provost has stationed us here to keep an eye on things."

"*En garde*," Geoff says, lunging forward, his stick brandished at an imaginary foe.

"Oh dear, what havoc I have wreaked. I can only apologize."

"Well, you have brought a hurricane down upon us," Doug says. "But like all hurricanes, it will pass."

"Probably not before some considerable destruction takes place though," Geoff adds. He leans over his metre stick now and sighs. "Oh Roberta, we don't really approve of what you've done. It was a shock to everyone, and the whole theme is abhorrent, especially to homosexuals like Doug and me who bear the brunt of people's accusations about paedophilia."

"But we've got to support you, even though what we most resent is the money you're making on this," Doug says, pulling a smile onto his face. "Your courage in writing that letter to the editor has been ... well ... I think *inspiring* is the word I want. Geoff and I have been trying to keep our relationship quiet, and now—"

"Now we've decided to come out of the closet." Geoff puts a hand on Doug's shoulder. "Doug's right, you know. You gave us inspiration."

"Inspiration?" Roberta asks. "After what you've said about the theme of the damn book?"

"Yes," Doug says. "When you wrote that letter to the paper, well, we realized then that it's time to show the same kind of courage." He smiles at his mate, then turns back to Roberta. "Oh good heavens, we've been so busy talking about ourselves that I've forgotten to pass along a message from the Provost."

"Oh dear."

"Yes, it probably won't be fun. He wants to see you in his office. He phoned down to the Porter a few minutes ago. *Pronto* was the word he used."

But Roberta is not ready for *pronto*. In fact, she finds that her legs are suddenly so wobbly she can scarcely stand. She makes it up the stairs to her office though, where she locks the door and sinks into her comfortable desk chair. She spends a few minutes taking deep breaths. Then she exits her office and goes along the corridor.

Now, Roberta is sitting opposite Provost Witherspoon in his office. He moves two piles of books from his desk to the Persian rug on the polished wood floor, leaving a clear space so that they can see each other. He's in his academic gown, probably in readiness for his Divinity seminar at eleven o'clock. The light pours in from the large windows overlooking the quadrangle.

"Better have a glass of sherry," he says, taking a bottle of Bristol Cream from the bottom drawer of his desk, along with two small crystal glasses. Roberta notices how his hand trembles as he pours.

She accepts the sherry and takes a sip, trying not to down it in one gulp. "You're going to tell me something unpleasant, I know. Not that I don't deserve it."

"Well, my dear, your record with Trinity has been exemplary. I know that you have never in any way ... ah..." His voice trails off.

"Never in any way...?"

"Never in any way ... ah ... advocated incest in your class-room discussions. But the issue of your book becomes ... well ... a matter that casts a cloud over the college."

"I'm sorry to cause this trouble."

"There are always people who will lay charges. We have only to think of Socrates and..."

"And how a so-called democratic society accused history's wisest man of corrupting youth. It's scary. But I cannot compare myself in any way with Socrates. That would be the epitome of hubris."

"Yes, well." The Provost pauses, and a blush creeps into his round cheeks. "I'm afraid the Governing Council of the University has been down my neck this morning. In fact, I've had a half-hour conference call with six of them. They've been quoting Morris Shadwell. You remember him? That chap who got in trouble? What was his euphemism for paedophilia? Quite a ... a ... bizarre phrase."

"'Intergenerational sex' was his term."

"Well, the Council has pointed out to me that your book affirms Shadwell's view that this ... er ... 'intergenerational sex' ... can involve intense pleasure." The Provost suddenly bangs his glass of sherry down on his desk, spilling some of it over the polished surface. "Dash it, Professor Greaves, how could you? How could you?"

"Provost, I intend to take whatever comes without self-de-fence. So tell me the worst now." Roberta drains the last of her sherry. "Please, let's get it over with."

"My dear. You are to be suspended from teaching in the college until the end of the year. Then, your case will be reviewed. By that time, this kerfuffle will probably have blown over. These things do pass, you know."

"I guess I saw it coming. Starting when?"

"Now." He stands up. "The retired professor who took over your classes when your husband passed away will have to be in your office until the exams are over. But in the interests of fairness to our students — I made this clear to the Governing Council — you will mark the final papers from home, of course. And you'll receive payment of your usual salary, which goes without saying...." The Provost's voice trails off, and for a moment, Roberta fears that he will break down and weep. Like most inarticulate men, he has deep emotions. She remembers his tears when Carl recited "Crossing the Bar" at James's funeral. But he gives a huge sigh, looks at a pocket watch on a gold chain, and pulls his academic gown around him. "Well, my dear, my fans await me for my last seminar of the season: Deuteronomy, chapters five through twenty-six, in which the law of Moses is set down for the second time. Riveting ... *ha, ha.*"

He rises and holds the door open for Roberta. In the corridor outside his office, he shakes her hand. "You're a good person, Professor Greaves. I'm sorry to be the conduit of bad news. So sorry."

"You did what you had to do, Provost."

"You'll be all right, my dear?"

"Yes, I'm just going to my office now. I'll clear out my books and leave detailed information for my replacement." She turns away afraid that if she says more, she will start blubbering. She moves down the corridor towards the solitude of her office.

But a few seconds later, a shrill voice coming from behind stops her in her tracks. "Roberta, what on earth are you doing here? You're the last person I expected to meet. Though I did see you being pushed up the front walk by that little sycophant, Muna Mehta. Probably thinks she can con a few marks out of you."

She turns to confront Joan Wishart, who's holding her morning cup of chamomile tea in her tiny hand. The woman's eyes are scrunched up, and her words come sputtering forth. "You're a fine one to do such a thing, to write such filth. You, the head of the Ethics Committee. As if that disgusting Ovid story wasn't enough, you had to go and rewrite it for the mindless mobs—"

"Please, Joan, I've had enough for one day. Just leave me alone."

The woman moves in closer and takes a deep sniff. "And drinking sherry with the Provost, what's more. Despicable. When I think about how this institution has declined in my lifetime, I—"

But Roberta turns away from the woman and rushes to her office. She opens the door and slams it in Joan's face.

32.

A T LEAST, I'VE STILL GOT my poetry workshops, Roberta says to herself as she heads towards Major Street for her volunteer work. The kids still need me, though I may be deluding myself. At least they need Charlie's food. And strange though it seems, I need them. She feels almost upbeat as the north wind pushes at her back and propels her forward.

Her cellphone rings. She hauls it from the depths of her shoulder bag. It's Marianne, of course. For about the tenth time in three days.

"Seen the bestseller list in *The New York Times?*"

"I'm trying not to read any papers for a while."

"Well, gotta tell you this: You're in twelfth place. In less than two bloody weeks. *You even beat out Nora Roberts!*"

"You're impressed, I can tell."

"*Nora Roberts!* Lordy!"

"To think that six months ago, I had no idea who Nora Roberts was, and now she and I are neck and neck for the race towards 'Worst Novel of the Decade.'"

"Cut the sarcasm, Roberta. I'm totally not responsible for bestseller lists or any of the crap you've got yourself into. And while you're listening, I may as well say that I'm damn sick of my phone ringing all the time with some chump wanting your email or your phone number and then giving me grief when I won't tell them."

"Okay, okay, Marianne, apologies."

"It'd be so much easier for me if you did the social networking that every other writer does."

"I've told you I have no intention of twittering or blogging or doing any of that stuff. Why would I want to connect with some sicko who's telling me it's the best fucking book he's ever read? I'm signing off now. I'll phone you later." Roberta stuffs the phone back in her bag.

She swallows the bile that's risen in her throat. Stay calm, she tells herself. Think about the afternoon's lesson. She's planned to reinforce the concept of metaphor by asking the kids to write a poem that begins "Life is..." Maybe she can get them started by talking about clichéd metaphors. "Life is a bowl of cherries," or better still, "Life is a crock of shit," which would get a laugh from Big Chris. Then from there they might segue into something more original. She'll have to supply some ideas. As she walks along, she comes up with "Life is stand-up comedy/ And sometimes the jokes aren't funny/ But you've got to keep laughing...."

She is still mulling it over as she comes through the front door to the familiar smell of overcooked cabbage ... and something else today ... is it stale wieners? Vile, anyway.

The staff counsellor Annie is struggling to get a window open. She spots Roberta and says, "Our volunteer from the food bank just brought over some potatoes for tonight's dinner. Well and good, but half of them were rotten. Phew. And now, I can't get this damn window up. It's been painted shut for years."

"Let me help you."

"No, I'll cope."

But Roberta puts herself alongside Annie, and, on a count of three, they manage to get it up. "I never thought that city air could be considered fresh," Roberta says as she and Annie lean in and inhale.

"Oh goodness, Roberta, I forgot for a moment, I've got to talk to you. In my office, okay?" Annie gestures towards a squalid little glassed-in space in the corner.

She closes the door to the cubicle, shutting out the stench of the potatoes, but engulfing Roberta in a miasma of perspiration and stale tobacco, probably from Annie's previous client. The Arborite table with a computer and printer leaves barely enough room for two small plastic chairs and a grey filing cabinet. Roberta seats herself in one of the chairs and sets her briefcase down on the cracked tile floor.

"I've been thinking about Hester," Roberta says. "You were going to see if you could get her some place to stay and a job somewhere."

"Done. I found her a bedsit in that hostel down the street. Pretty basic, but there's a hot plate and a small fridge and a lock on the door. I had enough money in the kitty here for a month's rent. After that, I think she may be able to manage it. She's got a part-time job at Wendy's. Trouble is, she hasn't the faintest idea about shopping for food or cooking, but I'll work on that."

"What a relief." Roberta pulls out some bills from her bag. "This is for anything extra she may need. Just don't tell her where it came from, please. Which Wendy's is it?"

Annie takes the bills — five twenties — and tucks them under the edge of her mouse pad. Then she takes them out again and hands them back. "Sorry, Roberta, I can't take your money. And I can't tell you where Hester's working."

"Why on earth not?"

"Because you can't volunteer here anymore." The words come out in a rush.

"Please explain." But Roberta is beginning to realize what's coming next.

"I don't know anything about Ovid, but I've been reading all the flak in the papers about your new book, and well, we're dealing with vulnerable people in this place and..."

"You think I'm going to endanger them in some way." Roberta can feel the blood rushing into her cheeks. "You can't be serious."

Annie rubs her hands over her face. "I can't take chances. I've talked this over with the chaplain and the major donors, and well, we all agree. I'm sorry. But take Hester, for example. She's been assaulted by her mother's boyfriend, I told you that. I shouldn't have. It was confidential info. But I thought I could trust you. And now you've written this book, and I know, I know, I haven't read it, but it seems to be the very sort of thing we've got to protect the kids from." Her voice trails off.

"I'm teaching them poetry, for God's sake." The phrase is out; she's taken the Lord's name in vain. But what the hell. "I want them to write about themselves and through the creative process to come to terms with life's complexities. Isn't that one of the reasons you let me volunteer here in the first place? They're making progress. They're actually planning to hold a poetry slam in a month or so, and they're going to get their friends lined up to attend. I'm just starting to get somewhere with them, and now you're telling me I'm finished here. What's going to happen to my program? Do I do today's lesson or not?"

"Look, I'm trying to get a replacement. I should have phoned you. But I just can't let you go down there today. No way. I'll make an excuse. They don't need to know why you're not working here anymore. We'll just say you've found yourself too busy to continue."

"No."

"No?"

Roberta stands up. "I'm not going to scuttle out of here like some kind of cockroach you found in a cupboard. If you want me to leave, I guess I'll have to. But I'm going downstairs now and tell the kids the truth. They deserve that."

Annie pushes her chair back. "I'll have to go with you."

They go down the stairs to the room where the kids are waiting. They are already devouring Charlie's lunch. Today, it looks like club sandwiches on a big serving plate, and there is a square chocolate cake in the middle of the table. It's a lot more solid-looking than the Roman Ruin.

"Hey, Roberta!" they say as she enters the room. "You're late," Moose adds. "We thought you'd fucking decided not to come or something."

"Nah, I knew you'd show," Bat says. "Sandwich?" He pushes the plate over to Roberta.

She sits down. Annie stands behind her. Now they're all staring at the counsellor. "What the fuck are *you* here for?" Hester asks her. Today, her face is clean, and she's actually taken the ring out of her nose. Her dog Scrappy seems to be enjoying a piece of chicken from her sandwich.

"Roberta wants to tell you something and I'm here to listen," Annie says.

"Annie tells me I'm not going to be allowed to teach you today," Roberta says. "I'm deep in what Moose might call 'a crock of shit.'" She tells them about *Mira*, that it's an update of an old story by a long-ago Roman writer. "I needed some money fast," she says, "and it seemed like a solution to some huge debts I had to settle."

There's a silence as if they're trying to process what she's said. Then Moose speaks up. "This kid has sex with her old man for fun? People are going to believe that? I don't fucking believe it."

"It's not like he's forcing her or something?" Big Chris asks.

"Hey, I think I read about it in *Toronto Weekly* while I was sitting on the corner," Bat says. "But it was wrote by someone called Renee Meadows, they said."

"*Rainy*. That's how you say it. Renee Meadows. Me. It's a fake name, a stupid joke I once thought might be funny."

"But I'm not getting it," Big Chris says to Annie. He stands up, puts both hands flat on the table, and leans forward. "What's this dumb book got to do with Roberta not teaching us?" He's a big guy and his tone is pugnacious.

Annie steps back. Her voice is shaky as she explains.

"You're saying Roberta is, like, a *perv*?" Big Chris shouts. "You're saying *that*?"

There's a rumble of voices, a chorus of "what-the-fuck" and other favourite expressions.

"Look," Roberta says, "it's not Annie's fault. Annie's like a lot of people. She thinks I'm promoting paedophilia. You know me, and you know I wouldn't do that. But I wrote the damn book. And now I've got to face the consequences of my own stupidity and other people's stupidity." She cannot resist adding that last bit. She gets up from the table. "Charlie will send you the food every Wednesday, so be sure to come here and eat it. And Annie's going to get someone who'll go on with the poetry. So you'll be able to have the slam and invite your friends. And I'll try to come and hear you if I can."

"It's not about the bloody poetry, you know? And it's not about food or nothing. It's about this bitch here trying to get us to fucking believe you're a *perv*." As Moose says this, his ears get red.

"She calls herself a fucking counsellor, but she doesn't know *nothing*," Hester says. She stands up, slams her chair into the edge of the table, and walks over to Annie. Scrappy is beside her, his ears laid back, his hackles up. "If you think Roberta's a *perv*, you'd better get yourself a bloody shrink to fucking tell you what's up."

Annie turns and runs towards the staircase.

"Wait," Big Chris yells. "There's one thing that's gotta be said before you scuttle out of here." He bangs his fist on the table. Everyone falls silent. Annie pauses on the third step. "Every day I come in here, I see that sign inside the front door. Something about this place being dedicated to the glory of God or some shit like that. And you know what I think? I think it's run by a gang of two-faced shitters, excuse the expression. And you're the worst."

Now the whole group is banging the table with their fists and chanting, "Two-faced shitters." Scrappy starts to bark and growl.

"Wait a minute," Roberta calls to Annie. "Come back here,

please." She waits until Annie creeps back down the stairs and stands beside her. "Now look here, all of you. I appreciate your support. I do. Your trust in me is the best thing that's happened in all the time I've been coming here. But I need you to support me now when I tell you this: Annie's probably going upstairs to phone the cops or the security people. Right, Annie?"

Annie nods. She is pale and the wrinkles around her mouth seem etched into her face.

"I don't want her to do that. You'd all get into trouble and that would make me feel even worse than being called a ... a ... *perv*. So before I go, you've got to promise me one thing. You'll stay here and finish your lunch, and then you'll go upstairs and leave quietly."

The rumble of voices has quieted. They're all looking at her. "Promise?"

"Yeah, okay," Big Chris says. "We promise." The rest of them nod.

"Good. And Annie, *you*'re going to promise here and now in front of me and twelve other witnesses that you're not going to call the cops or the security people or anybody else. You'll walk upstairs now with me, and then you'll go into your office and stay there."

Annie bobs her head though Roberta can see her reluctance.

Roberta looks at the group around the table, taking her time to nod at each of them in turn. "Goodbye. I'll miss you."

She and the counsellor climb the stairs. "Thanks for that," Annie says. "It looked bad for a moment. I was worried."

"Please. Shut up a moment." Roberta stands at the top of the stairs, listening. "They're keeping their promise. Now for God's sake, Annie, you keep yours." She walks to the front door. As she opens it, she turns back for a minute. "Know what? I think Big Chris summed things up nicely. You and the other so-called Christians in this place are a bunch of two-faced shitters."

Out on the street, she tries to take deep breaths, but the north wind smacks her face and she has to turn her head away from its force. She's crying and her nose is streaming into her scarf. She pulls out a tissue and tries to wipe up the mess, but the sobs come and she can't control them.

She sure as hell has learned a lot in a short time. She foresaw the descent from her pedestal at Trinity, yes, but to fall from the paradigm of perfect professor to pervert in the space of a few short days? Well, she couldn't have foreseen that. She's hit the bottom of the pit.

33.

IT IS SEVERAL WEEKS into Roberta's suspension from everywhere, and in sheer desperation, she's taken to walking each morning in High Park, an oasis of four hundred acres of trails and woodland and ponds in the west end of the city. She's acquired a pedometer and resolved to put at least ten kilometres on it every day.

The walking regimen was Carl's idea. In fact, he gave her the pedometer. "Sticks and stones may break your bones, but names will never hurt you," he said to her after she told him about Annie's decision not to let her near the street people. "It's the dumbest bit of doggerel in this wide world. But please, dear Robbie, try to remember that you're *not* circumscribed by her ideas. *She's* the *perv*, not you. Now, I'm going to suggest something. A brisk walk every morning in High Park. You'll find all kinds of things to take your mind off your problems. I used to go there on days when Claire was in chemo. I'd just walk, walk, walk, and I'd be so tired by the end of it that my mind would be emptied of all the sludge that had accumulated."

"In Summerton, it was always food that was the panacea," Roberta told him. "A banana split cured me of my childish sorrows."

"Well, if a banana split would help you, go for it. But I suspect it wouldn't cure you as quickly now as it did when you were ten. Try the High Park remedy. I'll join you on the weekends."

So Carl is with her on this Saturday morning. They've just

had a quick cup of coffee in the Grenadier Restaurant, and now they're striding downhill, past the cherry trees that are starting to flower, to the path along the edge of Grenadier Pond. Carl is wearing hiking pants with a zip pocket on the leg and a sweatshirt that shows off his broad shoulders.

There's an Asian man down at the side of the pond, almost hidden by the rushes. He has a fishing pole, and he throws it down when he sees them coming. By the time they're on the path, he's got his binoculars up as if he's there merely to bird watch.

"Not sure of the rules and regulations for fishing in these parts," Carl says, "but I suspect that guy's doing something fishy, pardon the pun." They march along for a minute or two, then Carl adds, "I used to fish with my dad when I was a kid; we used to go to the creek in Bolton just before midnight so that we could put our lines in at exactly twelve-oh-one on the first Saturday of May, as I recall."

"You went fishing with your dad? I did too. He'd come home after office hours, throw his white coat in the washing machine, then pull on his old windbreaker, and we'd be into the Olds and away. Mother never went with us."

"Too busy doing the wash, no doubt? I wouldn't have wanted to be a woman in those days."

He takes her hand, squeezes it. "Go on about the fishing."

"Daddy and I would stroll along the creek, stop by a deep hole, usually under the bridge, and then he'd put a worm on my hook. I was always too squeamish. Then we'd throw our lines in. I didn't really want to catch anything. I'd just leave the line dangling and sit reading my book. Daddy used to laugh when I got annoyed if there was a tug on my line.

"And after we'd caught a few speckled trout, it was time for the picnic. There was always fresh home-baked bread, crisp beans and radishes from our garden, and a delicious pudding called gooseberry roly-poly. It had to be steamed several hours, as I recall."

"No wonder your mother didn't want to go fishing. Probably just wanted a few hours to herself to flake out on the sofa."

"Maybe. Because when we got home, Daddy would gut the fish, and then she'd coat it with some buttered crumbs and fry it up for us. I've never had fish since that's been as good. You know, Carl, as I'm telling you all this, I'm realizing just how much I took my mother for granted. Things keep coming back to me. The gooseberry bushes in our backyard, for example. She had to pick the berries in order to make the roly-poly. I sure as hell wouldn't have wasted all that time on a picnic lunch."

Roberta and Carl are halfway around the pond now. They have been walking at top speed, and they're both huffing and puffing.

"Let's take a time out and look at the ducks," Roberta says. "I don't know a damn thing about ducks, but it's an excuse to stop." By this time, they have both flopped onto the grass by the side of the pond.

"What was *your* mother like?" Roberta asks Carl.

"I don't remember her at all. She died of meningitis when I was two. So there were just Dad and I. He was in the war, you know, came home, went back to university, became a successful dentist, got married, and expected to live happily ever after. But it didn't turn out quite that way. Suddenly, he had to be father *and* mother to me. He did it all, and I think it must have been a tough, lonely life for him. But I didn't lack for anything, and I'm thankful for his care." He pulls out a bit of chickweed from the grass. "He drinks too much now, and I think, so what? But I worry about him. He's in Holland now for the Liberation ceremonies. I phoned a couple of his Legion buddies, and they're keeping an eye on him. I want him to be safe." There's a pause, then he says, his voice soft, "I love him."

"You never wanted to have children of your own to love?"

"I guess not having what you'd call a 'normal' life with a father and a mother and siblings, I never felt a yearning to have a family. And Claire was … acquiescent; I suppose that would be the word. Anyway, we had an unspoken agreement not to have children. Perhaps we would have been happier with kids." He pulls up some more weeds and throws them on the grass. "Water under the bridge," he says, pulling Roberta to her feet. "But Claire might have been happier as a mother. I never bothered to find out."

They finish their walk around the pond, have another cup of coffee, and head north to Bloor Street.

"Are you okay, Robbie?" Carl says as they part.

"Yes. In fact, I've sorted a few things out this morning." She stands on tiptoe and kisses his cheek. "Thanks."

He blushes but looks pleased. "That was nice. Let's do it again soon."

She is not sure whether he's referring to the kiss or the walk in the park, but suddenly, it's all good.

The house is quiet when she gets home, except for the muted strains of Beethoven's *Ninth* coming from Ed's room. He's probably working on research for one of the tiresome cases that old Peabody dumps on him. Charlie is at The Fig Leaf, of course, Saturday being one of the busiest days for the restaurant. So her timing is good. She goes to the phone in the kitchen and punches in a familiar number.

"Mother? Please don't hang up on me. I've just got to tell you that I'm sorry I never thanked you for all you've done for me over the years."

"What's brought this on?" The voice is grumpy.

"Well, a number of things. I'll mention one. Carl and I were reminiscing this morning, and I told him about all those great lunches you used to pack for Daddy and me when we went fishing."

"Why all this ancient history right now?"

"Oh, Mother, can you forgive me?"

The line goes dead for a moment. Roberta thinks maybe her

mother has hung up. Then she hears Sylvia's voice, strained but determined. "Before you say one word more, I need you to know that Neville has moved in, lock, stock, and barrel. 'Stock' includes Polonius."

For a second, Roberta wonders who the hell Polonius is. Then she remembers. "Better keep the windows open then. Or at least, get the fan running night and day."

There's a giggle. "Come and see us, dear. Soon. We'll have lunch."

34.

A S THE GO TRAIN PULLS INTO in Summerton, Roberta reflects that she is better prepared for this visit than she was a few months ago. She doesn't expect to find her mother in bed with Neville this time (she's phoned in advance as a warning), but she's geared up for the cohabitation: Neville's presence in Daddy's favourite chair, Polonius's farts. What she's not sure of is the reaction of the locals to the news that she is Renee Meadows. They'll know about it. Everybody reads *The Gazette*.

It's a cloudy day, but she puts on her big sunglasses and the green broad-brimmed hat that shades her face. She heads down Victoria Street. As she passes Nora's Nimble Needle, the door opens and Nora Dorsey hails her. She has a loud voice, so there's no escape.

"Hey, Roberta — or is it Renee? You didn't think that disguise would get past us, did you?"

"Well, I hoped, but I should have known better."

"Speaking of which, you do know now about your mother and Neville? No surprises like last time? I told my daughters that—"

"Will you join me for a glass of wine at Finnegan's, Nora? We could talk there."

Roberta has become aware of an old woman nearby who has turned her pink permed head in their direction.

"Lead on, girl. My daughter can look after things for a while."

The pub is next door to Nora's shop. Roberta remembers when it was a non-licensed restaurant owned by the "Chinaman" as everyone called him back then. Only her parents called him Mr. Yu. The place had a long Arborite bar and a number of tall chrome stools on which people perched to eat the sausages and mash the "Chinaman" served them.

Now the Arborite bar has been replaced with mahogany veneer coated with layers of urethane to make it impervious to spills. There's a huge mirror opposite, flanked by mahogany shelves filled with pottery steins. Hunting scenes matted in green hang on every wall. Roberta is glad of the recorded music — a quavering Irish tenor singing, inevitably, "Danny Boy" — which will cover their conversation.

They find a leather-padded booth at the back, and a girl in a green apron asks, "Two Guinness for you?"

"Okay by me," Nora says. "But this fine lady from the city needs a glass of white wine."

The drinks arrive, and Nora takes a swig of her ale. "Expect some nastiness over that novel of yours," she says. "The owner of The Bookmark told me she's sold seventy-five copies since your letter came out in the paper. People in town have sure got you pegged as the kid, but they're having some trouble placing the publisher guy who's the stepdad. Poor old Herb Philpotts who used to publish the *Summerton Economist* has come in for some grief. Remember how he always had a picture of you on the front page when you won those writing contests and scholarships? Not that Herb was exactly what you might call a *crusader*. Not like your father, anyway."

"I know you were a fan of my father. You knew him well, didn't you? Better than most of the other women in the town?" She hears the edge in her voice as she says this.

Nora drains half her pint in one long swallow. Then she says, "So your mother told you?"

"Yes. But I want to hear your side of it."

Roberta waits while Nora gulps the rest of the Guinness and

sets her glass down with a thump. "Your dad, he was kind to me. He was the kindest man I've ever known. He helped me out with Janeen once."

"I know about that. When I was a child, I overheard him telling my mother about the abortion. But he warned me not to tell anyone about it, and I've kept it secret all these years."

"I guess I've got to thank you for that."

"And now you can return the favour and tell me about your affair with him."

"To understand it, you have to know about my husband. I was pregnant when we got married. It was called a shotgun wedding in those days. And afterwards, he started to abuse me. He thought he could slap me around, but he didn't get away with it. I walloped him over the head with a frying pan, and that was the end of that. But his words were brutal. He never stopped reminding me that he'd been forced into marriage. Not that it stopped him from taking his pleasure with me any time of the night or day.

"So when Janeen got knocked up, I had to do something. I didn't want *her* to have a shotgun marriage. So what solution was there? There were still no abortions then. Nothing legal, that is. Just those back-alley monsters with coat hangers and plant poisons. But your dad came to the rescue. I loved him for his gentle way with me and the girl. So I guess — when I saw him looking at me with those eyes — I fell for him. I kept going to his office for problems I didn't really have. It was just an excuse to get to know him better. And then, when some of the Eastern Star ladies were giving him grief over the condoms in Budge's Pharmacy, I was the one who supported him. I know he appreciated that. We got close. I don't know whether he loved me or not, but he..."

"In a town like this, how did you get away with it?"

"The knitting, that's what."

For a moment, Roberta thinks Nora is still talking about back-alley abortionists. She heard Daddy talk once about the knitting needles they used to puncture the amniotic sac. "I'm not following you."

"Knitting, you know? Your mother wanted to learn to knit, and I used to come over to your house in the mornings when you were at school. People got used to seeing me head there with my bag of wool and needles. Sylvia was a quick learner, and she wanted me to show her all the tough patterns I could think of. So I did." Nora signals the girl for a second Guinness.

"Then?"

"Well, some days Sylvia would be out of town on the train, maybe visiting you in Toronto or shopping or something. Your dad would cancel his morning appointments and stay at home and we'd..."

"Okay, okay, I get it." Roberta finishes her glass of wine. "I should be getting home. Why don't you stay and finish your Guinness, Nora? I'll settle the bill with the girl."

"Just one more thing, Roberta." Nora fingers the silver-and-gold pin she's wearing on her ample bosom. "See this? Given to me by the Masons after my son-of-a-bitch husband died. He was a Mason, like every other male in this town. The Widow's Brooch, it's called. 'Conferred on all worthy Masonic widows' is the wording, as I recall." She gives a snort of laughter. "Know what? I wear it just to spite that so-and-so, may he rot in hell."

"I don't blame you for what you did with my father," Roberta says. "I understand now. Thank you."

"Your mother, that's who I can't understand. How could she take up with a nitwit like that Neville?"

"Sorry, Nora, but I can't stay around to hear you criticize Mother." Roberta stands up. She pays for the drinks at the long bar and turns at the front door to look back at Nora. She is gazing into her second pint of Guinness as if turning over in her mind all the memories their conversation has evoked. There's a strength about the woman that Roberta admires: Her determination not to let Janeen suffer; her repudiation of her husband's physical abuse.

From the pub, she turns left onto Osborne Road. It's one of the early streets in the town, lined with churches and stone or brick houses with large lots. As on all her other visits to Summerton, she must pass the Wesley United Church with its silly flashing sign. Today it says, "TANK ON EMPTY? COME IN HERE AND FILL UP."

The young pastor — she's forgotten his name — is just getting into his car in the parking lot. When he sees Roberta, he gets out and comes over to her, blocking the sidewalk so that there's no escape. "Roberta," he says, leaning in a little close for comfort. "I confess to having read your book. It's terrible, I have to say. And I know you need help." He points to the sign. "Your tank's on empty, for sure. Please come into my office for a minute, and we'll talk. I know a counsellor who may be able to help you."

"I'm not proud of the book," Roberta says. "But I don't need a counsellor, thank you."

"Oh, my friend, admission is the first step to recovery. Anyone who writes a book about a child seeking out incest needs help. Is there something in your early family background that needs—"

"No, nothing in my background. You're new to this town, so I can excuse you for silly presumptions. You didn't know my father. You don't know what a good man he was. I loved him, but incest? God, no. My novel is based on Ovid's story."

"Ovid?" What's-his-name's high forehead is glistening with sweat. Has he not heard of Ovid? Or maybe he's not made the connection between *Mira* and "Myrrha"? Roberta steps onto the grass bordering the sidewalk and moves past him.

"Thanks for your concern," she says. Then, she adds, over her shoulder, "But it's misplaced."

She rushes on, up the block, then, on impulse, turns right at the corner and goes down a grassy path into the graveyard of St. George's Anglican Church. She hurries towards the family plot, to the tombstones of her father and James. Someone has hoed neat little patches in front of each of them, and purple violets are in full bloom. It must have been Mother who did this. Roberta has not been able to come here before, has not even checked out the granite stone that she ordered after James's death.

It's quiet in the churchyard. The only sound is the soaring notes of a pair of cardinals in the towering pine trees that shade the graves. She stands looking at the granite memorials, and the tears come. She cannot hold them back. Aloud she says, "I loved you two more than anyone else in my younger life, more than my mother, perhaps even more than my sons. Wherever you are, can you hear me? I forgive you your trespasses. And James, my darling James, can you forgive mine?" The stones are close together and she stands between them, one hand on the top of each. The clouds have dissipated. The sun strikes her face, warming her tears. She feels them drying on her cheeks.

Back on Osborne Road, she checks her face quickly in the mirror of her powder compact. Not great, but good enough. She thinks, I can explain the red eyes easily enough: spring allergies, conjunctivitis, or eye fatigue. *But Mother may not notice anything. She will probably be too keyed up about my reaction to the new living arrangements.*

This time, she bangs on the brass door knocker so there will be no surprises. Her mother appears instantly. She looks pretty in a loose orange linen shirt, tan pants, and stilettos. Neville hovers just behind, fully dressed this time, thank God.

"You're late, dear," her mother says. "We've been holding lunch. But there's still time for a drink on the back porch. I've got some crackers and some of that hummus you like."

"Great." She's not about to say that she's already had a drink with Nora at the pub. But she does mention the visit to the churchyard. "It was nice of you to put in all those violets," she says.

"It was Neville who did it. He loves gardening. He's planning to help me with the roses this summer."

"Mmm, I smell my favourite chicken casserole," Roberta says as they move through the kitchen to the huge cedar deck at the back of the house. But as she says this, she inhales something less pleasant. Sure enough, Polonius is lying under the kitchen table. He struggles to his feet to greet her, his stump of a tail wagging. She scratches the top of his broad nose.

"Let's put him outside for a while, Sylvia," Neville says. He throws the kitchen window open and gets out the dog's leash.

Well, Roberta thinks, he's an old dog. He won't last long. And Neville appears cognizant of his digestive problems, so that little bump in the road to cohabitation will undoubtedly smooth out.

Neville uncorks the Sauvignon Blanc, fills glasses, and passes the hummus and crackers while Roberta's mother sits back in a comfortable Muskoka chair. "Neville has been a big help these last weeks," she says to Roberta. "That book of yours has caused such an uproar. I can't go downtown without everyone asking me about it. And we've actually had reporters here. Neville answers the door and tells them to get lost."

"And Polonius backs me up," Neville says. "When he hears that I'm angry, he growls and raises his hackles. They usually skedaddle down the front steps without much preamble."

"That damn book has lost me my job at Trinity, at least temporarily, my volunteer position with the street kids, and now you're telling me that you've been harassed, too. Oh my God, it's too much."

"It's been mostly fairly minor stuff, dear, like our local paper and *The Simcoe Star*. The new publisher of the *Summerton Economist* actually asked about you and poor Mr. Philpotts. Annoying and stupid, but manageable."

"But just this week, we had that critic from *The Gazette*," Neville adds. "Oh, what a muddy-mettled rascal he was! I recognized him at once. He used to sit in the front row at Stratford, and I'd be in the middle of a soliloquy, and I'd look down and see him making notes, his face all screwed up as if he were suffering agonies. Off-putting, to say the least. I could never bring myself to read that horrible man's reviews the next day."

"John Schubert. I know him. Carl calls him El Creepo. What was he doing here, for God's sake?"

"He wanted an interview with Sylvia about your relationship to Sylvia's 'first husband' — that's how he put it. Oozed charm from every pore, at least for the first minute or two."

For a minute, Roberta gets sidetracked, noticing how Neville sinks into a sonorous baritone whenever he gives a quote. For her mother, that quirk must surely be off-putting, to say the least. But then she realizes what Neville has just said. "What did you do?"

"I said, 'No thank you,' and he got nasty. He actually put up his hand to give a push at the front door to get in, but Polonius gave a most impressive snarl and dived for his leg, and he retreated just in time. Then he went down the front steps muttering something about my being the worst Claudius he'd ever seen on the stage anywhere."

"What a wretched thing for him to say." Roberta is surprised to find herself feeling genuinely sorry for Neville. "I've caused you a lot of grief with that novel."

"Sylvia's told me about you and your father," he says. "And she knows there was nothing sick about your love for him. She also mentioned that you were strapped for money after your husband's death and writing the book brought in some moolah. So that's all I need to know." He reaches for her mother's hand and holds it. "But don't you want to know what I thought about it?"

"Go ahead, tell me the worst. After that generous drink you poured me, I can take it."

"Well, it's not exactly what you'd call a bedtime story, but I thought it was a lot like the story of Little Red Riding Hood and the big, bad wolf. There are so many interpretations of that narrative. But I'll just mention one. You know Stephen

Sondheim's *Into the Woods*? Especially the song 'I Know Things Now'?" Roberta and her mother nod.

"Red Riding Hood," Neville says, changing again to the deep, polished tones of a professional actor, "is a girl hungry for sexual awakening and the wolf figure — or the father figure in your story, Roberta — is the only male around to help her find this fulfillment."

"Oh, darling, what a good analysis," her mother says, smiling at Neville. "Put that way, it doesn't seem so bad."

But it is bad, Roberta thinks. *It's Ovid's sick fantasy that I stupidly adapted.*

Neville carries the drinks and food inside, and they sit down to lunch. Besides the chicken casserole, there's a broccoli salad with tomatoes and feta cheese, and, yes, gooseberry roly-poly. "I had plenty of frozen berries," her mother explains as Roberta takes a second helping, "and it seemed a good way of using them up."

When Roberta gets home in the late afternoon, the house is empty. For a minute, she remembers the days when she would rush home from work to pick up Charlie from daycare or take Ed to the library for his project on ancient civilizations or get the block of frozen food into the oven while James made a salad or poured out the glasses of red wine. Now, it seems there's no one to care if she comes home at all. It's liberating — or pathetic. She can't decide which. Probably the latter. But thinking over the day in Summerton, she recognizes one fact: Her mother is happy, and that makes her happy too.

But she needs to tell someone about the day's events. She phones Carl.

"How did it go with Neville?" he asks.

"Better than I expected. This time, I didn't have to see anything of their sex life, thank God. But I did see another side of him. He's helpful. He did all the serving for lunch for one thing, and apparently, he thwarted the invasion of the media, including El Creepo, who came all the way to Summerton to dig up some dirt on me. And speaking of dirt, he's going to do the hard work in that garden, which has got altogether too much for Mother to handle in recent years. I only hope the romance stays in bloom. She's got a half-acre of lawn and two hundred and fifty roses that need pruning."

"Hmm, don't know about *romance,* the sex side of it, anyway. How much will the old boy's back be good for? None of my business, of course. What else did you notice about the guy?"

"Well, he does love to show off, but Mother doesn't seem to mind that. You know, at Christmas, Ed described him as a 'pain in the butt,' and it's true in a way. But he's a man with a good heart. I like the way he's so protective of my mother."

"And that four-footed farter, what about it?"

"I think I'm beginning to like Polonius, too."

"Robbie, perhaps you should get right into bed now. I'm afraid that you've either had too much to drink today or the fresh air of Summerton has addled your wits. Take an aspirin, and call me in the morning."

35.

A FEW DAYS LATER, as Roberta finishes dressing, she hears *thumps* from the kitchen. Coming downstairs, she finds Charlie standing in front of the counter. It's Monday, his day off from The Fig Leaf, and he's got some brown things in a clear, heavy plastic bag that he's put on the floor, and he's stomping them into bits.

"What are you doing?" she asks.

"What does it look like, Mom?"

"Like you've lost your mind, that's what." Then Roberta sees a cellophane bag on the counter. There are one or two Oreo cookies left in it. "Ah, now I get it. You're smushing the Oreos."

"Yeah, I've tried food processors and rolling pins in the past. But the booted foot is always available and always efficacious. See?" He gives another hop or two onto the bag and then holds it up. The Oreos have metamorphosed.

"I'm impressed. Not only by your vocabulary, but also by your tiny, perfect crumbs."

"It's Dad's expression and Dad's idea. He could never be bothered messing with the rolling pin — got crumbs all over the counter — and the food processor had to be washed. 'The booted foot is always available and always efficacious.' That's what he used to tell me. And I use it — as long as there's not a health inspector hovering on the horizon."

He pours the crumbs into a bowl, adds melted butter, mixes it all together, then presses the crumb mixture into the bottom and sides of a pie plate. Finally, with one swift motion, he flips open the fridge door and sets the pie plate on the shelf.

"I miss Dad."

"In spite of everything ... I miss him too. I went into the churchyard when I was up visiting your granny. I put my hand on his tombstone and asked him to forgive me. And you know, while I was standing there, the sun came out. Maybe he heard me."

Charlie comes to the kitchen door where Roberta stands. He puts his arms around her and presses his cheek against hers. She can feel his tears. "Sorry I was grumpy when you came downstairs, Mom. What am I doing? Making a peanut butter pie for Mrs. Schubert."

"Sounds ghastly."

"It's actually good, as long as you don't worry about your arteries. I made it when I was at George Brown. We did a course on regional dishes, and this one is a Kootenays special. And Mrs. Schubert likes rich, sweet things. I think this'll be a winner. I saw her yesterday taking the garbage to the curb, and I thought, Christ, it's time I did something nice for her. I remember the fun she and I used to have in High Park. I've still got that headband we made from Canada goose feathers."

In a minute, he's got the hand beater out and he's blending cream cheese, sweetened condensed milk, and peanut butter with some whipped cream he must have prepared earlier. Roberta watches him from her chair in the breakfast room.

"Big Chris has a message for you, Mom. All the Mission kids want you to come to their poetry slam next week. It's at the Wing-On Funeral Chapel — in the basement. Mr. Fig Leaf, aka Mr. Wong, says they can have the room free of charge. It's his brother's chapel, and since Mr. Wong likes Big Chris, he set it all up."

"Never again will I laugh at the name of the place. I swear it."

"So you'll go?"

"Absolutely. As long as I don't have to darken the doors of

the Christian Mission and speak to that counsellor again. Did Big Chris tell you if she got a replacement for me?"

"Yeah. A graduate student, female, who Big Chris says just wanted an opportunity to get something fresh on her resumé. The way he described her lesson — there was only one — it went something like this: 'Close your eyes, let your astral body take flight, then move your hand across your page, and write down the good karma that blows into your fucking mind.'" Charlie gets out a lemon and squeezes some juice into his mixture. "Stop laughing, Mom. I haven't finished. After they'd done this for ten minutes, they spent the rest of the lesson reading aloud the immortal words they'd just written. Apparently, Hester's inspiration went like this: 'Piss off piss off piss off piss off.' Big Chris says she kept reading this phrase until the instructor lost it and screamed at her to stop. So that was 'Amen' to the classes."

"I'm sorry. There was talent in that group. I'm wondering if they will have enough poems for the slam?"

"Big Chris tells me some of them have been working on additional poems in the patterns you showed them. He wanted me to ask if you'll go down on Friday to the Wing-On Chapel and help them rehearse. 'Get us on the fucking path again' was how he put it. He's coming in to The Fig Leaf tomorrow for an answer."

"Tell him I'll be there. Two o'clock as usual."

"Done. And I'll tell him to call in on Friday for some sandwiches."

Roberta watches Charlie put the filling into the Oreo base. He adds a few squiggles of melted chocolate, and the pie is done. Then each of them takes a spoon and licks a side of the bowl.

"Yum."

"Yum."

While Charlie takes the pie over to Mrs. Schubert, Roberta makes herself a cup of Nescafé and sits in the bright morning light of the breakfast room leafing through *The Gazette*. She cannot stop herself from reading the bestseller list, and she is not completely surprised to notice that *Mira* has moved to fourth place. Marianne told her there had been a spike in sales since the real identity of Renee Meadows came out. But it's served its purpose: The debts are disappearing bit by bit, and the creditors have stopped bothering her since they have seen that she is serious about paying. There will be enough royalties to cover the advance. But the label, *pervert,* may stick for a while. And her job at Trinity may be forever lost. She is going to have to get a new life. Euripida's story of Galatea's rebellion against Pygmalion could be updated into a play. It has universal appeal. She thinks of Ibsen's success with a similar theme in *A Doll's House*. And there's the modern translation of *The Cretan Manuscripts* that Paula Piper is still interested in, according to Marianne. A couple of reputable manuscripts will go a long way to reinstating her in the good books of the Trinity hierarchy.

She hears the squeal of tires in Mrs. Schubert's driveway. The sound is all too familiar. Looking through the breakfast-room window, she sees Schubert's big black car in flight. She hadn't even realized he was at his mother's place. What has happened? Is Charlie okay?

There's a slam of the sunroom door at the back of the house and Charlie comes in. His face is flushed, but he looks happy. *Thank God.*

"Success," he says. "I scared the fool, and I don't think he'll try anything more."

"I didn't know he was at his mother's, Charlie. If I'd known, I would have asked you to wait. I don't want you involved in his skulduggery."

"There you go, Mom, treating me like I was six years old again. Please. I'm grown-up. I know what I'm doing."

"Okay, okay, just tell me what happened."

They go into the breakfast room. Charlie takes her cup of

Nescafé and dumps it into the sink. He puts a filter in the coffee maker and grinds some beans.

"Please, Charlie, don't treat *me* like a six-year-old. Let's hear the story."

"Mrs. Schubert liked the pie and cut herself a piece right away. Then we sat and chatted for a bit. While we were talking in the kitchen, The Skunk arrived. You know how he talks. 'Mater this, Mater that.' Anyway, he was there to look over her perennial bed at the back of the house. 'Those hosta plants, Mater, have got to go.' Then he was out the back door. I excused myself and went out too.

"There he was in one of those shirts with the hand-stitching, Brooks Brothers or something, peering at the hostas and clucking away. When he saw me, he says, 'Oh dear boy, you *are* kind to Mater, but that pie, *devastating*. Her arteries, you know, could go *splat* and I'll have to deal with it.' No way, I wanted to say, they'd go *thunk*, but I didn't want to engage. Anyway, he blathered on for a few minutes, doing what you'd call the *noblesse oblige* thing, then I cut him off."

"Good for you. But what did you say?"

"You know how you told Ed and me that he was harassing Granny? Well, I put an end to that. And I'm pretty sure I put an end to him harassing you, too."

"My God, Charlie."

"I went into Plumtree, Pogson, and Peabody mode, just like Ed does, and here's what I said." Charlie clears his throat, and hooks his fingers through the pockets of an imaginary waistcoat. "I understand, Mr. Schubert, that you have physically assaulted a child of sixteen. No, don't deny it. She has told my mother everything. The victim is now considering steps that may possibly lead to criminal charges against you. She is also seriously considering civil action for battery that would include a claim for punitive damages. To address her loss of self-esteem, she has had to pay for costly psychological treatment—"

"Hey, where did you get all those fine words, *battery* and *punitive damages,* and the like?"

"From Ed, of course. We talked it over. One of us was going to go and see Schubert in his office, but opportunity knocked and I took it." Charlie pours two cups of coffee and sets one in front of Roberta.

"But what did he say?"

"Well, he pointed out that *your* 'dear little book' shows that young girls can be predators, too, and that he could say in court that *he* was the victim, that *he* could make his own claim, *blather, blather, blather.* I let him go on, and when he'd finally run down, I pointed out that a case of assault — if it hit the media — would not exactly do his public image much good. He totally dried up on that one. So then *I* did the *noblesse oblige* thing. I said that you were picking up the girl's counselling bills at the moment and were prepared to see her through this without a court case, provided *he* stopped carrying on his ridiculous behaviour, harassing my frail old grandmother, and generally conducting himself with no sense of decency."

Roberta laughs. "I can imagine your granny's face if she heard herself described that way. But my God, Charlie, do you think this bit of verbal blackmail worked?"

"Undoubtedly. But just for good measure, I added, 'Govern yourself accordingly.' Ed said every letter he sends out ends with that sentence. Well, you heard the roar of his car, didn't you? Those fancy tires of his took a beating."

Roberta sips her coffee. "I've been wondering. How much of this do you think that sweet old lady knows?"

"Mrs. Schubert? Not much is my guess. He's a good son, in his way. He condescends, but he keeps an eye on her. The hostas thing, you know? And though you may find this hard to believe, he's kind to her. She offered him a piece of pie when he came in, and he said, 'No thanks' quite nicely. Didn't give her the artery alert or anything. My guess is that he doesn't want her to know anything about the bad stuff he's into."

"My guess is she'd have to know about *Mira*. It's been in the papers."

"Maybe not, Mom. I don't think at this stage in her life she'd ever get through a newspaper. She had a huge magnifying glass on her kitchen table when I went in. She'd been trying to read the Lee Valley catalogue. So I read some stuff about gardening tools out loud for her and helped her fill out an order form. Visually challenged, as they say."

"I'm conflicted: I don't want Mrs. Schubert to be hurt, but I would like that son of hers punished in some way for what he did to Hester. Verbal blackmail is all very well, but he should be brought to trial as well. I can't do anything — I promised Hester — but maybe she will pursue things someday."

Charlie carries their cups to the dishwasher. "Know something, Mom?" he says, turning to her. "You're not as uptight as you used to be. You actually said the dread word *blackmail* without batting an eye, to use an expression of Granny's."

Roberta remembers her father's words from long ago: "Sometimes you have to do things that are wrong in order to set the world right again." Aloud she says, "'To every thing there is a season.'"

"When you go on like that, Mom, you sound exactly like Neville."

"I'll let that remark pass as well — without batting an eye." She picks up the newspaper again. "But in my own persona, I just want to say this: My two sons are the best of the best."

As she reaches for her reading glasses, she sees Charlie's wide grin.

36.

IT'S THE NIGHT OF THE POETRY SLAM, and as Roberta comes into the basement room of the Wing-On Funeral Chapel, she sees that her poets have worked hard for the event. They've grouped chairs around small tables and placed lighted candles on each table. There's even a spotlight and a makeshift stage.

"The room looks wonderful," Roberta says, clapping her hands. "A coffee house, no less. And whose idea was it to cover up those windows with coloured paper?"

"Mine," Sheena says. She's a short, skinny girl with a sallow complexion. Usually, she seems mournful, but tonight she's smiling. "But the spiders in the cracks spooked me. So Bat killed them, and then I stuck up the paper. It's awesome now, eh?"

"Sure is," Roberta says.

"Me, *The Exterminator*," Bat says. "I got the idea from Robert Ginty."

Roberta never stops being surprised by these kids. "That's an old movie, Bat. Where did you see that one?"

"Found it in the dumpster of a house that was being totalled. And watched it on the Mission's DVD player when that fucking Annie was gone home for the day."

Charlie has sent over trays of biscotti and oatmeal-raisin cookies along with lots of coffee in a large urn. "Will you replay your Robert Ginty role beside the coffee urn, please?" Roberta asks Bat. "Just to make sure no illegal substances get added to the brew."

"Hey, no sweat, man," Bat says. "I'll kill any prick who tries it." He places himself beside the urn, a short, tough little guy with an attitude that probably fools everyone who doesn't know him.

The audience is arriving now. Roberta looks them over. Mostly young friends of her poets, dressed in clothes that may have come from Goodwill or Value Village. She notes the flair with which they've managed to transform the castoffs. One young man has knotted a scarf around the knee of his jeans. A girl has painted her toenails bright orange to match a bright orange hoodie that has a broken zipper.

There's also a sprinkling of volunteers, social workers, and parole officers whom she's seen at the Christian Mission. Thank whatever gods may be that Annie has not shown up. Roberta has asked Carl to come, but he's not in the crowd. He did say he had a pile of test papers to mark, so maybe he's giving his night over to homework.

She turns back to the front of the room where her kids are fidgeting with their papers. "I don't think I can do this poem, Roberta," Lori-Lyn says. She's a tiny waif and her stick-like fingers are trembling. Lori-Lyn, Hester's pal, who performs fellatio on strange men in parking lots. There are so many kinds of courage.

"Deep breaths and coffee with lots of sugar will set you up," Roberta says. "I'll get the coffee for you while you're doing the breaths." As she turns towards the coffee urn, she nods to Big Chris who's emcee for the evening.

He's scraped his face raw for the occasion, and in his black jeans and black turtleneck, he looks like a combo of biker thug and Beat poet. Roberta can see the threads where he's tried to fix a tear on the shoulder seam of his sweater.

He goes to the stage area at the front of the room where the kids have set a couple of chairs facing the audience. There's a podium with a microphone that they must have borrowed from the chapel upstairs.

Roberta has just given Lori-Lyn her coffee and taken her seat at the back when a tall, solid figure comes through the door. It's Carl. Of course. When has he ever let her down? He waves and moves to the only vacant seat; oh, no, it's beside Hester and Scruffy.

Carl has probably made Hester's day. Roberta can read her mind. There he is, within spitting range, a fucking trespasser from Martha Stewart Land in grey flannels and a cashmere sweater. And a tie. Oh, please.

The girl has on what Roberta's mother would call a "get-up." Platform-soled running shoes, and a two-piece black lace outfit — bra and long skirt — with matching dyed black hair, black lips, and dead-white cheeks. She treats Carl to a black-rimmed snarl in response to his "Good evening," while he, unperturbed, rubs Scrappy's ears and receives a wide grin and a wave of his feather-duster tail. Once again, Roberta wishes Heather would take a few PR lessons from Scrappy.

Each kid performs three poems. At the rehearsal a week before, Roberta gave a basic lesson in presentation skills: "Memorize it! Slow down! Speak out!" She's happy now with the results. Even Hester has decided to take part. Her haiku, "Condom Breaking," is a hit with the audience, and she scuttles back to her seat, unsettled by the laughter and applause she receives. Scrappy rubs his head against her leg.

The social hour afterwards is a success. Charlie's cookies are excellent, and to Roberta's surprise, Hester stays long enough to eat one of them. Roberta moves up beside the girl. "Things going better for you now, Hester?"

"Fucking wages they pay me at Wendy's. But they let Scrappy stay in the back kitchen, unless the fucking inspector comes, then I gotta get him out into the alley." She makes a move as if she's about to bolt out the door, but suddenly she turns, actually smiles at Roberta and says, "Got a lot to thank you for. I know you put shit-faced Annie onto getting me a room. That's worked out good. And get this, I know a cop now.

Comes in all the time for a large double double, and if I'm heading home late at night, he gives me a ride. In his big fat cruiser. Whoa!" She reaches towards Roberta as if to touch her arm, thinks better of it, and heads for the exit.

Roberta watches her go, feels the tears start behind her eyes, then follows the advice she gave to Lori-Lyn, takes a deep breath and turns back to the crowd. She sees Carl coming towards her.

"Dear Carl," she says. "I'm delighted you came. Sorry you got stuck with Hester."

"Her companion was pleasant. And I enjoyed the poems. Most of all, I enjoyed their pleasure in what they were doing."

"What will happen to these kids, Carl? Will poetry help them get their lives together? Or will they be back on the streets asking for spare change? I worry about them getting busted by the cops." But as she says this, she thinks of Hester and the good cop who keeps an eye on her. Maybe the girl will summon the courage to tell him about John Schubert, and El Creepo can be brought to justice. Aloud, she continues, "Good middle-class citizens can't stand the notion of street people. Can't stand the dirty sleeping bags and filthy clothes. It's the Pygmalion thing again, I'm afraid."

"Never underestimate the influence of a good teacher, Robbie. You've introduced them to fine words, and you've got them creating good words of their own. I'd say you've given them a different view of the world. And they've given you a different view of the world too." He smiles at her. "That word *busted* just rolled off your lips as if you were 'to the manner born.'"

They're laughing together when Big Chris comes up to them. "Guess you're Carl," he says, extending his large hand in salutation.

"Good fella," Carl says. "How did you know my name?"

A flush rises above Big Chris's black sweater. "Uh...uh..."

"Come on, tell me. You're clairvoyant or something? Or has Roberta been talking about me?"

Suddenly, Roberta remembers: the corner of St. George and

Bloor, Valentine's Day. "I guess you'll have to tell him, Chris."

He clears his throat, makes several passes at creating a sentence, then suddenly the words spill forth. "I was, like, on the street corner, selling these Valentine poems to any sucker who comes along, and all of a sudden Roberta's there. And I, like, ask her, 'Wanna buy a poem?' and I think she was just being nice to me, but she buys one. 'How do I love thee?' — stuff like that. You know it? And I'm putting special inscriptions on them, see, so I'm, like, 'Can I put something on the top of this, Roberta?' And she tells me, 'To Carl, I love thee freely.'"

Big Chris's face is bright red now. "Oh fuck, Roberta, I've loused things up. Sorry, sorry."

"No, no, Chris," Carl says. "You've given me some good news. Thanks."

Big Chris takes out a square of heavy white paper — it looks as if it came from a hotel washroom — and mops his face. "Just so I didn't louse things up.... I wouldn't do nothing to hurt Roberta. Fuck, Carl, if I hadn't of had Roberta's poetry classes, I'd never of had the good luck that came today. I was picking up the cookies and stuff for the slam, and Charlie says to me, 'You're a reliable guy. I have a job for a reliable guy.' And long story short, I start Monday, cook's apprentice. How about that?"

"That's great," Carl says.

"I'm so happy, Chris," Roberta adds. "You've always been my favourite person."

She takes his large, rough hand and holds it for a moment, smiling up at him. Bless Charlie's kind heart. And bless Big Chris. He's helped her in ways he couldn't even imagine. Maybe, just maybe, he can put his life together. And maybe, just maybe, she can put hers together too.

She realizes that Big Chris has moved away and that Carl is staring at her. Smiling at her, really. His blue eyes gleam in the candlelit room. "Got a suggestion, Robbie," he says. "Why don't you do what you have to here, say goodbye to the kids and all that, and then we'll walk up to Bloor Street and grab a glass of wine?"

37.

ROBERTA AND CARL STROLL hand in hand along the north side of Bloor Street, past the familiar places where, not so long before, she made her daily morning dash from the subway to Trinity College. They're headed to the Park Hyatt Hotel, but Carl pulls up short in front of the InterContinental. Two uniformed doormen look at them hopefully.

"Let's stop here," Carl says. "It's probably got a quiet bar and washrooms that don't smell of embalming fluid. And I want to order some wine right now and put you across from me at a tiny table, so we can have a good talk."

"As long as you're paying, my lad. I've only been in here once and they stiffed me twenty dollars for a not-so-great club sandwich."

"Then remember the joys of Visa," Carl says. "Let's live it up."

They enter the revolving main doors and turn left for the bar. But as they pass the washrooms, Roberta says, "Give me a minute, will you, in one of those toilets you've been touting?"

She's just had an idea. It came to her a few minutes earlier when they passed the Medical Arts Building where she got the Valentine poem from Big Chris.

She's carrying the black bag she always carries. She surely had it with her on Valentine's Day. It's a large, satchel-like thing — "my suitcase," she calls it — with many zippers and compartments. On bad days, she can never find a thing in it. At the counter in the washroom, she rummages, unzipping and searching. In one seldom-used compartment, she finds an old subway transfer, a Starbucks gift card, and yes, there it is at the bottom: Elizabeth Barrett Browning's poem, "How Do I Love Thee?" She takes it out and puts it in a side pocket of the purse where it will be easy to find.

Then she looks at herself in the huge, unforgiving mirrors over the sinks. Not bad. She's glad she took time to iron the green linen shirt that matches her eyes. She pats down her wavy hair that has blown about in the spring breeze, and applies fresh lipstick.

Then she joins Carl.

They settle into comfortable leather banquettes and Carl orders a litre of Sauvignon Blanc and the cheese platter.

He smiles at her and raises his glass. "To the end of our winter of discontent."

"To springtime," she responds, clinking her glass against his. "To rebirth and renewal." There are tiny purple and yellow violas on each table, and she looks over them, seeing Carl in a way she had not been able to in the flickering light of the Wing-On Funeral Chapel. The slate-coloured sweater cools his ruddy cheeks and brings out the deep blue of his eyes, and there's something else....

They drink their wine, eat the cheese, and smile at each other over the violas.

"Your braces," she says, finally getting it. "You've had them removed. I've always liked your smile, but now it's dazzling."

He leans across the table, takes her hands in his, and squeezes them.

She pulls the poem from her bag then and puts it in front of him. "I've had it all these weeks," she says. "It's the one I bought from Big Chris, the one he inscribed for me."

He looks over the first line on the page, saying aloud, "To Carl, I love..." He stops and shoves the page aside. "Who are the other two?" he asks. His voice is a growl, and he's turned his lips downwards into a grimace that fortunately seems more fake than genuine. "Out with it, Roberta. I have to know the truth, however devastating."

It is not the romantic moment she planned. "What are you talking about?"

He shows her the page. She reads, out loud: "'To Carl: I love *three* truly....' Oh my God. Big Chris's mistake. He was trying so hard with his calligraphy. I just put it in my purse and never even noticed." She bursts into laughter.

"Forget the excuses, Robbie. I'm still waiting for an answer. Who are the other two?"

"Charlie and Ed, of course." She points to the poem. "But come on, read the rest of it. The other lines refer to you alone. Isn't that enough of an answer?"

"It'll do nicely, thank you," Carl says, changing the fake grimace into a smile. But he doesn't read what's on the page. He looks into her eyes and recites from memory:

> *I love thee to the level of every day's*
> *Most quiet need, by sun and candlelight.*
> *I love thee freely, as men strive for Right:*
> *I love thee purely, as they turn from Praise.*
> *I love thee with the passion put to use*
> *In my old griefs, and with my childhood's faith.*
> *I love thee with a love I seemed to lose*
> *With my lost saints, — I love thee with the breath,*
> *Smiles, tears, of all my life! — and, if God choose,*
> *I shall but love thee better after death.*

His voice, a deep bass, is soft and compelling, and for a moment, there are just the two of them in this wide world. When he finishes, his eyes glinting with tears, he says, "When Big Chris told me that story tonight, I couldn't believe what I heard. Why didn't you tell me sooner?"

"I guess there was so much going on in our lives, I didn't know for sure that I loved you. Or that you loved me. And I didn't want to rush things, to push you into something you weren't ready for."

"But we know now, don't we?"

"Yes."

They sit in silence for several minutes, legs entwined, and drain the last drops from the wine decanter.

When they finally struggle to standing position, Carl says, looking down at the floor, "I've undoubtedly had too much to drink because there's something relevant to the moment that I'm trying to remember. What was it that the Porter in *Macbeth* had to say about drink?"

"'It provokes the desire, but it takes away the performance.'" She puts her arms around him, luxuriating in the feel of his broad shoulders and slender waist. "Shall we check it out?"

They go to the reservations desk. "No, we haven't booked," Carl says, staring down the supercilious clerk. "We just need a room."

"You want help with your bags?"

"No bags," Roberta says. "All we want is the key card."

In their room on the twenty-first floor, Roberta makes a quick call to Charlie and Ed. "I won't be home tonight," she says to Ed who answers the phone. "I'm with Carl."

"Go for it, Ma," he says and hangs up.

In a moment, they have moved to the bed. "If I'd known about tonight, I'd have worn everything with Velcro tabs," Roberta says, as their trembling fingers fumble with zippers, buttons, belts, hooks, and ascot. At last, there's nothing separating them.

Later, much later, she whispers in his ear, "I think the Porter got it all wrong."

At daybreak, they get up, shower together, prepare cups of coffee from the packets on the shelf, and dress. "I don't think the kids will notice I'm wearing yesterday's clothes," Carl says. He runs his hand over this chin. "But I may have to make up something to explain the stubble and the unmarked tests."

Then he adds with a catch in his voice, "Oh Robbie, I won't forget this night."

Roberta puts her arms around him and holds him tight for a minute, then stretches up and says, "I love you," into the hollow of his throat.

"And where do we go from here?" he asks.

"I'm thinking about Elizabeth Barrett Browning," she says. "When she and Robert met, she was a semi-invalid with an injured spine. He took her away from a wretched father and a wretched life and gave her new hope. In fact, he saved her."

"And...?"

"*You*'ve given *me* the will to move on. I don't believe in that silly word, *closure*. But you've helped me cure *my* broken spine; you've helped me put the pieces together again. In spite of all the messes I've been in, especially with that wretched book, I feel hopeful now."

"I sense there's a 'but' coming," Carl says.

"'I love thee freely,' my darling, you know that. But now, I must strive to find Right, just as Elizabeth says."

"And what does 'Right' involve, Robbie?"

"I want to write a script. Perhaps it could be a take on Euripida's tale of Galatea. The story of a strong woman who faces the challenges of a tough life would go far towards wiping out memories of that sad little story of Mira and her stepfather. I'm going to think about it. What I know for sure is that it's got to cover the things I've learned in the months since James's death. When I get it done, I'll have sorted out the complexities of my life. Or, as Big Chris would say, I'll have made it less of a fucking mess."

"And when you do find Right, will there be a place for me in your brave new world?"

"Count on it."

ACKNOWLEDGEMENTS

This novel has undergone several metamorphoses since its inception at Humber School for Writers over a decade ago. I thank Richard Scrimger for his witty and perceptive commentary on its progress all those years ago. Since then, I have received valuable advice from Canadian novelists Barbara Kyle and Gail Anderson-Dargatz. My West Coast writing group—Laurel Hislop, Annette Yourk, and Carolyn Gleeson—also contributed their insightful wisdom during this long writing process. Laurel Hislop made useful comments on the finished manuscript.

I am indebted to many other people as well. Among them is Mandy Birch whose knowledge of horses and eventing enriched the opening chapter of this novel. Irma Fiacco gave input on the Italian references. Regan Olinyk helped me with the financial aspects of Roberta's husband's life. John Birch offered advice on the legal issues raised in the book. Hugh Birch introduced me to the street youth in the KYTES program to whom I taught poetry for several years and from whom I gained insight for the creation of important minor characters.

Carolyn Thompson gave constant feedback, and her belief in the novel sustained me. I am also grateful to Sylvia McConnell who encouraged me in the process and to my husband Nicholas Birch who undertook a hundred mundane household tasks so that I could sit at my keyboard.

Finally, my thanks to the folk at Inanna Publications—especially Luciana Ricciutelli, Renée Knapp, and Val Fullard—for their support and help in getting the manuscript out to a wider world.

CREDITS:

"Crossing the Bar" by Alfred, Lord Tennyson and "How Do I Love Thee?" by Elizabeth Barrett Browning are taken from *Representative Poetry, Vol. II* (University of Toronto Press, 1946).

An award-winning educator, Ann Birch was an associate professor in the teacher-training programs at York University and the University of Toronto. She was Head of English in several Toronto high schools, and author of the best-selling text, *Essay Writing Made Easy*. She holds a post-graduate degree in CanLit and is currently a fiction writer and editor. Her first novel, *Settlement,* was published in 2010.